BELLICOURT TUNNEL

THE CROWNING BATTLE
OF THE GREAT WAR

A NOVEL

JERRED METZ

Singing Bone Press

BOOKS BY JERRED METZ

Prose

The Angel of Mons:
A World War I Legend

The Last Eleven Days of Earl Durand

Halley's Comet, 1910:
Fire in the Sky

Drinking the Dipper Dry:
Nine Plain-Spoken Lives

Poetry

Butter in a Jar:
Days in the Life of Iola Thomas

Brains, 25 ¢, Drive In

Three Legs Up, Cold as Stone:
Six Legs Down, Blood and Bone

The Temperate Voluptuary

Angels in the House

Speak Like Rain

Bellicourt Tunnel

The Crowning Battle of the Great War

Cover illustration (front): Courtesy of the Australian War Museum
Back: The Thirtieth Division in the World War
Metz, Jerred, 1943 –
    Bellicourt Tunnel: The Crowning Battle of the Great War

ISBN 978-0-933439-19-1
Library of Congress Control Number: 2018913959

Singing Bone Press
Singingbonepress@gmail.com
jerred.metz@gmail.com

Jerred Metz's *Bellicourt Tunnel: The Crowning Battle of the Great War* take its readers out of the trenches, across a machine gun-infested battlefield and towards the heavily-fortified Bellicourt Tunnel. Although a work of fiction rich in detail, the novel reads like first person accounts written by hardened combat veterans. A riveting tale that is tough to put down and a fine tribute to the brave American doughboys of 1918.

Mitchell Yockelson, *Borrowed Soldiers: Americans under British Command, 1918*

Jerred Metz's latest novel on the Great War focuses on one of the last great battles of the four-year blood bath that helped bring the terrible toll in deaths to an end. Using original documents and photographs, he developed a fictional group of South Carolinians who train for the battle of their lives. They witness the horrors of battle and the ultimate destruction of the enemy's greatest defensive line, Bellicourt Tunnel. As he does so, Metz brings in famous people from his first novel of the war. Historical figures Sir Arthur Conon Doyle and Winston Churchill play roles as witnesses to the carnage while the fictitious British corporal, Tommy Atkins, comes back to life to lead them to the front. By using historical figures and fictional characters, Metz tells a story of World War I in a new, captivating way.

Fritz Hamer, Curator of History/Archivist, South Carolina Confederate Relic Room and Military Museum *Forward Together: South Carolina in the Great War*

Dedicated to the Soldiers of the 30th Division
Second Battalion
118th Regiment
Company "M"

"I had not expected to see any more actual operations of the war, but early in September 1918 I had an intimation from the Australian Government that I might visit their section of the line. Little did I think that this would lead me to see the crowning battle of the war."

Sir Arthur Conan Doyle
Adventures and Memories

"The greatest battle of the war, in many respects."

Colonel Holmes "Buck" Springs,
Commander, Divisional Trains
(field transport)

"Place of misery. Who, even with words set free, could ever fully tell, by apt relating, the blood and the wounds that I now saw? Every tongue would assuredly fail because of our speech and our memory that have small capacity to comprehend so much."

Dante Alighieri
The Inferno
Canto twenty-eight

Acknowledgements

Works of historical fiction depend as much on research as do works of history, though deviations from fact are permitted. First, there is almost always a cast of characters the author creates, and they are not persons known to history. I selected American Privates and a few British Sergeants and a Lance Corporal. Second, historical characters may appear where they were not in real life. Events, dates, and conversations may be accurate, and they may not. The story is the central matter.

Nevertheless, I wish to acknowledge the wealth of information that came from conversations with historians and archivists. Columbia, South Carolina is blessed with Joe Long, Education Director, and Fritz Hamer, Curator Historian, both of the South Carolina Civil War Relic Room and Military Museum, who shared their knowledge of the Thirtieth Division and their interest in the story I was telling. Mike Lott, National Guard Museum for the Thirtieth Division in Columbia also led me to documents and artifacts related to the events. Elizabeth Sudduth, Director of Irvin Department of Rare Books and Special Collections, Thomas Cooper Library, University of South Carolina, and the Bruccoli Great War Collection, was a guide to material in the collection. Nick and Tony Bird, Bird Battlefield Tours, and The Imperial War Museum, led me to important information. Mitchell Yockelson, of the National Archives and author of *Borrowed Soldiers, Americans under British Command, 1918,* encouraged the work. His book was fundamental to my understanding of the Division's role and work in the war and in the Battle of Bellicourt Tunnel. Jim Legg, Military Archaeologist, University of South Carolina, made his collection of documents about the Thirtieth Division in World War I available to me. We met frequently for lunch where we shared our enthusiasm for the subject, and he answered my many arcane questions. Bill Froke sent me current books that informed my understanding of facets of the war that were new to me. My wife, Sarah Barker, and editor Cecile Willgoss, paid attention to the novelization, the storytelling. Great thanks to all. Friendships grew through these connections.

I value that as much as the studious information and guidance.

TABLE OF CONTENTS

INTRODUCTORY

Corporal Tommy Atkins and the Revenant
(souls returned from death)

On August 23, 1914 in the first battle against the Germans in the Great War the British Expeditionary Force, facing double the number of enemy, was in peril of annihilation. At the moment the Huns were to cross the Nimy Bridge at the Mons-Condé Canal, St. George at the lead and a horde of cavalry angels swarmed down from the sky, repelled the Germans. So they say at Mons in Belgium. Among the British, soldier Lieutenant Maurice Dease, gallantly commanding two machine gun sections at the bridge, wounded three times, died—and his spirit rose to St. George's side in the sky.

And St. George brought lowly Private Tommy Atkins—one of Dease's gunners, killed by shrapnel that pierced his throat—back to life to fight on through the war.

At the Battle of Ypres on November 11, 1914, five soldiers, a British Vickers machine gun section—the Ruffians—were killed, leaving Tommy Atkins, behind to fight. Later, at moments of dire need his mates—now angel soldiers—would appear, take bodily form. Private Paul Carmichael and the godly Private Sidney Godley might help him repair the gun, hand him a part. They could march along to the trenches, full kit. Even Captain Leckie, the doctor, wounded at Mons and dead six days later in a prisoner of war hospital. Privates Willard Catchpole and Louis "Ziggy" Palmer, escapees from the burlesque and leg-show, would cheer him up, sing a London stage ditty, replacing the romantic and sentimental lyrics with ribald lines to make him blush.

The Americans

Machine Gunners of Company. "M", 118th Regiment

The 27th and 30th Divisions of the American Expeditionary Force arrived in June, 1918 for training near the Front in France. Corporal Atkins was Lead Instructor for Lewis machine gun sections, Company "M", 118th Infantry Regiment, 30th Division, American Expeditionary Force, South Carolinians from Sumter, Columbia, Mountain Home, and St. Helena Island. They would fight attached to the British Fourth Army. While they first fought in the Ypres-Lys offensive, Atkins and his instructors trained them for leading the attack at Bellicourt Tunnel and breaking the Hindenburg Line, a military and spiritual barrier. Because of the assignment's importance, Atkins initiated the two teams into the "Golden Arrows of God."

A mystical order within the secret "Messieurs de St. Georges" in Mons, Belgium, the "Golden Arrows of God" carried out orders dictated by St. George to the Hierophant, the order's leader. Officially identity of its membership of a dozen was known only by the Hierophant. Though this could not be so. The people knew they were men of power and honor, learned and wise, and whose ordination came from St. George himself. No one ever spoke about who the members were, but the people were wise enough to know. In manuscripts from the 1400's the order was already described as an ancient and powerful organ for spiritual and brotherly good and in direct communion with the City's patron saint.

By Signs they Knew Him

Yet, as the Bible says, by signs they knew him. So it was with Instructor Lance Corporal Atkins. In Tommy Atkins were none of the usual marks of greatness—beauty, carriage, charm, voice, eloquence.

Their first sight of him drew forth trust, admiration, and hope from the Gamecocks and Swamp Foxes. Inwardly they bowed to Instructor Thomas Atkins, he, worthy of high regard. But how they knew, none could fathom.

Slowly, through their own senses, through faint impulses, they felt the otherworldly in Atkins. More than once, when they caught him in peripheral vision they saw his face shine. Once, for an instant, it flashed bright as the sun, and all saw. A slight thrill of the breath all the way to unprovoked joy rising in their hearts—signs they received of the workings of Atkins power.

Atkins' spirit comrades will help these Americans in battle.

Just as Tommy Atkins and his mates were new to war four years ago at Mons and Ypres, so are these South Carolina boys fresh to battle, full of fight, bravery, the will to win, and willing to die. The Lewis gun teams and all the Americans left behind the ways of home. They lived in tents and barns and stables and in the open.

In the last weeks of September, 1918—historians would later call it The One Hundred Days, or The Advance to Victory—these boys, these soldiers, were leading a new life, an ocean away from home, among ways of life they had never seen, a war that wore the body and stunned the senses, the mind, the imagination. The machine gunners saw destruction and misery, breathed the stench of life's raw elements, putrid decay and rot. They heard the guns and explosions, breathed burned gunpowder and explosives. The cooking was not their mothers'. They had to learn the British Army way of doing things.

Now, at the Battle of Bellicourt Tunnel angel warriors will prepare and help the Americans in one last great battle.

(I recommend that you now read the Cast of Characters 193-196)

Book I

LANCE CORPORAL THOMAS ATKINS ❖ 1

CHAPTER 1
The Last British Soldier Killed in the Great War:
Angel of Memory, Grief, and Tears

Nimy Bridge, Mons Canal
Mons, Belgium

November 11, 1918

On Monday, November 11th, before the "cease fire" sounded, the mighty successors of "the contemptible little army" were in Mons, a spot that was consecrated ground to them. By the most remarkable coincidence in history, the war on the British side ended where it began.

In the last week of August 1914, five British divisions retreated from Mons. In the first week of November 1918, five British armies marched back to Mons. It was the most tremendous recoil in history.

The new British soldiers wished to stand victorious in the Flemish colliery city (Mons) where their old Regular little Expeditionary Force of 86,000 men had opened the war against overwhelming odds.

"The War Illustrated" 23rd November, 1918, "Star of Mons in the Ascendant"

Edward Wright

Before All the Falderal

(In the words of Lance Corporal Tommy Atkins)

I was Private Thomas Atkins, later, Lance Corporal. Some think my name a pseudonym, not my real name. Others sing about Tommy Atkins, all the privates, our dedication, duty, and sacrifice. Yet others say I am the soldier the generals had in mind when they picked the name for the sample Army Registration Card. I am none of those. I am plain Tommy Atkins, son of Ezra Atkins, cobbler, and Margaret Atkins (nee Gilbertson), home at Woburn Buildings, my father's place of business. We lived behind Father's shop. Always the smell of leather, polishes, dyes, rubber, machine oil. Before I enrolled in the army, above us lived a Yeats fellow, a man of great renown, I was told. Never read a word of his, though. We've passed one another on rare occasions, a nod, a touch of the cap brim, a muffled greeting. My father cobbled several pair of his boots.

I came of age to enlist six months before the war began, time enough to train then ship out before all the falderal. Before angels fought beside us. They saved the B.E.F. from annihilation, saved the few of us in the early days of fighting. That was years ago. My two uncles, military men, my mother's brothers, convinced me there was a fair chance for a young man who stepped into line before the war began. For they knew that war was soon to come. I would stand for promotion better than those who came along after the storm broke. I thought I was headed for an office post like my uncles', not knowing how low I stood on the ladder of skill and aptitude.

I stepped forward, took the oath, received the King's shilling, greeting, thanks, and letter of appointment. Sign your name and you are Tommy Atkins to the Army thereafter, one of the thousands of pieces the generals move about so the King can have his way. Then six months of training and travail.

The moment training started, I could tell that I had made a dreadful mistake, so far from my element. Gone were the conveniences of life I was accustomed to. I knew nothing of the world. Little more than a schoolboy in the company of hard men, I was the butt of pranks, tricks, jokes, japes, and capers. Why, they had it in for me in ten minutes. Last in mess line, ignored, assigned the lowest, menial jobs.

But the Army said I was made of something. I could not bring igno-miny upon my family's name. I had the good sense to knuckle down. It wasn't easy, didn't appeal to my taste, didn't suit my nature. I made it through. I'd never be promoted on the strength of my qualifications. At the time I was too dim to realize it. What had my uncles been thinking? Me in charge over men of that sort? Once they saw the failure I was, and not wanting the family's names disgraced, my uncles must have pulled strings so that I would be lost to view.

Little by little the men eased up. Finally, they helped me along and said I was a good lad, but near an idiot and how did I ever get in the Army?

The Vickers occupied the backwater of the British Army. At the start of the war years ago it was thought of as only a weapons used for defense. Later, of course, it became valued as a potent offensive weapon. I was stuck on a Vickers team, what that little piece of hell turned out to be. None of high rank paid the weapon any attention. Maybe good for defense, and little good for that. Its clack and clatter and roar foretold a life of noise. Bullets fly so fast, they were invisible. Except for the destruction, the cas-ings flung about were the only sign that they had been fired.

Everyone on the Vickers team saw as soon as I came on that I was a creature made for mockery, a butt of jokes. Slight of build, short.

Talk I overheard about myself:

"He reminds me of a rabbit the gardener finds in his vegetables, brains with his hoe."

"Brains of a marrow. A natural talent for the role of a vegetable in school dramatics."

"Cheerful, he lacks the sense to know the world. Naïve."

"His face with all the features of a darning egg—pug nose, thin lips, chin lacking, expressionless, pale eyes."

"Hair? Flops about when it is dry. Plastered, sticks like wallpaper to his head."

"Ears something to behold—handles on a jug. Rheumy blue eyes, red-dish hair that glistens when it gets the pomade."

"Moping look."

"Too young to shave."

From what I overheard, my personality matched my face. I wouldn't know. I was not one to look within. And thus, I learned the world's opinion of me, or at least my chums'.

I began as a gear humper, scout, range taker. A Six—that is what I was—sixth on the team, the lowest position on the squad, but important even so. Everyone could fire the gun. Even me. I carried two boxes of ammunition, a rifle, and my kit. At first too much for a shrimp like me. My shoulders and back were always sore. I wasn't built for this kind of work.

A team was usually six. One fired, Two fed the ammunition, the rest carried the weapon, ammunition, spare parts. When we were in battle we lowly ones spotted, kept water in the canister to cool the gun. Jumped at orders. After what happened at the Nuns' Woods they must have taken pity on me. I jumped from Six to One. Not the usual route, but that's what happened.

In the Nuns' Woods

North of Menin Road

Four Miles from Ypres

11 November, 1914

The Germans attacked from three directions: north-east, east, and south-east. Nine days and nights we spent in the woods and nearby. Sometimes it was quiet, but often our side or theirs would be ordered to attack for no good reason, feign a night raid, a sniper catch some poor fool with his head sticking up. There were points that one side was keen to hold, the other equally keen to gain. The movement of our two guns was all within the range of the wood and surrounding farms and villages.

20 November, 1914

It had happened at Mons, at Le Cateau, everywhere, wherever we would turn and fight. In some places a platoon, a company, a battalion would march along and it was quiet as Sunday morning. At the same time the next village over, or a nearby neighborhood, or around the corner, or down the road, rifles and machine guns cough and sputter, a shell explode, a barrage would fall. Suddenly it was as if the gates of hell had burst open wherever the fighting was going on.

Soldiers say when your time is up, you're in for it. So it was for us.

I was hauling the canvas bucket from a brook. Our teams gave ourselves names to distinguish ourselves, to pump ourselves up. We were the

Ruffians. Our partners, the Victors. Our crossfire killed Germans when they tried to cut through the line we held. A scythe cutting hay comes to mind. I didn't have time to shout, "Run!" A bolt of brilliant light, a blast, a rain of hot steel. A second followed, a third. Cries of anguish. Curses. Alive one minute, dead or dying the next. Me, a tear in my tunic, a nick on my left shoulder. I dropped the water bucket, ran about, checked each man for signs of life. All gone.

No need for medics. Burial team was all.

Life still in him, but fading, was Carmichael, Gunner Three on the Vickers. The boy left the circus sideshow for a life in the Army. Killed. Left behind a life of melancholy when he was killed at Ypres. Thereafter he was confident, relaxed, sported a jaunty air. He made life in the Army nearly tolerable for the newly-enlisted Tommy Atkins four years ago.

I held his head up, rested it on my lap, so he could have some ease. We looked over the scene, stunned. The men were dead. At first, there were waves of light rising in summer heat. Then a golden mist, then a shimmering, like the tips of ripples on a ruffled pond. Each man became an orb of light, like Dease months ago. They hovered over us in the air. As if they spoke through a phonograph, voices remote and thin, they sang "For He's a Jolly Good Fellow." I heard one say, "Farewell, brother." "Carry on, Atkins." "Dease awaits us," Another said, "He is above. Calls with open arms." I swooned, but was awake. "Do us honor, Atkins," the sound now crackling like a worn recording, "Golden Arrow of God." Then, from my eyes pinpricks of golden light, shot forth golden arrows. The arrows became eagles flying straight into the distance, the future, bullets from my eyes, from the Vickers machine gun. My own flesh melted away. I was skeleton, yet standing, as if I did not need flesh or sinews or muscles. I saw the doom to come. Then I heard a mortal voice. Carmichael. His voice fading with each syllable, he said, "I see their souls rising. I join them." His dying words. Another brother gone. Like a swarm of golden bees spiraling off, his soul joined the others.

My brothers. My strength. Uncles mistook me. Parents, dull to any notion of me. What does a cobbler and his wife know of the world? Leather and last, nails, sinewy thread, wax, and polish. The Ruffians raised me, made me. Victors, too.

I would not abandon the gun, had to stick with it. Too heavy to carry myself. Too precious to leave. I enlisted soldiers coming by. Not to shoot, but carry the gun along. Keep it from the Germans, prevent being killed by my own Vickers. For surely they would turn it on us as I hurried off. Collected all the ammunition we could carry. In shock and grief I left, hoping the burial crew would take Christian care of my friends.

Not the End of the Ruffians and the Victors

Whenever I fought at a moment of need, the spirits of the Ruffians or Victors would appear, but in full bodily form, if you can imagine. Gabriel Jessop or Carrew Nancarew might help me repair the gun, hand me a part. Catchpole and Palmer might march along to the trenches, full kit, singing a London stage ditty, its verses replaced with ribald lyrics to lighten my heart, make me blush. "How's old Vicki holding up? Had to piss in the canister to keep her cool when there is no water about?" Catchpole might ask.

I answered, "You uncouth old fool. Besides, I am Gunner One now. Not my task."

Or at night under the glory and glare of tracer bullets, looking across No-Man's-Land at the Somme. At the Christmas Truce, December 24, 1914, the Victors and Ruffians, all eleven killed, filed onto the field, made up a proper football squad, played against a German team. For all I knew, the Germans might also have been departed dead playing.

The Victors broke out a case of brandy, the Ruffians, wine. We drank with the Germans, toasted St. George. The Germans raised their tin cups to St. Michael. Our hearts begged the saints to signal that we would not fire another shot, the war over, all to return home to families. We ate sausage spread with dark mustard spread on rye bread, pickles, and roasted potatoes. We served up plum pudding with hard sauce and mince pies. That night my angel brothers reverently carried the dead and tenderly moved the wounded to aid stations.

I awoke next morning to gunfire and bombardment. My heart, filled with joy and hope the night before–last night a heavenly miracle–shriveled to a walnut-hard center of grief and regret.

Since July at Passchendaele the battlefield had been raked with every known kind of armament. My crew and I arrived in muddy October. Every day the shrieks of the horribly wounded, the groans and cries of the dying, filling the interstices of quiet between the explosions of the bombs, the clatter of machine gun and rifle fire across No-Man's-Land. I was wounded, spent the night huddled in a cold muddy bunker. My dear Lieutenant Dease came to me. He told me that the "Golden Arrows of God" went about their duties, some escorting the souls of the fallen to the gates of Judgment and pleading for redemption for the souls of those who died sin-stained, curses in their dying mouths. Catchpole and Palmer entered the minds of those despondent and fearful, inspiring them with courage and hope. The rest, Hardy and Lang, Paul Carmichael, Sergeant Sanders, were perpetual mourners. Angel Lieutenant Dease tenderly tended my wounds. They healed at his ministering touch.

Marching Northwest into Belgium

October, 1918

Somewhere in the last weeks of October of 1918—military historians would refer to these as the One Hundred Days—we fought through places where I had fought four years before. After all I had been through, all the places I had been, all the fighting I had done, all I had seen and suffered, I would not have guessed that I would tread the same roads, fighting westward and north instead of east and south. Le Cateau, the Forest of Mormal again. Mons again. The same places again, but vastly different, mightily altered. Wreckage and destruction everywhere. In place of fields lush with the bounty of the earth, and freshly harvested fields, and centers of industry, mining—desolation. Crops harvested to feed the Germans. Coal, mined for Germany. Iron smelted into German rails and weapons and ammunition. No hearty natives and their smiling children. Now the dispirited, abused, insulted. The aged, the crippled, the ill, old women, emaciated widows and children. The fit men dead, in prison, war camps, or enslaved, working for the Germans. Devastation. The people barely survived on the little food the enemy allowed. The German occupation of four years drained the life from the people.

Then, splendid Mons again. Burned out shells of buildings on both sides of the Rue de Nimy. Years of rain and snow and heat and cold turned them into menacing skeletons, bones of the dead. City of St. George, of whose "Golden Arrow of God" I am one. His care in battle my shield. In the cold of winter, my warmth. In the heat of summer, my shade. How many I killed to his honor, I cannot count. The soldiers the bullets reach too far to make out. Bullets from many rifles, shells and shrapnel from artillery.

The twin guns–one died, one lived, at least in name. The Ruffians called their gun Hun-Killer, then it got killed. Victoria, Victory, Vicki, Vixen, variously named, long ago scrapped along with the dead Victors and Ruffians who served her. Thereafter, Atkins named every gun he served Victoria, Victory, Vicki, Vixen.

The war's end in sight. I felt it coming, heard it was on its way. Rumor. The German army falling to ruins. I had a good sense for it, having been in since the beginning. Something of an expert. Signs everywhere.

By now I was little more than a ghost of myself. Vicki, and me, Tommy Atkins, trudging toward victory. New cells replace old ones many times in our bodies over a lifetime. Though I am Tommy Atkins with all his memories, experiences, beliefs, not a shred of me is the Tommy Atkins that I began in jolly old, good year of our Lord, 1914. All the bully beef and plum jam and tea, rum, preserved meat, cheese, biscuit, tea, sugar and salt—that have passed through me and changed me. New atoms and molecules.

It is true for Vicki as well. No part of the gun original. A new barrel every twenty thousand rounds. Every part repaired till worn useless, finally replaced. Even the tripod base is new. I kept the original reciprocating key, worn and useless. Strung it on the chain about my neck with my identity number disk. Scratched the names of my original five brothers-in-arms with a steel stylus. Where they are I'll never know. But their names are here with me, close to my heart, graven in my memory as deeply as an inscription on a gravestone. I cannot count the number of gunners Two, Three, Four, Five, Six who fed Vickers thereafter. Dozens in the course of the war. Their names and faces, a blur.

The future lay before me. What to do? Stay in the army? Return to ordinary life? I would not know what to do. Prepared for no profession, no trade. I stink of blood and gore, death.

Me and the Vickers, Victoria, Vicki—Victorious. After Ypres in 1914 I was made Gunner One, later promoted to Lance Corporal. No promotion beyond that ever came. Any chance, though hinted at, lost in the miasma of bureaucracy. It didn't matter to me. I came to manhood in the war's first months. In the years since I came to something vastly different from the boy I had been. I had absorbed the spirits and personalities of those who had taken me in hand–the sarcasm and wit of William Catchpole and Ziggy Palmer, the common sense of Carrew Nancarrew, Paul Carmichael's intelligence, and the saintliness of my beloved Lieutenant, Maurice Dease. Qualities also of the Victors, Sergeant Sanders, the clever soldiers, Hardy and Lang, and the rest.

But now I was little more than a ghost.

Winters. Freezing in the trenches, benumbed with cold. Summers sweltering in the sun. The inescapable stench. My brain now seared with pictures from which it will never be free.

THE AMERICAN SOLDIERS ❖ 1

118TH INFANTRY REGIMENT

CHAPTER 2

Three Cousins Enlist

The Tradition of Military Service

Especially among families in the South whose ancestries go back to earlier days in America, there was a tradition of military service. It would be common for a young man in 1915 to have fathers, grandfathers, even great grandfathers, relatives, neighbors who fought in wars from the American Revolution through the Civil War. Accounts of exploits in the War of Northern Aggression stirred patriotic sentiments. Boys were enthralled by stories of grave, great battles. Tales of honor, bravery, gallantry, sacrifice, and valor were the substance of a Southern boy's life. It was the foundation of the culture—society, church, school, social institutions of every sort.

Elliot Joiner, Donald Barton, and Ezekiel Able, cousins—their great-grandfather fought in many a Civil War battle. Before him, ancestors fought in the War of 1812, and before that, the Revolution—Charleston and Cowpens. Veterans on their fathers' sides, too. For them soldiering was a duty, an honor, a tradition they carried on. Keep the tradition alive. Serve the family name. Honor the ancestors.

In 1914 there were still a quarter of a million veterans alive who had fought in the Confederate States Army. The cousins, and their whole generation, grew up amongst them. Enthralled by their stories.

In this they were typical Southerners, South Carolinians. It was nearly universal.

Those who came to America in later generations might not hold things this way.

Donald Barton Argues with His Father about Enlisting

(The First Cousin)

Donald Barton, Private
Sumter, South Carolina
July 25, 1917

Donald Barton's first name honored his mother's Scottish heritage. His father owned the rest of him.

Mr. James Barton brokered cotton, timber, and tobacco in Sumter, South Carolina, the county seat. Barton Freight Hauling profited mightily, and was at the heart of the town's wealth and power. Barton offices, warehouses, sheds stood along the firm's railroad siding. It carried produce and dry goods from Florida to New York City, the whole East Coast.

As much as he disliked his father—Donald thought of him as "Sir Sneering Barton," the tyrant—the young man resembled James Barton in temperament and outlook. Donald treated others the way his father treated everyone: Sneering condescension, perpetual smugness bespeaking a vast superiority. Everyone an antagonist unworthy of the match. Every conversation an argument he must win.

Added to this, Donald Barton had his own marks of personality. He believed people resented his good looks, his intelligence, position, his cleverness and charm. In everything people said to him he heard criticism and challenge, resentment and rebuke. Consequently, he "had it in" for everyone, everyone an adversary.

Yet he fought his father's domination. Donald realized if he enlisted in the National Guard as a private he would best and humiliate his father. James Barton never fought in a war. And his father would certainly want his son to be an officer, if he was going to join at all.

After dinner Donald asked to speak with his father. They went into Mr. Barton's study. "Sir, sit down and we can talk," said the rotund businessman, taking an easy chair.

"I prefer to stand," said Donald.

"As you prefer."

Even though the family's ancestors and their achievements meant little to him, Donald said, "Tomorrow I will enlist in the Guard. They will soon go to France to fight the Hun. I will add a link in the chain of our ancestors that leaves you out." He said, "Serving our country or cause, I am willing to make the greatest sacrifice, my life. You never defended the country or a cause."

"You can't deceive me. You don't do it for these reasons," said Mr. Barton. "You do it to vex me. To anger me. Your sarcastic tone profanes and belies the very words you speak. Your mother will weep when you are gone, but not me." He paused in thought. When he spoke, his tone was soft, almost pleading. "But if you enlist, at least enlist as an officer." He stepped toward the telephone on his desk. "I will arrange it. The Army needs officers. At least bring the family name to the fore."

Maliciously taunting, Donald said, "No. I will not. I will enlist as a common soldier. Your grandfather, your father, began as privates and rose in the ranks. I would refuse a commission."

James Barton retorted, "We have already risen in the ranks, as you say. Decline the privilege and you disgrace the name. Why bury yourself it in the muck of the ranks?"

His son shot back, "Name? What's in a name, Shakespeare asked? Call a turnip a watermelon, it's still a turnip. And rank. Private. General. Stars on the shoulder is the only difference. Except for the family name, I am nothing more than a lucky bastard, one step away from being a nobody, a merchant like you." Adding to his retort, his temper rising, Donald said, "And patriotism!" Booming voice: "My nation!" A loud whisper: "Right or wrong." Then, "The same for the Germans as for us." His voice now that of a typical Southern senator. "We are the ones who count. We wield the triumphal sword of God." In his own angry voice, "Patriotic guff. I've heard this all my life. Everyone in the South feeds at the same dish of grits and ancestor worship. We're like the Chinese. The difference: they fill up on rice. God, grits, and grandsons. That's your history and theology. I'm not enlisting for that, either. I just want to throw it in your bulldog face, like a wet cow turd."

Mr. Barton's face reddened, his anger just short of rage. "You're a damned fool. Look what I raised. A damn fool. You don't believe anything. Listen to me, you insolent pup. Ancestry is the cornerstone of our culture. Generation to generation. Who we come from. We act based on what they would do under the circumstances. Same with the Bible and religion. We undertake obligations in the hope that our ancestors would approve. I'm sorry I never got to serve. War purifies and sanctifies. Of all our rites and ceremonies, it is the foundation of virtue and worship and worth."

All the while, Donald smirked, taking this all in for the thousandth time. He had raised the point about which James Barton was ashamed.

Donald sneered and dug the blade deeper. "A fine speech, senator. Pure slops you could feed to the pigs. Ceremonies? War a ceremony? Are you insane? Salute the flag, say a prayer. Those are ceremonies. War is no ceremony."

His own anger rising, Mr. Barton growled, "You are my life's biggest disappointment. You will break your mother's heart."

The son all but spat when he said, "Don't give me my mother's broken heart, you bag of wind."

Father: "And it breaks my heart even to your blood and death."

Donald: "Not my blood and death! It won't come to that. Our ancestors lived to tell their stories of bravery and glory. I will live and tell what I did and saw."

The senior Barton said, his fist pounding the table, "You insult me, the family, our country." Pointing to the office door, like a creature from melodrama, he said, "Get out of my house. Get you gone!"

And Donald Barton packed and left, his parents never to see him again.

Young Barton was engaged to Dorothea Cline, daughter of tobacco and produce broker Elmer Cline, his father's competitor, in Manning, twenty-five miles to the south. They planned to marry the next December. It was now July 25, 1917. The President called the National Guard into federal service. Barton enlisted two days later. Miss Dorothea Cline, not particularly attractive, not a social figure, unaccomplished in any art. Mr. Cline, his father in-law to-be, would gladly take him into the business. Donald planned to abandon his father and prosper another man. Revenge. Donald offered to marry before he went off for training two weeks later. Mr. Cline declined the offer.

Father and Son Converse: The Able Men

(The Second Cousin)

Private Ezekiel Able

(In his own words)

Two sisters came along before me. My father was twenty-nine when I was born in 1896, his only son. Here I am, inscribing my name in the book of honor, Ezekiel Able. None of my father's brothers survived to marriage-able age so I am the only one able—funny word—to carry on the family name. There are other Ables, but we are not related. The Able blood will live on through my sisters, but if I don't come back from the war the family name will perish. And the business, too. Able's Naval Stores.

Like every boy raised in the South, I grew up on family stories of comradeship, noble purpose, bravery. It inspired us. With the prospect of war here was another occasion for noble purpose, bravery, to test our manhood.

My father called me into his office. I knew what he would say, and what I would reply. I was well rehearsed.

We had already talked about my desire to marry Margaret Dixon. We had attended school and Sunday school together since childhood. Our families knew each other through church and civil organizations. My father said, "Ezekiel"—ordinarily he calls me Zeke—"If I'm not mistaken, you want to know if Mr. Dixon would entertain a visit from you." My father did not know I had made up my mind to enlist.

I answered, "I was, but not now, Father. I am going to enlist. I will not marry before I leave. I might die or be maimed for life."

"Enlist? Why enlist?" Father asked.

I answered. "I've thought about it long before I decided. But decide I did. You read the newspapers and magazines. Anyone can see that we will go to war."

"It's clear to me, too. But need you enlist right now?" he asked. "A year from now the Army will still need you. The war will not end quickly, so I have been told."

Then he expressed his heart's desire. "I want you to marry and have a son. I'm sure God will bless you with a fine one. I want the promise of another generation bearing the family name."

"Bless you with a grandson. Ancestor to descendent." I clasped my father's shoulder, said, "I hope I can, but after the war."

He said, "There is no reason to argue. As they say, our country calls. The civilized world calls. My ancestors fought for their causes. The family name inscribed in the church roles, the family Bible with our genealogy written in brown ink."

I said, "My country calls and I will go."

Father was disappointed, saddened, but he knew I was right.

"Please tell Mr. Dixon. Should I meet with Miss Dixon and tell her what I've decided?" I asked. "For all I know, it might be her place to break our engagement."

"I will consult with your mother," my father said. "Maybe a letter. Avoid the sadness of parting."

"You mean awkwardness of it?" I replied. "What we would have to say to each other?"

"That too, I'm afraid."

I had no trouble enlisting. My father had connections with our congressman and senators through business and civic affairs. But I didn't need any of that. I showed up at the armory and signed up. I knew the recruiter. We were buddies from way back.

Easy as that.

Europe had been at it for nearly two years.

The next week I marched off to training.

The Cousins in Training

(The Third Cousin)
Private Elliot Joiner

Twenty years of age,
farm boy
(Camp Sevier, Spartanburg, South Carolina)
July 31, 1917

I knew Ezekiel and Donald. My mother, sister to their mothers, married into a not well-to-do family, my father a simple farmer with no money, little land, and that, poor. Cotton, mostly. I was not schooled nearly as well as they were, left school in the fifth grade. I knew my cousins mostly by word of mouth, family accounts. From what I heard, Donald seemed a bit wild, a bit off his rocker. Good report on Zeke. That's what we called him—Zeke, not Ezekiel. I found my way into the 118th Regiment, mule driver and wagoner. Good with livestock, mules, and farm horses, my service of great value to the Army, I'm told.

Unlike everyone else, Cousin Barton despised Zeke. Cousin Able, friendly, a kind word. Always good for a "hey, y'all" and a smile. Looked you in the eye when he talked with you. Didn't mind being the butt of a joke. He'll laugh along. On every examination in training his score was always among the highest. He was always ready to help a guy learn. All this inflamed Barton's hatred.

Hardly anyone liked Donald. There was nothing about him to like. At Camp Sevier we ran into each other once in a while. At Sevier he attracted a few toadies, flunkies, guys who cheered on his taunts and bullying.

Donald taunted Zeke, but Zeke paid it no attention which made Barton angry. I could tell he was frustrated to the point that he would come after Zeke and beat him up.

I talked to Barton. "You better straighten out right now or you'll end up in stockade and kicked out of the Army."

"Who the hell do you think you are, you sack of pig manure?" That was the way he talked, even to a cousin.

It didn't stop me. "Zeke done nothing to you. You think you can bully him into being afraid of you? Think you can get a rise out of him? Save your threats for someone you might scare."

Provoked he turned his hands into fists. I said, "What the hell's wrong with you?"

"Mind your own damn business."

"This is my business. You're a disgrace to the family. You should be ashamed of yourself. I don't want anyone to know I'm related to you. I'm glad we have different last names."

His parting words: "You think I want anyone to know that you're my cousin, you mule shit. Like I said, mind your own damn business. Keep your nose out of this if you don't want it bloodied."

I walked right past him, brushed his sleeve hard enough with mine, I came that close. He knew what it meant. The coward didn't do anything.

Privates Able and Jenks Braddock Meet Again

Ezekiel Able and Jenks Braddock met when they were assigned to units at Camp Sevier. Out of mutual respect for the work they did they formed a bond of friendship. While they cleaned their rifles they talked every day.

Before he enlisted in the National Guard, Jenks Braddock worked as a tapper for Able's father's company. The senior Mr. Able not venturing into the forests where his workers gathered pine resin to distill into turpentine, Braddock and he had never met.

"Haven't I seen you before? Your face looks familiar," Braddock said to the young Able.

"We tapped resin together for a while."

"I thought you looked familiar. My name's Jenks Braddock. What's yours?"

"I'm Ezekiel Able."

"Not related to the big boss, are you?"

"I'm his son."

"I'll be damned. I didn't know you were Mr. Able's son. Never knew he had one. Never thought about it. If he had one, I would figure he would be living the life of ease. What the hell are you doing here? When I knew you, you were—what was your name?"

"Clopton Havers."

"Yeah. I remember now. Clopton. None of us ever heard the name Clopton before. Strange as they come."

"My father gave me a made-up name for work. Clopton Havers was his boyhood friend. Sixteen years old. Killed in a sawmill. Logs rolled free and crushed him. My father always blamed himself for his friend's death. I don't know why. I thought the name bad luck. The boy met a tragic end. Even the camp boss didn't know I was the big boss's son. No one knew."

"But you were just a tapper. How come?"

"My father made me learn the business from the bottom up. That's how he started in it himself. He said if I grew up with the privileges of wealth I wouldn't amount to anything. He'd seen it many times. So had I, to tell the truth. That wouldn't happen to a son of his. I did the lowest jobs along with the Negroes. I needed to work, work that strained the muscles, wore the body out. Sweat. Exhausting toil. I needed to do tapper's job in the heat of summer. Even scraped rosin. Like you, I was covered in sap and rosin. I carried the heavy buckets. Worked at the boiler. Worked by the furnace distilling turpentine. He said I needed to hear what workers said about work, the boss, their hard lives. I wasn't spying on them. He already knew what they thought. If I didn't do all that, he knew I would have no reason to take into account the way they saw things when I became boss. Maybe that's why I enlisted as a private. I think I see things more the way the enlisted men, the draftees, the NCOs do, than the officers.

Jenks Braddock said the obvious. "You were in the money. What ever brought you away from the loot and the easy life?"

"That's what my father wants to know. It makes no sense to him. But it does to me."

"You're an unusual case," Braddock said. "Most guys like you would enlist as officers." Then, "Done with the oil? Pass it to me."

"My father came around though. Saw it my way. I said few men believe it, but I think you do. I am no better a man than the men who tap our trees or work the stills. Many of them are going to the war. I will be among them. Comrades."

"Maybe giving up his only son in sacrifice for the death he blames himself for," said Braddock.

"That may be part of it," Zeke said. "I don't know. My father told me, 'The business needs you. My agents and salesmen, bookkeepers, even tappers are leaving. Who will run the business? But I know you must go. So go with my hope for your safe return.'"

Braddock said, "Dummy, don't look down the barrel. If an instructor sees you do that, you'll be in for it. They don't like soldiers looking down rifle barrels. A waste for a soldier to kill himself looking down the barrel of his own rifle. Enough will die anyway. Besides, I need the pull-through since you're done with it."

The two talked. Able hoped he'd be assigned far away from his nasty cousin. To his friend Braddock he said, "With thirteen companies, better than ten to one odds. Pretty good chance we'll end up in different ones. But I hope you and I can stick together." In spite of the odds, Able and Jenks Braddock were assigned to Company "M", along with Barton.

The likelihood of the cousins being given different assignments was still high. Different aptitudes, test scores, instructors' reports, the company having many different needs. In the infantry Able could be an ordinary rifleman, a hand bomber, a rifle grenadier, on an automatic rifle. He could be assigned to a machine gun section. But when they got to France and training both were made lead gunners for Lewis machine guns and in class and field practice together.

CHAPTER 3

William Spears and *The Master Book of Dreams*

Spears' Grandmother

When Private Spears was embarking for Camp Sevier from the Ye-massee train station, his grandmother pressed a Bible, a prayer cloth, and a copy of the pamphlet *The Master Book of Dreams* into his hands. Three inches wide by five long. Its cover thin. On the train he remembered her words. "Billy, God uses us to help and heal others. God, or Jesus, or an apostle or saint tells me what to do. I'm a vessel, a servant." She took his hand, kissed it. "Let these books guide you. Read your Bible. If God brings you home safely and if I live so long, I will teach you to serve the Lord. Blessings, grandson. God first, then your country."

He carried the little book in his kit. He had often consulted it and found the meaning to dreams guided him to wise choices and decisions, wisdom and insight, answers to hard questions.

At Camp Sevier the Lewis Gun Team Reads in the Book

Jenks Braddock spoke up. "I'm from the Piedmont where people are sensible and sane. You Low Country folk, with your ghosts and goblins. I think your beliefs rise up from the bad air there. Miasma from the swamps and marshes."

"Miasma? What's that? What are you talking about?" Spears was used to being ridiculed about his beliefs, but it irritated him nonetheless. "My grandmother and her mother, and our people back to antiquity know these things. Mamaw taught me how all things are connected."

Braddock said, "At the coast is swamp glow. I've seen it myself. Folks think they see ghosts and wraiths in mist and fog. Cloud lightning. Maybe that's when they come out. I don't know."

"That ain't how it is. Mamaw sees the Other World. She works with yerbs, incantations. Chants, she calls them. She's a healer. She has the gift of vision. She gave me this," he said, bringing a booklet out of his kit. Exasperated, he said, "*The Book of Dreams*. Mamaw swears by it. Not swears like in religion. She trusts it. So do I. She puts people's minds at peace. She trained me in remembering my dreams. I see things in them. The book tells what the dreams mean."

"Like our training manuals?" said Braddock.

"Now you're getting it. It takes training and practice."

His friend Braddock took it, thumbed through. ''The Devil's book."

Private Hans Schmidt, gunner assistant, a Swamp Fox, said, "Can I look at it?" He flipped through the pages. "No table of contents? No index? How do you find what you are looking for?"

"It's alphabetical." Spears said, "What's important in the dream—I study what it means." He turned the pages. "It's tricky. Sometimes I dream about one object and the book says it means the opposite. Sometimes it means what I expect. Sometimes the meaning is completely unexpected. It's inspired, my mamaw says. It doesn't follow logic."

Braddock asked, "Can I see it again?" He turned to the last page, read in silence then said, "Gee whiz. Let me read some." Aloud, in halting speech he read aloud.

> Z. Zebra Seeing one: disappointment in something you have waited for a long time. Riding one: travel.
> Zeppelin: Your ambitions are beyond your reach.

This one must be recently added, unless the Master knew about the zeppelin before it was invented.

> Zigzagging: you must be alert and firm minded so that you can deal with things rapidly.
> Zinc: You will build a new life on a firm foundation.
> Zipper: You are impatient and want everything to work smoothly and quickly.
> Zodiac: A terrific storm or widespread disturbance.
> Zombie: You will be haunted by a horror story.

> Zoo: Prosperity, and a romance starting with
> a chance meeting, perhaps at a zoo.
> Zulu: Danger has been threatening your hap-
> piness, but you will be released.

Who dreams about a Zulu?" Jenks Braddock shook his head in disgust. "Who the hell ever dreams about any of these things? Did any of you ever dream about a zipper, a zombie, or a zoo?"

Schmidt joked, "If you do, you'll know what it means," and laughed at his own humor. Then he read:

> Zwieback: You are worrying over your
> health, but this will be a temporary condition,
> if you take care."

Braddock shook his head, concluded, "This is pure foolishness. I believe some faker or fool must have written it."

Even so, slowly, a few of the gunners came to Spears and in private complaining about terrifying dreams and nightmares and asking what they meant.

BATTLE PLANS ❖   1

CHAPTER 4

The Hindenburg Line and the New Doctrine Governing Offense and Defense

The Siegfried Line affords the most favorable conditions for a stubborn defense by a minimum garrison. It is therefore adapted to the requirements of obstinate close combat.

Grundsatze für die Führung in der Abwehrschlacht (*The Conduct of the Defensive Battle in Position Warfare*)
Concluding remarks of the orders
For the Spring Offensive, 1918

Permanent Trenches for All

After the first battle of the Marne—an important river in northern France—in September, 1914, the Huns built permanent trenches with dugouts deep in the ground, turning the war from mobile to static. Then the Allies did the same, dug in and entrenched. By the time the digging was finished, the trenches ran four hundred-fifty miles from Calais, France on the English Channel to Alsace, at the Swiss border. The battle lines wound their way across the countryside from the sand dunes and flat, reclaimed sea level land on the Belgian coast in the north, to the mountain peaks at 4,500 feet above sea level in the Vosges mountain range at its southern end. Laid end-to-end, the systems of trenches would run 25,000 miles— 12,000 occupied by the Allies, and 13,000 by Germany. The Western Front remained that way until the German Spring Offensive of March, 1918.

From First Ypres, in October, 1914 until the end of 1916 and the catastrophe of the Somme the armies in the west fired from the front line trench, massing soldiers to repel the enemy crossing No-Man's-Land. Their enemies bombed and machine-gunned the Germans. The generals saw multitudes killed, masses wounded in the trenches. Germany had few conscripts to take their places. They needed to abandon the tactic of static trench warfare.

Then after four years of pursuing the same failed strategies and tactics, Russia declared a ceasefire in the last month of 1917. The Bolshevik government of the new Soviet Russia signed the Treaty of Brest-Letovsk with Germany on March 3, 1918. With Russia out of the war and German troops now free to fight on the Western Front, and with fresh soldiers arrived from the United States, ingenious ideas, devices, and strategies sprang to life in the minds of planners and staffs on both sides.

The German central command devised new tactical and strategic doctrines to carry out mobile war when, up to then, the war had been trenches and trench fighting. Taking the battle to the enemy, the plan brought the soldiers out of the trenches, spread them over the battlefield, hid them in concrete pillboxes, to carry on open warfare.

The Hindenburg Line and the New Doctrine

The Imperial Army's new doctrine claimed that an attacking force—French, British, Americans, anyone—would "fight itself to a standstill and use up its resources while the defenders conserve their strength." Thus would the German Army wear the Allies down, bringing either victory or an armistice on terms good for Germany.

Both sides abandoned the fruitless frontal attacks and adopted the strategy the Germans developed, tested, and used the year before. Instead of filling the front line trench with soldiers and firing from there, which they knew Allied artillery would bomb, the Germans left it nearly empty. The main force would fight from the second line and in zones in front of it and behind. There were four advantages to the strategy. Now, enemy shells would fall on empty trenches, wasting valuable ammunition. Since bombs dig craters, Allied shelling would create obstacles. The allies' soldiers would have to watch the ground, pick their way around, slowing their advance. The enemy's shelling makes them better targets. And, a fifth advantage: German soldiers would be alive and fresh to fight when the allied soldiers would cross the first line.

Now the Germans would fight in small, scattered groups, moving in any direction in an instant, using the land as an element of defense. This served defense, offense, counter-attack. When the Allies began an artillery barrage the German troops would move to anywhere on the battlefield where enemy shells were not falling, preferably advancing onto No-Man's-Land. So it was at Bellicourt Tunnel.

Simple tricks like this called for radical thinking, and made a great difference.

To support these changes command shifted to the squad or platoon, now the basic tactical unit, instead of from the battalion. If the enemy penetrated the outpost line, these small, forward crews would counterattack immediately, not having to wait for orders from above. They were independent, led by lieutenants and sergeants.

Then when the British, or Australians, or whoever the enemy was, overran the second line, as they might well do, German artillery would shower them with shrapnel and high explosive shells, killing many of the remnant and making it impossible for reinforcements to reach them. Machine-gun posts and field artillery would wipe out any who made their way across the battle zone. Without doubt, a small number. Then, German artillery would unleash a counterattack.

The German plan for attack also changed. Operation *Michael,* the first major battle of the *Kaiserschlacht,* the Kaiser's Battle, employed the changes.

Instead of the main purpose of an attack being to kill the enemy, it was to destroy the means of making war. The best German soldiers, trained as storm troopers—an innovation—would rush forward, pass through the Allied defenses' now weakened points, and destroy or capture enemy headquarters, communication, command, and transportation centers, artillery emplacements, and ammunition and supply dumps.

Then, infantry armed with rifles, light machine guns, mortars, and flamethrowers—*Flammenwerfer*—would attack Allied strongpoints which the shock troops had passed by.

Finally, the less skilled and least able would follow, mopping up as they went.

In the first and main attack the storm troopers' rapid advance worked well. But speed and ruthlessness being more important than care and safety, many more were killed or wounded than otherwise would have happened. Mopping up worked poorly. The soldiers who followed were ineptly led, their best officers now fighting as storm troopers. The battle *Mi-*

chael raged for fourteen days until the Germans ran out of food and supplies. The operation petered out, as had so many before.

Even so, the Germans had come extremely close to victory. The British and the French were fortunate to withstand the massive attack. If Germany had won the battle, they would have won the war. Schmidt said, "Aw, nuts."

In January 1917 infantry commanders began training in how to apply the new doctrine. Manuals went into great detail, covering a multitude of contingencies and circumstances.

The Allied Armies Changed Doctrine, Too

When Supreme Allied Commander General Foch brought the Allied Armies under unified command and the commanders of the Allied Armies saw the new German system in operation in 1917, they applied what the Germans taught them to plan the Great Advance. New weapons, new tools and techniques to surprise the Germans made their way into training and onto the battlefield, something the opponent had no ready defense for.

Even this late in the war, each branch of the Allied services—artillery, infantry, tanks, air corps—operated almost independently. Under the new Allied plans, instead of artillery attacks with no infantry, or infantry with no artillery, or artillery without machine guns, tanks with no infantry, and so on, the services would fight together. At Le Hamel Lieutenant General John Monash, commander of the Australian Corps and a brilliant military strategist, used combined arms tactics. The infantry, artillery, armor, and aeroplanes, and the new Mark V tank attacked together.

Most importantly, until now each national army—the Belgians, the French the British, even the Commonwealth countries, and now the Americans—carried on its own war against Germany. From now on the Armies would fight as one Army.

Now, simple ideas, small changes, improved the Allies' abilities. For the first time, before the battle of Le Hamel Australian infantry and tanks trained and lived together. Now colored markings on the tanks' sides told the infantry which tank to follow. Carrying as much as a thousand soldiers could, for the first time the RAF dropped medical supplies and rifle ammunition by parachute to the advancing troops. Supply tanks hauled stores swiftly to the troops as they advanced. For the first time officers used pigeons, Lucas lamps, and wireless to communicate with command. These changes, combined, contributed to the victory.

Up until this point in the war the British began battles shelling trenches for hours, even days, before sending the infantry across No-Man's-Land. The idea was that the bombardment would kill or wound many Huns in the trenches and destroy barbed wire and the trenches, too. This was rarely what happened. First, the bombardment told the Germans an attack was coming. And the rooms—much more than simple dugouts—hid the Germans twenty feet below the ground, kept them safe from the shelling. So, when the British infantry attacked, the Germans climbed the steps from the dugouts, mounted the fire steps, and rifles and mortars and grenades greeted the enemy. Beginning with the battles of Le Hamel and Amiens the Allies began the fight without bombardment, caught the Germans unprepared.

In these battles all branches attacked at once.

LANCE CORPORAL THOMAS ATKINS ❖ 2

CHAPTER 5

The Three British Instructors

May, 1918
(Four Days After the Division landed in France)

The Regiment boarded railway boxcars in Calais. They rode the "forty-and-eight" *Quarante ou huit,* written 40/8 on the side of the boxcar, good to carry forty soldiers or eight horses. The boxcars they rode had carried both. The familiar, pleasant smell of horse was strong.

The British Army Instructors
Get Ready to Train the 118th Regiment

At Recques in France, their first training camp in Europe, the Gamecocks and the Swamp Foxes met their instructors, Sergeants Ballwin, Brentwood, and Corporal Atkins.

Sergeants Harold Ballwin and George Brentwood grew up together, the same road, same school, same church. They enlisted—"pals"—in 1916. Still alive and wanting to fight. Tommy Atkins added them to his trainers' cadre. All strapping, splendid British soldiers. Each had been wounded, unfit to serve at the front. None talked about his suffering. Ballwin's face was scarred, shrapnel. The wounds that disabled Brentwood were not visible. Brentwood's left hand, mangled beyond repair. Atkins walked with a slight limp. Strangely enough, he accidently shot himself in the foot with his sidearm. And the trouble it got him in. Almost court martialed, being suspected of wounding himself to get home to Blighty.

Each of these soldiers would have rather been with his unit in the field than having to train these dullards.

In the mess tent, drinking tea, the instructors talked about what the Americans knew, what they thought the Americans would be like as they laid out the course of study and practice the Doughboys would endure.

Said Sergeant Ballwin, "America did nothing to get them ready to fight."

Brentwood grunted. "Ignorant of the art of war."

Ballwin: "What they did in Texas will do them no good here." He went on. "No good at all, I'm sorry to say. That Mexican War of theirs was a cowboy fantasy. From what I hear the Regular Army soldiers tramped around the desert trying to catch this Pancho Villa, chased him for nearly a year. Nothing came of it. And the so-called soldiers who we're to train stayed behind in Texas. Pershing didn't want them anywhere near the Regular Army."

Brentwood took up the theme. "Ballwin, who knows what they did there? Lived like sports, a lark. A good time was had by all."

"Get on with it, for God's sake. My tea's already gone cold." said Atkins.

But Ballwin just went on. "I went to America in 1910 to find a cousin sent away years ago, a 'remittance man.' He was out west. I got off the ship in New York City and stayed three days. It was hoodlums and gangsters I was afraid of, pistols and revolvers. A policeman stopped me. 'Say, I been watching you run past doorways and building entrances, peek around corners. What's all this duckin' and divin'?' I told him New York is full of criminals. I'm looking out for them."

" 'Yeah, there's criminals,' the policeman said. 'The city's big. There ain't that many of 'em.' He didn't talk like an educated man. 'You'd have to be in the right neighborhood to run into them. Even then, they ain't on the street shooting everybody who passes by. There's more of 'em in the movies than in real life.' "

Atkins asked, "What's your point? Get on with it."

"I'm getting to it," said Sergeant Ballwin.

"Please," Atkins said. "We've important matters to talk about."

Sergeant Ballwin was not ready to move on. "Excuse me. Can you spare a drop of rum for the tea? My throat's dry."

Atkins poured a splash. "Any for any?" They all took a spot. "Now get on with it, for God's sake," Atkins said. "You got me using the Lord's name in vain."

Harold Ballwin said, "All right. I worried that bandits and gunslingers or Indians with bows and arrows would kill me. When I got off the train in Cody, Wyoming I expected every man to have a holster hanging from his belt and shouldering a rifle. I stayed away from the middle of the street, walked close to the buildings, didn't look anyone in the eye. The men wore cowboy hats, all right, and point toe boots."

"Damn it, what's your point? Do you have one? We have work to do," echoed Brentwood.

"I'm getting to it. My point is, I thought I knew what to expect, but nothing was the way I expected. The cinema is different from the way things really are. My point is these Americans might turn out different than what we expect," said Ballwin. "We don't really know what these boys will be like. We'll soon find out. Hope for the best. Anyway, we have to train them."

Atkins: "All that, to tell us what we already know. My God. When you lecture better stick to the lecture text. You'll drive them nuts with your drivel."

The two sergeants were ready to chuckle at their own banter when Atkins said, "They damn well better understand. And learn. Their lives depend on it."

Said Ballwin, "So do ours."

"You don't know it, but so does the war," said Atkins.

And Brentwood and Ballwin had the same thought. St. George. Atkins alive after being dead. He knew something. But they were mum.

At first it was hard for the instructors to distinguish one Southerner from another. They wore the same uniform and the hats obscured their faces. But even with heads bare there was almost a family resemblance. Similar features, about equal in height—though taller than the English and French and Germans. Their American faces had not yet taken on individual character. No lines of worry, fear, or grief yet creased their brows. These would appear in the next several months. Soon the instructors got to know them.

And their speech. It sounded like grunts and growls and moans and monotones with no pause separating one word from another. It took a while to understand them. The same held true for the Americans. They knew the English spoke the same language they did, but the sounds did not add up to words that they could make out. In time each side could understand the other.

Corporal Atkins' Teaches about the Lewis Machine Gun

Corporal Atkins began. "I grew up on the Vickers machine gun. Four years its Gunner One. Now I'm with you on the Lewis automatic machine gun."

He got right to it. "Serve the gun. Help it do its work. It's your salvation. You will learn everything about the gun, every part, name, and function. We will teach you how to kill the Hun." He removed the gun from its leather case, pointed to each part. "Forty-seven cartridges, top mounted circular pan magazine. Bullets laid in by hand. Blade and tangent sight for down-range accuracy. Bipod support for the barrel."

The gun's dimensions and capabilities. "Length: fifty inches, barrel, twenty-six. Weight: Twenty-eight pounds, half as much as a Vickers, more portable. Muzzle velocity: half a mile a second. Effective firing range: half a mile. Maximum firing range: two miles. Rate of fire: six hundred rounds a minute. Ten a second! Continuously fire—the air-cooled Lewis could go through six canisters in a minute. But this is not how you fire. The gun case stores cleaning materials, oil, spare parts. No special tools or equipment needed."

He was quiet for a long moment, glared at each man. "Do you remember what I just said? You damn well better. What you know and what you don't know is sometimes the difference between life and death." And went on. "You damn well better listen, or you'll miss something important and find yourself dead on the battlefield. Worse, your pals, dead and wounded, because you weren't listening." Then, back to the gun.

"Loaded, ready in an instant. Fires in any direction from any position, from any kind of mount, rest, or cover. A foot soldier can fire the gun from any firing-point infantry can reach. But the Lewis tends to jam. You need to learn quick repair."

He passed the gun around. "Heavy for a light gun, light for a heavy one."

"Now, if you're ready, gentlemen. Each member of the section will carry three hundred bullets for the Lewis, seventeen pounds. A drum magazine weighs two. Half a dozen in a canister. Another twelve pounds to lug. Plus one hundred rifle bullets: six pounds more. Double that for the steel clips. You will be burdened."

They learned every part by heart, took the gun apart and put it back together. Finally, they did it blindfolded.

He looked over the group. "You are able men, strong, young, and full of fight. This will prepare you."

Then, "Each team six soldiers. The gunner carries the Lewis ready to fire in a case like this one. Assistant carries a leather case with six loaded magazines. The others advance, observe the field, and load magazines when you are on the enemy. As few as two, one to fire, one to carry and load the bullets can operate the gun, if that's all you have. Fritz calls the gun the Belgian Rattlesnake."

Tommy Atkins and the others taught how to fight as a team. Everyone became interchangeable parts of the section.

In the Classroom Brentwood's Specialty was Trenches

On a slate board Sergeant George Brentwood drew a castle battlement, its squared openings at the top for the archers. He said, "Most trenches are made this way, too, but not to defend a castle. The trench is crenulated or zigzags every several yards." Then he drew two parallel lines and an arrow down the middle. "You can work out what explosions along a straight line would do. Kill and maim many."

Then he pulled down a trench map, pointed with his stick.

Grumbled Donald Barton, "A map, for God's sake. At least we have something to look at." Sarcasm. "Listening to this blockhead. . . ." His voice trained off in disgust.

The instructor acted like he did not hear the comment. "You can see the differences right away. A bomb explodes in a trench. The crenulations block the explosion. Only those within a few yards can be hit. See?"

Barton yawned and stretched, showed off his boredom. But Brentwood and the other instructors observed Barton, noted what they saw. Sergeant Brentwood said, "Trenches run in all directions—spurs, isolated strips, taking advantage of features of the land, concealment, elevation, surprise. Some stretches need more, some less. Rivers, canals, valleys, ravines, cliffs, ridges, escarpments, mountains, forests, swamps. Nature does the job there."

"You'll work in the training trenches. You have no idea how much digging you'll do. Almost every day, even when you get to the Front. Maybe you thought the digging you did in camp was just to keep you busy. No. You'll go from blisters to calluses. Some call you Doughboys. The Australians are Diggers. Figure it out. They know digging, all right. So will you."

The Americans found the instructors' humor insipid, their manner stiff. Muttered Barton, "At least the drill sergeants at home cussed when they were mad. These guys just keep talking. If he don't liven things up I'll die of boredom. The other trainers just as bad."

After the lesson Otis Mankins, the Gamecock who totes ammunition, spoke up. "I know what zigzag is, but that other word? Cremated? It means burning a corpse. What does it have to do with trenches?"

Jenks Braddock asked Gunner Assistant Spears, "William, is he the village idiot?"

William Spears said, "I do think so." Then to Otis, "You saw what the instructor drew on the board?"

"I saw it, but I don't know what it means."

Braddock scratched the same design in the dirt with his boot. "Spears, you explain."

Private Spears said, "Crenulated. Crenulated. Crenulations. See?"

"Not really," pleaded Mankins. "I know what cremated means, but not this other word."

"Cremated will do you no good." Exasperated, Spears said, "You'll find out in the trenches."

"I thought you'd help," Mankins said, discouraged.

The boy from St. Helena took pity on Mankins. "Well, we tried. You're beyond hope. Don't bother us. We've got to study the subject ourselves." And they trudged back to their tent.

Week after week the Infantry's Lewis gun teams spent the day the same way. Lectures every morning, field practice in the afternoon, study at night. So it was, day after day, day after day. Slowly, they were getting the idea of what fighting in war called for.

Ballwin on Barbed Wire: A Primitive Tool in Today's War

Before he delivered a memorized talk, Sergeant Ballwin made an attempt at humor. "Barbed wire came from America. You 'folks', as you call yourselves, invented it. So far, it's your country's biggest contribution to the war. Barbed wire does wonderful work. Keeps the cows in." He paused for laughter that didn't come. Then, "Primitive tool, but not a primitive weapon in this industrial war. Day and night factories in Germany, England, and France spin barbed wire."

On the bench in front of each trainee, a yard's length of barbed wire. The men do not touch them until ordered. Ballwin said, "Every strand cut from Hun lines at some battlefield. Hun barbed wire. Hold it. Look it over. Pass them around. Different types. Different purposes. You can tell what they were made for. Touch the points. Some pierce. Some slice. Catch, snag, snare. Be careful. Don't let the Hun's weapon wound you here in the classroom." No one realized this was another little joke.

Then Ballwin turned on a projector, half-dozen slides showing the ways armies use wire and stakes. "Barbed wire is your enemy." Next picture: thick fields of it. "It forms a blockade. Like a river or mountain. In your case, it will be a canal you can't cross." Next picture: "It draws an attacking force to sited artillery and machine guns. Puts you in the line of fire. Makes you a fixed target."

"As simple a defense as could be. No need for technical repairs like mechanical weapons. Cheap compared with artillery and machine guns. They cost a lot to repair. Just being dug in on the battlefield is enough. Barbed wire easy to keep up. Don't need parts, skilled mechanics. Don't need hospitals for barbed wire to be treated for wounds. You don't feed it. No paymaster. After it's staked it's what an American called 'free for nothing.'" He paused, letting what he said sink in. "You must wonder how men get through barbed wire. We will teach you. You damned well better listen and study and learn."

The strands of wire and the pictures and lectures and field practice and all the courses every day for weeks prepared the Americans for the battlefield.

Brentwood's Second Lesson on Trenches

Sergeant George Brentwood taught the Americans about each kind of trench. He described each kind. "Firing trenches. Steps on the side facing the enemy. You stand on it to shoot. Obvious, isn't it?" Then, "The parados. Dirt piled on the trench's back side to mask your head's silhouette." Next, "Communication trenches. They connect firing trenches with the rest of the battlefield, the system. Soldiers haul ammunition and guns, rations, run back and forth."

"Saps, shallow diggings sunk into No-Man's-Land for observation, grenade-throwing, and machine gun emplacements." And so on. The training went on for hours. After the basics, they learned details. At this state in their training the Americans listened attentively and scribbled notes.

Brentwood taught, "This is a pick and shovel war as much as rifle and bayonet. Soldiers dig in sand, mud, clay, chalk, and rock." This led him to dirt. "Dirt is the oldest weapon, rocks and sticks. Flying rock kills. Sand and clay bury and smother. Soldiers drown in mud. Trench walls collapse and trap Huns in their dugouts. Shell holes and trenches harbor poison gases. You could breath a whiff before you realize it. Too late. Dirt and sticks."

After class the gunners practiced shoveling dirt the British Army way, learned more than shoveling. Training lasted weeks. Always practice, something to learn.

The Company trained for trench fighting and open warfare, as well. All they learned took getting used to.

Ballwin on Maps

"Every soldier needs to know where he is and where he's going. Learn to read maps." With his pointer Sergeant Ballwin guided the men through the ninety miles of German defenses. "The *Flandernstellung* (Flanders Position) reached from the Belgian coast to Lille in France. The *Wotanstellung,* the Wotan Position, began at Lille and reaches Sailly, goes behind the 1915 battlefields of Loos, Vimy, and Arras in 1917, and the 1916 Somme battlefields. The *Hundingstellung* runs from Péronne to Etain, north-east of Verdun behind the Champagne battlefields of 1915. The *Mi-*

chelstellung protects Etain to Pont-à-Mousson behind the St. Mihiel Salient." Then they studied local maps of the sector they would attack in detail.

Sergeant Ballwin ended with these words. "No wonder they think themselves impregnable. Your job, prove them wrong."

"Flypaper" Barton

Atkins walked with Gamecocks Gunner Assistants Beau Baylor and Miles Mason. The others were coming behind. "I hear you talk about someone named Fly-catcher."

"No, sir," Baylor said. "Flypaper."

"Who is that?"

Private Mason said, "Barton. That's who."

"Behind his back? Why?"

Baylor said, "We all have nicknames for each other. A way of needling, keeping things light, but keeping each other in line."

"You didn't answer my question. Why behind his back?" Atkins asked again.

"Are you kidding?" Private Mason answered his own question. "Barton would cuss anyone who called him Flypaper to his face all the way to Kingdom Come! When he's angry his English magnifies. King of cussin'. And he'll knee the guy in the nuts. Hard."

"The cussedest cusser," added Baylor, an echo. "Sir, a strange question for you. In the United States of America we use fly swatters. How do you kill flies in England?"

Tommy Atkins replied, a touch of the snide in his reply. "I've not been home for two years. Things may have changed. Maybe it's come along since then. I'll ask in my next letter home. When I lived at home we used swatters, too." Then he turned it into a lesson. "But here, boys, we endure the flies and vermin if that's what you're getting at. You get used to them, like everything else you find disgusting, or finds you."

Mason: "It's not what we were getting at. No, Donald ain't the swatter, sir. No. He's . . . I'll explain. You buy a sheet of paper coated with arsenic and something sweet flies like to eat. Put it on a counter or sill. Wet it. The flies lick it and die. The poison kills them. Well, that's the kind of flypaper he is."

Atkins did not reply. He was thinking about how this applied to Donald Barton.

Baylor: "Put it where a kid can't get to it, or a dog or cat. Make 'em sick. Maybe kill 'em."

"What we mean, sir, is he's piezin," said Mason. That's why we call him 'Flypaper'. He's no good. But I think you're going to put him up to lead us."

Around the corner came Barton. "I heard you. Flypaper, am I? I've got far worse names for you. I keep 'em to myself, because they would make you weep."

Baylor spoke up. "We don't mask our opinion of you, just as you let us know what you think of us. It shouldn't surprise you."

"I knew you'd pick some stupid name you'd use behind my back."

"Listen to the Devil's sophistry," muttered Private Mason. "Parries with words."

"What did you say?" challenged Barton. "Speak up."

"The Devil's sophistry."

"I'll bet you don't know what sophistry means, you numbskull. You can't accuse me of something you don't know the meaning of. I plead not guilty by virtue of you don't know what you're talking about." Barton laughed at his own jibe. No one else did.

To Atkins, Mason said, "Sir, honest-to-goodness deceit. Twists things around."

Then to Barton: "A blowhard and boaster. You're poison. Other than that, you're a fine fellow, ain't you, Flypaper?"

Barton to Atkins: "Listen to him, sir. Only someone with these qualities could describe them with such sure knowledge. Don't you agree, sir?" To Mason, "And you, you can call me whatever you want."

The men wondered what there was about Barton who they could see was going to be put over them when Atkins picked the squad leader. Whatever it was, they couldn't tell what it could be. In any case, they were soldiers enough to follow every command, every order, no matter who it came from. If it was Barton, they knew they could handle it.

Keep Your Damn Head Down

Taught again and again, because he knew the temptation was so strong, Tommy Atkins told them right before they went down into the training trench, "Learn it now, and never forget it. Keep your damn head down. Develop the habit from the start. Make it second nature. Never give in to the temptation to look over the parapet. Never. Starting this minute. I know you are dying to see what is out there, see what's going on. And die you will if you look. This very minute snipers are anxious to put a bullet through your head. You're an easy target. Any hunters here? I hear a lot of Americans hunt. Not like at home in England, where its reserved for the nobs. Sharp eye and good aim." Then, "This looking up. It's almost irresistible. But don't be like Mrs. Lot."

Private Mankins asked, "Sir, Mrs. Lot? Who's she?"

Atkins said, "Lot's wife. In the Bible. "

"Pillar of salt?" asked Mankins.

"That's the lady," said Tommy Atkins. "Warned not to look back. She did anyway. Never minded. Point is, stick your head above the parapet, a German will shoot your fool head off. Curiosity killed the cat. Curiosity kills the soldier. Don't think that it hasn't happened. Many times. And on both sides."

By the end of training the Americans had the beginnings of an idea of what fighting in trenches and No-Man's-Land would be like.

After the First Several Weeks' Training
July 11, 1918

Phase A of II Corps training began on June 10 at Recques, France. On June 27 Phase B began near Poperinghe, Belgium eight miles west of Ypres, for two weeks, Phase C planned to start August 10. But the Corps took to the battlefield before it finished phase B. "A pity," Sergeant Brentwood said. "They need more training, a great deal more. There is too much they don't know."

But they went to the Canal section of the Ypres-Lys Offensive, the Fourth Battle of Ypres. In early September the two American divisions finished their work and continued training for the attack at Bellicourt Tunnel. The instructors for the 118th Regiment considered their progress.

Said Corporal Atkins, "That Australian, General Monash, gave the 27th and 30th Divisions, the poor souls we're training, the place of honor in the assault."

Harry Ballwin: "I know. At first I thought he was putting the freshest troops in front."

"Freshest meat?" joked Sergeant Brentwood. Then, "Too many of them poor boys will get killed."

"Or the soldiers who least suspect what they are being put into? They plain don't know enough. They'll make a lot of mistakes. " Ballwin lit his pipe and took a puff after each phrase. "These doughboys are itching for a fight, as they put it. Ready to throw themselves into the fray. Show everyone what they can do. Teach the Germans a lesson. This is what the Americans say."

Fish in a Barrel

At Tincourt
September 23, 1918

The British instructors stayed with the Americans, teaching them, drilling them, getting them ready for what lay ahead. Among themselves, the trainers discussed the war. "We'll soon have the Hun on the run," said Atkins. "And he has no place to go but home with his hands up."

"Yes. The Americans have an expression, 'like shooting fish in a barrel,'" said Ballwin.

Sergeant George Brentwood: "What strange things American do. If I had fish in a barrel, I would catch them with a net."

Ballwin couldn't tell if Brentwood took the idea seriously or if he saw the joke. When George spoke Ballwin could tell Brentwood was playing the dumb American, imitating Otis Mankins's voice, pitched high, and his accent, his dialect. "Bullets would wreck the barrel. Fish might not be easy targets."

Ballwin joined in the play. "Anyway, I think the concussion would kill them. You don't have to really hit one."

"I don't think they shoot fish in a barrel," said Brentwood.

"Of course they do," argued Sergeant Ballwin. "Otherwise they wouldn't say it."

Putting on a don's voice Brentwood said, "Overstatement. Hyperbole, it's called. Ever hear of it? You went to school, didn't you?" Then he harrumphed, cleared his throat, and said, "Shooting fish in a barrel means something is easy to do. That's all."

Steering the talk back to the subject, Atkins said, "My point. In this battle we have the advantage. You understand."

Still playing the fool, Brentwood's opinion. "If we have the advantage, let the Generals surrender. Then let's declare victory and go home."

Tommy Atkins: "Can't. The Germans can't surrender. You'd have to call it a draw or stalemate."

Said Ballwin, "I wish the High Ups would think of this, and do it, too."

"They think about it, all right. That's high level wishful thinking," said Atkins.

His talk turned serious again. "The war will go on till one side runs out of bullets and soldiers to fire them. This will be the Germans, and soon. These American boys will spell the difference. They may not be very good, but they'll draw a lot of fire. But don't fool yourselves," went on Tommy Atkins. "This is no 'fish in the barrel' game. The Kaiser still has good armies. The one across the way is top rated. They'll defend the line to the last man. And they might just hold it. They'll have cunning tricks, too. Don't you think they won't. And we will have to figure out what to do."

The Lewis Gunners Divided into Two Teams

Corporal Tommy Atkins divided the Lewis gunners into two teams, Ezekiel Able to lead one and Donald Barton the other. Atkins sent Barton's lackeys and stooge elsewhere. He told Sergeants Ballwin and Brentwood, "I'm giving him Jolly, Miles Mason, and Beau Baylor and a couple of others." Atkins said, "Barton will see that he better not try to push these three boys around. He will have to change his way."

Brentwood said, "Or they'll change him."

"Straighten him out if he needs straightening," Ballwin joked.

Corporal Atkins said, "When they find out whose team they're with the boys will hope he tries his ways. I'm sure they would like to have a run at Private Barton. If they were mean, and they are not, they would provoke him. They are too much the soldier. At first sign of the old Barton, though, I think they will knock the vinegar out of him."

"Strike the person in command?" his face a scowl, Sergeant Ballwin said.

Tommy Atkins replied, "Of course I don't mean hit him. Of course, I hope Private Barton behaves the way a soldier in command needs to. That might do it. That's what we're hoping anyway. That's what we're counting on. He's courageous and will lead. We'll see, won't we?"

And the meeting was over.

CHAPTER 6

Thomas Atkins, Instructor

(According to Kendall Haydon)

Tommy Atkins' Leather Folder and How We Got to Know Him

Instructor Tommy Atkins wasn't the gruff old sergeant we expected. Far from it. He seemed no older than us, twenty or twenty-one. Some of us older than him. Slight. Short. Except for his weather-beaten face, he looked like a kid. He spent four years outdoors, every season, every kind of weather. A man in his youth, hard-worn. Unlike some of us and the Australians, he wasn't the least bit coarse. One of the few who fought at Mons and Le Cateau and, four years later, fights still. Lance Corporal now, he had seen more war than any of us could ever imagine. He had been home once in all that time. When we met him he seemed nothing special.

We didn't hear, but we did. Somehow it comes to our ears. I don't remember when we first heard these things. None of us knew anything about an Angel of Mons, or any other angels. We rarely heard the angel mentioned, once or twice, and only bits and snippets. No details. It wasn't like they were trying to arouse our curiosity. Was this a jolly to hoist on the dumb Americans? Tommy Atkins has something to do with an Angel of Mons? I doubt it.

Then far-fetched yarns about Tommy Atkins—glorified, gilded—travelled from soldier to soldier. Tommy Atkins died and returned to life with a message, died and was reborn. A seer, a prophet, he embodied the divine. He was an amulet. It came to pass, you might say, that British or Australian soldiers would walk close by him and, seemingly by mistake, touch his tunic, usually his insignia. They thought they had touched immortality, the possibility of life in the hereafter, for the soul at least, if not the body, as we heard had happened to Atkins.

One day Private Schmidt couldn't restrain himself, got up the nerve to talk about this with Instructor Sergeant Brentwood. "Do you believe St. George saved Corporal Atkins? Brought him back to life? I don't see anything special about him."

"We know about it. All about it. Don't talk about it."

Schmidt, expectantly: "At a private moment I might ask him."

Sergeant Brentwood scolded the American. "Private, number one. There are no private moments in the Army. Do you forget? Number two. Private, you dare not speak about it. If he wants to tell you anything about himself, which I doubt he does, he will do it on his own. Speak when you're told to speak."

"Aw, nuts. We all talk plenty," retorted Schmidt. "But don't worry. I won't pester him."

"Pester him? You better not even mention it. You'll have hell to pay if you do. "

Then one day when we were alone with Atkins, Hans Schmidt, still wanting to know, said. "I hate to raise a private subject, sir. I was told not to mention it, but we are curious, naturally."

"Let me guess," said Atkins.

"Guess?" said Private Schmidt, surprised.

"I don't have to be a mind-reader, now, do I?"

"No, sir."

Atkins said, "You were told to not bring it up, not to ask me about the Angel of Mons, weren't you? But you did."

"Sorry, sir," said Schmidt. "Forget that I asked."

Because Atkins could see that we were going to make decent soldiers, and were honorable men, the Lance Corporal told us what had happened at Mons four years ago. He opened a leather folder. Inside were postcards of the Angel of Mons, pictures of the angels from magazines, two from a book, *The Chariot of God.* He told us about his encounter with the Angel of Mons, dead, then alive at St. George's doing. "The artists who made these were not at the battle. We had no artists with us. Of course, what happened on the battlefield changed every second, raged up and down the canal. What took place in one place was different from what happened somewhere else, even just a few yards away. See? These pictures show what artists imagined. They can't show the tumult, the noise, and warrior angels in battle."

Corporal Atkins had two musical scores, the angel on the cover and in the title. No lyrics. Just music. He couldn't read music, nor could we. But we understood the titles.

Corporal Atkins told us about the divine events that took place at the crucial instant in the Battle of Mons on August 24, 1914. The British were assailed in great force at the Mons-Condé Canal, and especially at Nimy Bridge. St. George himself, the size of an evening summer cloud, on horseback, raised his sword, bellowed his command, and a host of angel cavalry flew down from the sky to the field of battle. Fought with swords and pikes and maces, making a bloody mangle of the German cavalry. The horses tore off in all directions. Those hauling artillery and ammunition tore off with limbers, ran frantically through the German infantry. Angelic infantry rose out of the ground, killing a multitude with arrows shot from longbows, crossbow bolts from Crecy, and flintlock muskets of the Duke of Marlboro's battle at Malplaquet, not far off. The Germans were badly mauled, chastened from their belief that the British Expeditionary Force would be easily defeated. He concluded, "The angels' attack gave the British holding the vital salient time to withdraw to safety with far fewer killed and wounded, with the possibility of a definitive defeat right there prevented. We withdrew in good order."

Then he told us of his own war. "After Mons and Le Cateau it was march, turn and fight, pass through our own line, march, turn and fight until we reached the Marne. Back-peddling, slog-fighting. We dug shallow trenches, foraged, marched, hardly slept at all. We had enough food, thank God. One hundred twenty miles in twenty days. The Marne and First Ypres.

The Two Kendall Haydons

(recalled by the private)

After class one morning Instructor Atkins said to me, "Haydon, stay a moment." I knew the Instructor looked at me a couple of times as if he was trying to recall who I looked like, who I reminded him of. Or I thought he would commend or reprimand me, but I didn't think either was called for. Atkins began right off. "I knew a soldier whose name was the same as yours. He was a drummer in the Company band. We were friends, but briefly. He was killed a few days after we met. Did you ever meet someone you took an immediate liking to?"

"Sure I did. Especially good-looking girls. The same idea."

"In any case, the other Kendall Haydon and I liked each other right away. We enjoyed each other's company. We talked." Atkins paused in thought. "I sensed a connection between you and him right away. The name, of course. You spelled your names the same. Family connection? Do you know anything about that?"

I said, "My family came from England with the first to arrive in South Carolina. I'm not sure. Ancestors and relatives who stayed behind. Some moved to other colonies. Barbados, Bermuda? So it's possible that we are distant relatives."

"I have in mind a deeper connection between you. I am not sure how to describe it, but there is something about you that reminds me of him. Do you know what I mean?"

"Not really. But it's interesting."

"Ah, well. Maybe it will come to me. We'll see. But I sense a strong connection."

That night I had a bizarre dream and Atkins was in it. The dream stunned me, really in a way terrified me. The next morning I went to him and said, "In a dream last night I saw you fly, not with arms outstretched like a bird's, but standing upright, from a tree at the height on one side of an old quarry to the other. The quarry must have been one hundred yards across and fifty feet above the floor. Not only you. I saw what looked to be a whole company of British soldiers raised from the floor to the top. In the dream I was above the quarry myself, hovering, looking down, seeing all, knowing all. The dream was more vivid than life." And the Corporal explained what had happened in the quarry at Le Cateau. I had seen what had happened four years ago. I was astonished, to say the least.

The next night I had another bewildering dream and went to Atkins again, interrupting him at his report writing. I said, "The other Kendall Haydon came to me last night. I knew it was him. He told me before machine gun bullets tore him in half he saw you travel across the air. He said he died, along with many trapped in the quarry. But many others escaped. Then he took me to his grave. I prayed for him and all the others killed in the war, maimed."

Atkins replied, "Indeed. At Mons. No, Le Cateau. He died, along with many others. Once again, you dreamed what happened there." Then Instructor Atkins closed his eyes, as if entranced, and his speech sounded like poetry to me. "All of us caught in the quarry marched toward the south wall, blind to the possibility of climbing it. Suddenly we were ascending rock steps we had never seen cut in the quarry wall. So it felt beneath our feet. We trod a path our eyes could not see. The way the hand finds the mouth–we made our passage." Atkins paused. I knew I was part of a revelation. How could it be that I was seeing events of a distant place and time and meeting a relative, dead four years, as alive and real as me sitting here with Atkins. I felt a chance coming over me. Beyond doctrine and dogma and creed. Breathless, I felt I was picked for a special task, a role beyond that of common soldiering.

Atkins took up his account. "Half way up the wall, rope ladders descended from the top. Each rung called for less effort than the rung below, until we were floating upward. As if we had turned to cloud, to air, yet were still ourselves."

"In a moment's time others joined us in the light. Even the wounded were restored and swept up in a cylinder, a swirling cone, marching in air toward the wall."

"It would have taken hours for us all to climb to the top of the wall, if it would have been possible at all. German snipers surely would have picked us off, every one, let alone what artillery could have done. Yet here we were, ascending, surrounded by light. Vaporous forms guiding us."

To me it was like hearing scripture stories as a child. I was filled with wonder.

Then he said, "Our hearts expanded with joy. Down the line I heard a bandsman sing,

> "We are climbing Jacob's ladder,
> We are climbing Jacob's ladder,"

His fellow musicians joined in.

> "We are climbing Jacob's ladder,
> Soldiers of the cross."

"As if we were again in the world of Biblical events. And on and up we went. We came in on:

> "Every rung goes higher and higher,
> Every rung goes higher, higher,
> Every rung goes higher, higher,

Soldiers of the cross."

"Some with us had been killed in the battle. We could not distinguish between those who were alive and those who were not. We were not even certain ourselves."

"As we approached the wall's top a voice called each by name, rank, and serial number–the voice of a headmaster, an examining magistrate. As if they read from a questionnaire, a hospital admittance form, an insurance application. Separating the living from the dead."

Atkins' telling and Haydon's hearing these stories bound the two, a brotherhood forged in dream and vision held until death.

Battle Plans ❖ 2

Chapter 7

Bellicourt Tunnel

After the Germans were chased off,
the tunnel entrance from the side they entrenched

Bellicourt Tunnel. Also named St. Quentin. Also Riqueval tunnel. Built of a dozen layers of brick at Emperor Napoleon's command. Twenty-five feet wide at the top, sixty at water level. Fifteen feet within the north and south entrances the Germans built a concrete wall from the water level to the ceiling with loop holes for machine guns. They dug tunnels alongside and into the main tunnel. Laid narrow gauge tracks from depots and dumps far behind the line into the tunnel for trains to haul supplies and equipment to the Front, supply the installation with all its needs.

The main defenses of the Hindenburg Line were a short distance west of the tunnel. The canal itself posed the greatest difficulty. South and north of the tunnel stood steep bluffs, sixty feet high. The banks on the west side were infested with concrete dugouts. Royal Air Force pilots reported that from a distance it looked like swallows' nests, all up and down the face of the bluff, and far to the south. The east bank was filled with camouflaged machine gun nests and artillery far behind that.

A battle here could only be a set piece. The Germans did not know when or how the Allies would attack. But they knew it would be a frontal attack. They prepared a perfect battlefield on which to fight.

At Bellicourt thirty-five German divisions stood against fifteen British Fourth Army divisions, including the American 27th and 30th, plus many Australian divisions. Having many more troops, the German had a good chance of withstanding his opponent's attack. Concentrate the forces to hold the line.

The German plan made wise use of soldiers, weapons, ammunition, equipment, supplies, barbed wire, the trenches, the ground in front and between.

The Bellicourt Tunnel Plateau:
Except for This Narrow Strip of Land

The *Siegfriedstellung*, the Siegfried Position, starting near Arras, passed through St. Quentin to the Aisne River east of Soissons, and ended on the Chemin des Dames Ridge ninety miles away. The British called it the Hindenburg Line, after their nemesis, the Chief of the German Army General Staff.

Close to Bellicourt Tunnel, the Germans occupied the towns of St. Quentin, six miles to the tunnel's south entrance, and Cambrai, seventeen miles north, and the towns, villages, hamlets, and farms between, and the three miles of tunnel. A twenty-six mile front. They expelled the citizens, chased them out with no place to go, ate their food, confiscated livestock and crops. They destroyed houses, barns, sheds with fire and bombs.

Except for the Bellicourt Tunnel plateau, this small strip of land, the canal kept the Germans safe from the British, Americans, and Australians, and the French to the south. Yet this was the only place where an attack by land could even be attempted.

To a depth of fifteen miles on both sides of the canal the Germans destroyed everything that blocked the field of fire. Some villages along the outpost line they fortified for defense and offense. They cut down trees, orchards, hedgerows, filled in wells, or poisoned them.

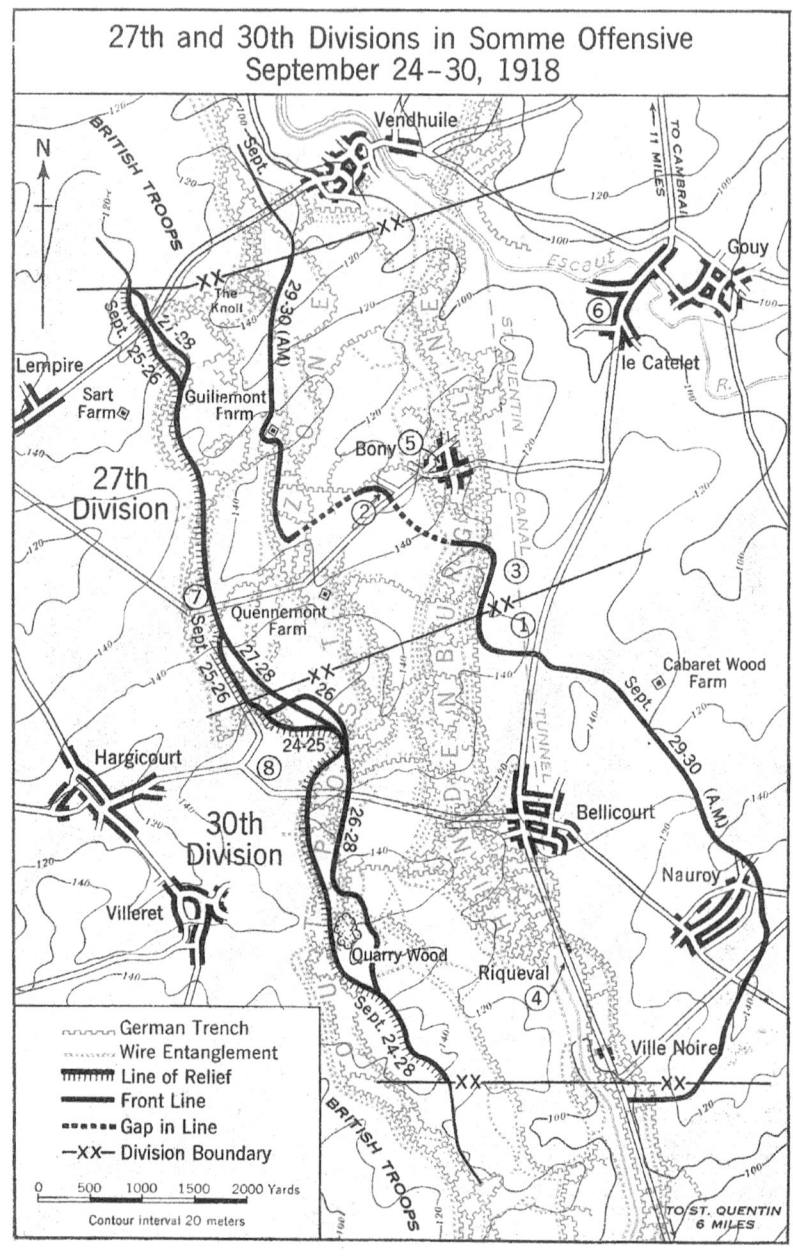

27th and 30th Divisions in Somme Offensive
September 24–30, 1918

Arial photograph of the entrance to the tunnel: September 23, 1918

The plateau over Bellicourt tunnel, heavily entrenched, three miles long and five deep, just behind the Hindenburg Line, used wide, long barbed wire belts, dug-outs, concrete pill boxes, and machine gun and artillery emplacements to withstand the Allies' attack. There were three deep trenches, the Hindenburg, the Le Catelet-Nauroy Line and the Beaurevoir-Fonsomme. The main trenches were two hundred yards apart. Three deep, strong lines. Interlocking communication trenches, and approach lanes from the back connected them. In front was a heavily fortified Outpost Line. And in front of that barbed wire fields—three hundred thirty feet wide, each strand loosely strung on wood pickets, producing an impenetrable tangle.

The vast fields of barbed wire at Bellicourt Plateau

The arrangement took advantage of the terrain's irregular features. Steep hills, chalk cliffs topped and faced with trees and brush, perfect for concealing dugouts and troops. Deep ravines, sunken roads. The Germans dug and fortified hundreds of dugouts in the canal's west wall in back of and behind the nearby hills. They dug passageways leading from the underworld to the battlefield sixty feet above.

Observers, the front divisions, occupied the mile and a half deep Outpost Line. Behind were two more trench systems—the Le Catelet-Nauroy Line and, behind that, the Beaurevoir-Fonsomme, their names taken from hamlets and villages they made part of their fortifications. The main line of defense was the second line, with dugouts housing most of the front division. Artillery observation posts and machine-gun nests were built in front of and behind the trench lines. The artillery stood farther behind the battle zone, the reserve battalion of each regiment behind that.

The Allies faced the *Siegfriedstellung,* the Hindenburg. On their maps the British cartographers marked the lines in color. At Bellicourt, Brown: The start line. Earlier in the war this had been a British trench. So the Germans had an old trench to work, improve, and develop. The old Hindenburg outpost line, the American and British objective was the Green Line.

Thus, it was the most heavily defended three miles of the entire Hindenburg Line. A dense network of killing grounds, it was the keystone of the Hindenburg system. Break through and Germany was on its way to being finished.

Strongpoints

In addition to the main trenches, three strongpoints were greatly important: To the northeast of the trench lines and from north to south, facing the Americans, the Knoll on the left, Gillemont Farm between, and Quennemont Farm to the right. From the Allies' position the ground rose slightly, a long, gentle slope that ends at a flat rise in the direction of the three points. To attack them, the Americans had to cross three miles of broad fields, empty of crop. The ground had been shelled earlier in the war, and often, and was cratered with shell holes. The Germans used the holes as forward machine gun nests. In spite of repeated attempts in the opening stage of the battle, first the British, then the American 27th Division failed to knock these nests out. From their position the British, then the Americans, were easy targets for German artillery and machine guns, being at the bottom of a long, open slope.

THE AMERICAN SOLDIERS ❖ 2

Chapter 8

Leslie's Magazine

Privates Hans Schmidt and Otis Mankins

(in the words of Private Schmidt)

For years we avidly read about the Great War in our patriotic newspapers and magazines. As early as 1914 we were told to get ready for war. Mentally, I mean. A cover of *Leslie's Illustrated Weekly Magazine*, June 29, 1916, struck me—a picture of George Washington with his words: "In time of peace prepare for war." Then in big letters, the first line red, the second, white, blue for the last:

**WASHINGTON
THE FATHER OF
PREPAREDNESS**

As plain as it could be. I took it to heart. I got myself ready.

The descriptions of great battles fired our imaginations, swelled the hearts. To take to the field of battle, to be part a world-shaking encounter, appealed greatly. The discipline, the camaraderie, the test of endurance. Struggling hand to hand with a hated Hun, rifle and bayonet, and killing him. We marveled at the new weapons—howitzers, mortars, machine guns. The message for me: enlist. Enlist and enjoy the adventure. And farm boys were eager to see something of the world. We joined up right away.

Once we got to Europe I didn't get to read *Leslie's*. My younger brother, Joseph, sent me the cover and a page torn from a copy of a *Leslie's Magazine*.

True Love *at* First Sight

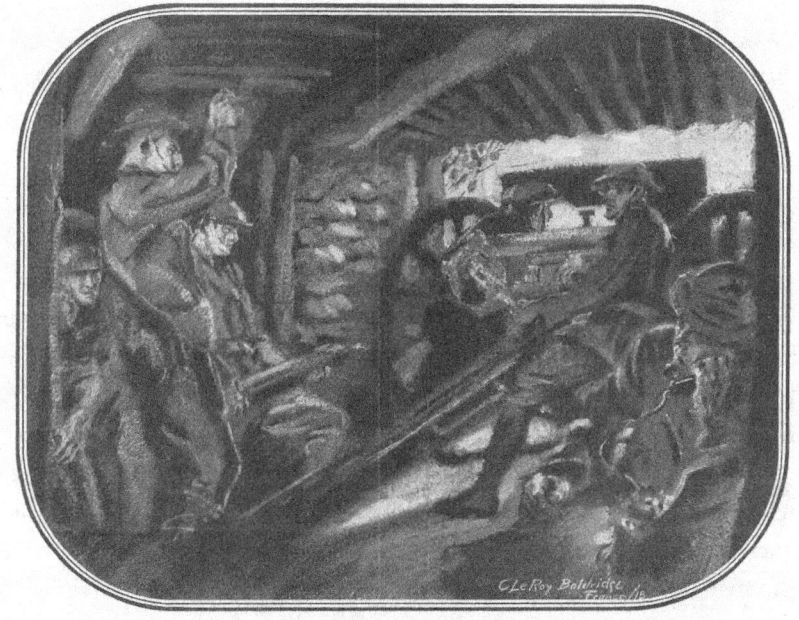

A United States Sergeant Gives the Signal to Fire the National Guard's First Shot at the Germans. Drawn with an A. E. F. Soixante-Quinze Battery.

He knew I was with the first of the National Guard to go over, so he knew it would interest me. I appreciated the full-page drawing under the title "True Love at First Sight."

The caption read: "United States Sergeant Gives the Signal to Fire the National Guard's First Shot at the Germans." Drawing of an A. E. F. Soixante-Quinze Battery, the old French 75, a gun that gave a good fight.

The American soldiers' love for the French gun.

> Miss Rosalee and Josephine
> Are ladies we have met
> Oh, don't get jealous, they just mean

In *Fransay*, bayonet.

> Now spiked pea-shooters, they may do
> For the dough-boys' wedded wives,
> But the wagon-soldiers are true-blue
> To the pretty seventy-fives.

> For us the rest are also rans,
> *Charlotte* is the only one,
> And her other name is *Swosontcans,*
> And, lord! How she hates the Hun!

But my brother Joe couldn't know the importance of that magazine's cover to me.

From some of the British we heard about the Angel of Mons, St. George. We were fifty miles from that town. Rumor, whispers, stories about St. George and angel warriors came down from the sky on horseback, fought the Germans and saved the British in the first battle the British fought.

But the cover: the angel St. George rode a white charger. He carried a white battle-flag, red cross in the center. The background—night-blue sky and stars. A lady angel leads him. Under the picture the words "Crusade of Mercy." So we were crusaders. Save the French, the Belgians, and the world from Germany. The message came rather late. Millions of soldiers are already dead and buried, or crippled for life. Some, useless hulks. None were what they had been before the war. And the poor civilians were no better off. Their pleasant, peaceful way of life destroyed. But us Americans, we were coming to the save those who remained.

The main thing: I realized that my seeing St. George, the Angel of Mons on the cover, was no coincidence. How fortunate to get this picture. As so much else did already, it elevated Tommy Atkins far beyond the ordinary in my mind. The stories we had heard, what Atkins had already told us, the cover mystified me.

BOOK II

BATTLE PLANS ❖   3

Chapter 9

Building the Defense for Bellicourt Tunnel

Construction and Destruction Went on Day and Night

When soldiers dug trenches in the midst of battle, which they often had to do, survival was ever present in their minds, not a well-devised plan for defense. The Bellicourt tunnel sector, twenty miles behind the battle-field, in pleasant surroundings, peaceful civilians, French citizens, in quiet villages, gave the army's civil engineers plenty of time to plan the lay out, construction, and use for defense in depth of trenches, the land between, and barbed wire, machine gun emplacements, artillery—field and heavy. Fritz applied new principles for fortification and defense, prepared positions ideally suited for observation, attack, invisibility, protection, and communication to the rear. The main line of resistance was directly behind hills and ridges, out of sight of the enemy and sheltered from artillery fire.

The engineers scattered the posts and machine-gun nests strategically in front of, in, and behind the trench lines. Elaborate trench system used the irregular features of the natural terrain. Steep hills, chalk cliffs topped and faced with trees and brush, perfect for hiding dugouts and troops, deep ra-vines, sunken roads. Other trenches ran off into branches and spurs, using ridges, depressions. And the Bellicourt Tunnel Canal. South and north, steep cliffs, sixty feet from the ground to the water. The Germans dug and fortified hundreds of dugouts in the canal's west wall and in back of and behind the nearby hills. Camouflaged machine gun nests and artillery far behind filled the east bank.

The laborers—some paid, most Russian prisoners of war, enslaved French and Belgian civilians—dug nineteen passageways leading from the underworld to the battlefield sixty and as many as three hundred feet above. The entry was thoroughly camouflaged. The passageways connect-ed with the trenches and the battlefield. Some of went as far as Bellicourt and surrounding villages. With its hidden exits and entrances, this world formed a communication and attack system. The engineers built wide, deep barbed wire belts, dugouts, concrete pillboxes, and machine gun, artillery, and infantry emplacements to fight the Allies off. Well equipped to thwart the enemy, the line at Bellicourt suited the terrain, an ideal trench defense system.

The Germans had all the material they needed to reinforce the ninety miles of defense. The works' construction used almost all the cement, sand, and gravel produced in occupied France, Belgium, and western Germany in 1916 and 1917. From October 1916 through the next March canal barges and rail cars carried 1,250 trainloads of engineering stores to the line. Barbed wire in massive rolls and iron pickets to hold them in place arrived from Germany.

Factory workers in Germany made parts to standard design for the steel-reinforced concrete dugouts for infantry and artillery-observation posts. German citizens and soldiers mined limestone, slaked it, made concrete. Others mixed and poured it into forms for pillboxes, underground dugouts, some covers twenty feet long and four feet thick, machine gun emplacements—every kind of fortification. German construction companies brought skilled workmen to assemble them in the trenches and twelve thousand German paid laborers.

Added to this, the Army had a plentiful supply of workers to dig trenches and build fortifications—50,000 Russian prisoners of war, and 3,000 enslaved Belgian and French civilians—sixty-five thousand laborers. The thud of spades digging the earth, the sound of iron pick axes on rock rang the length of the works. Day and night, day after day. The workers buried telephone cable six feet underground. Some sawed mining timber to brace the thick walls of the underground dugouts. Concrete strengthened the multitude of machine gun emplacements. They leveled land, laid ties and rails for trains to haul supplies. Many cut down trees to make a clear field of fire, easy to defend, demolished buildings, villages, farms.

In front of Fritz's outpost and main trenches, he strung two sets of three barbed wire fields, each forty-five feet wide, five yards apart—three hundred thirty feet wide all together. Five bands deep in some places. Each strand connected to iron rods, pickets, screwed deep into the ground, the many strands tightly strung, and four feet high.

The work went on unhampered, destruction and construction. A monumental feat of earthworks.

LANCE CORPORAL THOMAS ATKINS ❖ 3

Chapter 10

Winston Churchill Meets Tommy Atkins

Ploegsteert, Belgium
March 3, 1916

(In the words of Winston Churchill, Commander,
6th Battalion, Royal Scot Fusiliers)

Three Messages

Following the failure and tragedy of Gallipoli, demoted, demoralized, Winston Churchill resigned from the government, then became Commander, 6th Battalion, Royal Scots Fusiliers. In January 1916 his battalion took up position on the front line. There he lived in German officers' underground quarters. Carpeted floor, piano, radio, gramophone, telephones, running water, electricity. A filled larder, luxurious beds, grand furnishings looted from the French, a wine cellar—fine French and German wines— well-stocked. Churchill, unorthodox, popular. Battalion commanders almost never ventured onto No-Man's-Land. Churchill went out thirty-six nights in the three months he was at the Front. Soldiers didn't like going with him. Reckless. But he inspired the men to courageous action.

Tommy Atkins appeared only days before Churchill resigned his commission in March.

"Sir, a Lance Corporal, Atkins, requests permission to see you. Not from our Battalion."

For no reason Churchill could think of, he recalled his tea with Aunt Lady Jane Archibald, then meeting with Conan Doyle and Sherlock Holmes right after the battle of Mons in 1914. He knew the role St. George and his warrior angels played there and Le Cateau. He asked his adjutant, "What does he wish to speak about?"

"Sir, says it is for your ears only."

"Eyes?"

"Ears, sir. He was precise."

"Was he?" But to the adjutant's surprise, Churchill said, "Bring him in. Then leave and close the door." Ordinarily, someone took notes of the Commander's conversations. Private meeting? Secret information? But even Churchill was not sure why he told his adjutant to close the door. It was an involuntary choice.

Atkins entered, snapped to attention, saluted. "Lance Corporal Thomas Atkins, sir. Royal Fusiliers."

"At ease, Atkins. You have a message for me, then?"

"Three messages."

"From whom?"

"Although he is on the Other Side, Lieutenant Dease, who serves at St. George's side, instructs me. I am his agent, you may say."

"Other side? What other side? Is he a spy? Do you bring me information about the enemy?"

"No, sir. Long ago you learned of the Angel of Mons, sir, know what happened at the battle."

Strange, Churchill thought. That is what brought Aunt to mind, the thought unbidden. "I know about the Battle of Mons. Indeed."

"The Angel of Mons, sir. I said the Angel."

"So you did. I misheard."

Atkins explained his connection to the Angel St. George and the angelic intervention that saved the British Expeditionary Force from destruction on that first day of battle.

"This is fascinating. I am sure the occult circles would like to hear your account. Now, what is this about? Be quick."

"I told you I have three messages."

"From whom?"

"I just told you."

"Yes. So you said." Churchill was distracted. He had heard enough about the Angel and wanted to hear no more. "Well, get on with it, then. I don't have all night."

"The first message is the angel St. George will fulfill the promise of victory he made at Mons, sir."

"St. George told you that? That is your message?" Sarcasm just short of vitriol. "Is that what you came to tell me?"

"Yes, sir."

"What does that mean, pray? I hope you've not left important duties to tell me this. Mons? What has Mons to do with it, I wonder. Thus far you talk only nonsense. I credit the Army, the Navy, the R.A.F. and the Home Front, and the French and Russians if we win the war. Even so, I have seen enough to know that there was another dimension engaged in this war. I know second hand about the Angel. You say you know first-hand. I do not discredit what you say, but I must tell you His Majesty's Government allowed the belief in the angel to flourish only because I encouraged it. Our ardent propagandists gave the rumor wings. It grew and flew. All to the good for morale at the Front and, even more, at the Home Front. But my belief in angelic help is weak. Yes, my aunt told me about the Angel of Mons, showed me a letter from her niece. Yes, Conan Doyle and Holmes told me about the Angel. But since then the angels seem to be bystanders, if they are there at all."

"Not bystanders at all. Though I am not here to argue. Just a few moments, sir, and I will be done. A second message."

"Go on, then. Be quick."

"Bellicourt Tunnel, sir. A battle will be fought there. While it will not go well for the Allies that day, the Americans will break a sacred cord that will signal success to come."

"Sacred cord? More poppycock? You are an annoyance."

"The Hindenburg Line. They will penetrate the Hindenburg Line. Minor military significance. It is bound to happen somewhere. But greatly important in the spiritual domain. At Bellicourt St. George and the Angels will contend with the Adversary. Angels will have a hand in this great work."

"And Americans will cut a cord? They are, as Americans would say, already late to the party. If they don't fight damn soon we will damn well need a miracle to win. I am not one much for angels in war. The Germans are strong and growing stronger. Unless America sends us a million soldiers ready to fight, I am afraid Germany will be the victor. I hope you are right and I am wrong, but I see little reason to think so. Forgive me if I doubt, but my doubt is borne of experience and knowledge. My doubt is a habit formed of much disappointment. Gallipoli, for example. The War Council griped and complained about my plan and its disastrous result. But what of their plans? They were as flawed as mine. French Generals Mangin and Neville? Forty-eight hours to Allied victory at Arras? A fiasco after the first day. Our own General John French? No better. We are all failures. As are the Germans. No? You've heard the expression 'two wrongs don't make a right.' In this war 'two rights don't make a right.' You have yet another message?" In truth, Churchill was enthralled by the conversation. Though he dare not let on. He knew he had yet something significant to give to his King and the Empire. This boy must be the key.

"Only numbers," Atkins said. "Just three numbers. One zed six. I do not know its meaning. Perhaps you do. One zed six. Or perhaps you will know it when you hear it. Such things happen. Listen for it, sir. If you see it written by hand or in print act on it."

Churchill said, "Corporal, how cryptic. One zed six is it? I've been closer to the war than almost anyone from well before it began and cyphers are the work of the Intelligence Office. Report your mystical number to them."

Tommy Atkins: "You may argue. But I have seen the truth of the angels and more. I know you will find a path yet to contribute to victory." That very thought had just passed through Churchill's mind. "Indeed, I believe it lies in the three numbers. We shall see. Until then, serve your men well, and your King. I shall do the same."

Atkins went on. "Before Mons I had no reason to believe, sir. The spiritual and mystical, the angelic, divine, St. George, other angels. Yet St. George sent me back to life and I have been his servant ever since. I am not here to persuade you of anything. The angels, the very Vickers machine guns crew I fought with and many others, are at work in the war. Now we part. I have others to speak with. May St. George bless you." Atkins saluted. Churchill returned the salute. Atkins pivoted on his heels, and was gone.

Churchill was astonished at the conversation. First, by what he had said, allowed himself to say, to a low-ranking soldier. Then, by what the young man said. The thoughts lingered like the scent of incense. A feeling came over him that what the young man told him was right. In spite of the bitterness the War Council's treatment after Gallipoli left in him, his heart filled with hope, a new resolve, and trust that England would prevail. He was sorry that he has been so contrary with this Tommy Atkins, and wished he could call him back to make amends.

Churchill, Minister of Munitions

By 1918, when Churchill became Minister of Munitions, the Ministry had a staff of 65,000, employed three million workers in 20,000 factories.

Yet, strangely, among the profusion of papers that covered his desk when he assumed the position was one with the number "1 0 6" and the word "fuse." Churchill knew what to do. At the Battle of Bellicourt Tunnel the 1 0 6 fuse was connected to the tip of shells for the first time. The bombs exploded the instant the fuse touched a strand of wire. The effect of the innovation produced a battlefield that was advantageous to the Allies. Thanks to Churchill's decision to approve the fuse. And Tommy Atkins' prophesy.

THE AMERICAN SOLDIERS ❖ 3

Chapter 11

The Chaplain

The 30th Division Captured Voormezeele, Belgium
September 1, 1918

Like the Soldiers Who Had Yet to Fire a Rifle

Like the soldiers arriving at the Front who had yet to fire a real rifle, let alone hold one, the Chaplain had just begun training for his role. Then suddenly he was First Lieutenant, Chaplain John Phelps, serving the four companies of 2nd Battalion, 118th Regiment. He joined the Battalion on the day the division won its first victory. Chaplain Phelps came from South Carolina, two years' graduated from Columbia Theological Seminary of the Presbyterian Church. Slight of build, a body not brought up on physical work, a seminary student's humble stoop. Bright blue eyes, spiked blond hair.

The first time he met Corporal Atkins they talked casually, not much more than introducing themselves. A week later Phelps asked Corporal Atkins if they could talk in private. They met in the Chaplain's tent. At the back of the tent was Phelps' altar—a stack of ammunition boxes and an embroidered tapestry the congregation of the First Presbyterian Church of Sumter gave him when he preached his last sermon there. Nearby, a table, a book, a Bible on top, and two chairs. "Please sit, Corporal." The Chaplain sat after Atkins did, fidgeted in his seat, paused, then: "If you don't mind. I hate to be so blunt. Since I arrived here I've heard about you. Though stories and rumors, I suspect. But it led me to think that you are wise and could help me."

The Corporal said, "What you've heard is likely true. What you haven't heard is probably stranger than what you have. But I don't know about wise. Tell me what's on your mind. We'll see how wise I am."

Phelps, worried about what lay before him, said, "Corporal, you've been in the war a long time. I am new to it. My work was easy at home. I thought things wouldn't be much different here, but they are. In Sumter I buried five parishioners in the two years I served there."

"Sumter?"

"Sorry. A town in South Carolina, a southern state, where I served as minister of the word and sacrament." The Chaplain went on. "Here 'M' Company already has at least three deaths a day. And we are not yet in the thick of the battle. In the days to come the numbers will increase greatly, I know. When I think about it, a month from now I may have buried twenty years' worth at home. It's easy to pray for one departed soul at a time. Not for the numbers I will have to pray over all at once." He went on. "I'm dumbfounded. I don't know what to say to the men. The usual words and phrases don't fit here. But no better words are coming to me. In the church at home daughters wanted daddy to stop drinking. Boys wanted to know if kissing their gal would anger the Lord. Of course, the bereaved need consolation from Scripture and a kind thought. But nothing like this, nothing dredged up out of the war."

Atkins tried to put the young man's mind at ease. "I know what you see around you is dreadful, fearsome. You will get used to it. We all do. For now, pray and meditate and read the Bible. The words will come. You will be surprised. Your prayers will do the men good. They want to be encouraged, made to feel brave, know what they are doing is for the good. It will also do the souls of the departed good."

Chaplain Phelps said, "It's a worry. But I hope you are right. You say the souls of the departed. We pray for them, too. But you seem to mean it in earnest."

Looking directly into John Phelps' eyes, Atkins said softly, "I do. You have heard stories about me, you say. I said they are more true than you would think. So I pray to St. George every day. I can tell you, he has something in store for you. I don't know when he will employ you or what he will have you do, but he will use you to some good purpose. I pray myself for guidance. You do the same. I appreciate your worry. In the meantime, do as I suggest. I am sure we will talk again."

The Chaplain was at once at peace and perplexed. St. George had something in store for him? He could not imagine what that might mean, what a saint had in mind for a mere John Phelps, newly graduated from Seminary? Or even if the saints were real.

The Changes War Wrought in the Soldiers
Concerned the Chaplain

A month later the chaplain mused to himself after a prayer meeting. He knew that these young men, these soldiers from South Carolina, North Carolina, and Tennessee mainly, arrived with old-fashioned church, school, and family morality. At home on Sundays they prayed in church, sang hymns, took sermons and homilies to heart. They read the Gospel. Reverent Christians in everyday life, they conducted themselves honorably. They held their elders and their ancestors in high esteem, especially those who had been valorous in war. "Yes, Ma'am" and "Yes, Sir" were expressions of genuine respect. Picnics, ball games, church dinners, camp meetings, evening strolls with friends. Before the war these were sources of pleasure for the boys from the South.

Chaplain Phelps saw that life in the war coarsened soldiers' speech and thought. "Fuck" or "fuckin'" became everyday words in the trenches and camps. Sometimes even between syllables: "ir-re-fuckin'-sponsible." "Dis-fucking–gusting." "Damn," "God damn," blasphemous words, everyday now. "Yes, ma'am" and "Yes, Sir" stayed at home.

The young chaplain concluded that war changed the American soldiers' outlook. One reason: they had seen so many dead, so much destruction and desolation all around, hopelessness in the French citizens chased from their homes. The greater change: they had seen their brothers-in-arms slaughtered, maimed, some hauled away, prisoners. The greatest change: they themselves had killed and knew they would kill more. They killed Germans, the Hun, all right. But these men were made in God's image, too. Was this all right with Him?

The men knew that war violated every rule they learned in church a thousand times over. One asked Chaplain Phelps, "Am I already on my way to Hell?" Another wanted to know, "Am I damned? What do you think, padre? I'd sure hate to be." The Chaplain preached God's mercy and forgiveness. The men of the Thirtieth Division, Second Battalion, 118th Regiment thought they would have to wait until the war was over, maybe until they died, to find out if they were blamed or forgiven. It even occurred to some that being killed or wounded was punishment for their own sin of killing.

Before they left home, young Phelps knew, there were things they wouldn't do, wouldn't think of doing. But things that would never occur to them to do, they indulged in here.

Others figured the chance of out-living the war, the chaplain realized, even any day's battle, was slim. Attracted by the novelty of the world they lived in, little by little many fell away from the life they had lived. Many left church morality behind across the ocean. They didn't think about it any more. Everything was permitted once they saw what went on here, what men did to one another. First smoking. Then a glass of wine. How good it tasted. Then a couple. Soon they got tipsy. They enjoyed the sensation and the comradeship, being one of the boys, already with stories to tell. How good to be away from the rigors of training, drills, marches, fatigues, and the horror of the trenches. An evening away from camp became a romp, a jollification. One thing led to another.

Of course the soldiers knew the Bible wants things a certain way. But they reasoned that if God could put up with this mayhem and slaughter, he would certainly forgive their little sins. Some came to live by the motto "Enjoy the fruits of heaven sooner rather than later. Later might be too late." Most believed God wanted them to marry as virgins. Now they were in danger of dying that way. Not far behind the line, brothels. Blue light for officers, red for NCO's and privates. Until then these boys had never seen a woman naked. Many learned sex was a wonderful pleasure. How good it felt. How thrilling. Many felt they could die as men now.

When the influenza epidemic struck, the medical officers told the men to smoke and drink all they want. This might protect them from the disease. They weren't sure it would work, but it was worth trying. Army orders. The soldiers were happy to go along. Drinking and carousing, gambling, blarney. Better than sitting around, brooding on influenza or death. All of this deeply distressed Chaplain John Phelps. Ideals, standards, morality, ethics, scruples, dying or dead in the men. He wondered how those lucky enough to return home would behave, how they would conduct themselves. He worried what life would be for them after the war.

Chaplain Phelps, Corporal Atkins, and
the *Cyclopedia of Illustrations for Public Speakers*

September 20, 1918

At St. Pol in France the day before the Regiment boarded trucks for their billet for Bellicourt, Atkins came to the Chaplain.

"May I speak with you, padre? Take a moment of your time?" asked Atkins.

"Please come in, Corporal. Sit down. What is it you want to talk about? What can I do for you?"

"It's not what you can do for me, but what I will do for you. If you will abide me for a few moments. If what I say offends you, please forgive me."

"This sounds most unusual."

Picking up the *Cyclopedia of Illustrations for Public Speakers* from the Chaplain's altar, Atkins said, "You are preparing yourself for the days of battle. Am I right?"

"Yes. Why"

"Inspiring words to share with your soldiers? You are taking inspiration from it yourself. Am I correct?"

"Yes, of course. The book was a graduation gift from my professors. I brought it to find passages to quote and preach on."

"A book wisely chosen, though you did not know it. It is a book of wisdom with many biblical passages, precepts, poems, little essays, much to think about, pray on. I have seen the book on your table I watched the page marker slowly making its way along. You are now on page 734."

"You opened my book without permission?"

"I did not open the book."

"Who did?"

"No one."

The chaplain was perplexed. What was Corporal Atkins talking about?

At that moment Atkins' eyelids fluttered, his eyes closed. When he spoke his voice was resonant, as if it came up from a well. Even the words struck the Chaplain as coming from an otherworldly place. "No one touched the book. You heard tales about me, fantastic feats. I told you there are many you have not heard. They can occur in any form at any moment. Without knowing that I could, just now, as we were talking, I saw into the book. These words came to me. Open the book to page 734 and three passages, 3249 through 3251." Atkins paused, listened to the inner voice. The Chaplain said nothing. Then Atkins gave Phelps instructions. "Read them, one a night. On the fourth night read them all again in order three times. Pray on each one. Read and take heart. Remember, one each night, beginning tonight before you pray." He stopped, as if listening again. He said, "Ah," as if he understood what he had been told. "I will explain why three passages. One leg or two would not steady a stool. Three will. The three passages are your three-legged stool. They will give you the strength, wisdom you need to ready your men for what they will engage in, what they will endure. As you said, many will die. Some within moments of being shot, or hit by shrapnel. I have seen hundreds die, maybe thousands. And many suffer long before dying. Wounds will plague many for the rest of their lives. You can ease their suffering if you prepare. Not relieve. Not end. Ease." Atkins paused. He slowly opened his eyes. He coughed, cleared his throat. His face, his gaze, remained somber. Now, in his own voice. "This book is your Apocrypha, your divining text."

Opening the book, Atkins said, "Here are the texts you will study and meditate on and pray on. Tonight read the first poem."

Today

Just this day in all I do
        To be true;
Little loaf takes little leaven;
Duty for this day, not seven,
That is all of earth and heaven,
        If we knew.

Oh, how needlessly we gaze
        Down the days,
Troubled for next week, next year,
Overlooking now and here.
"Heart, the only sure is near,"
        Wisdom says.

Step by step, and day by day,
        All the way,
So the pilgrim's soul wins through,
Finds each morn the strength to do

71

All God asks for me or you—
This obey.

The next night the Chaplain read the poem "Toil Accepted" and prayed on it, meditated deeply.

I ask not
When shall the day be done and rest come on;
I pray not
That soon from me the "curse of toil" is gone;
I seek not
A sluggard's couch with drowsy curtains drawn.
But give me
Time to fight the battle out as best I may;
And give me strength and place to labor still at evening's gray;
Then let me
Rest as one who toiled a-field through
all the day.

The third night he read "Toil and Providence." The words struck the chaplain as if meant especially for him.

It is common to attribute the great discoveries in science and industry to accident or sudden inspiration. But however suddenly discoveries are made, in some sense there are usually a result of long and patient toil and experimentation. Daguerre worked for many years trying to make the light print a likeness on glass or metal before an accidental hint gave him the clue.

At first Chaplain Phelps thought that he must discover Daguerre's clue. That would tell him what to do the next day, when the assault would be unleashed. The search was in vain. Then it struck him that all the training, the practice, the rehearsal, the earlier battles, though on a smaller scale, were the toil and experimentation. Tomorrow the clue would reveal itself, if not to him, at least to those planning the battle. He had been afraid that his own fear for the morrow, his own inadequacy in the light of what was to transpire, would be insufficient to prepare the soldiers spiritually. He now knew that the next morning, before his warriors went into battle, he would speak words of encouragement.

When he read the passages the way Atkins prescribed, the words consoled him. He had believed that the fight ahead was beyond the capability of the young soldiers he ministered to. They were new to the game of war, while many of the Germans were experienced, hardened. It was theirs to hold the day, while the Americans and their allies had to push through obstacle upon obstacle. Success in one day's battle would bring about growing confidence in their chances of further success and victory.

Chaplain Phelps was grateful for Tommy Atkins' instruction. He marveled at the British soldier's power. He could believe anything about him now. A man young in years, younger than he, skilled in leading young men into terrible battle. Four years as First Gunner on a Vickers squad honed the mind, calm in difficulties, wise in words and action. Atkins held the confidence of other soldiers.

The Night of September 28th and The Smell of Death

That night Chaplain Phelps prayed with the men who attended his prayer service, hoped he buoyed their spirits. He knew he was seeing some of them for the last time. But he knew, through Atkins, a divine act would occur, unlike other moments, other occasions in the war. Like few occasions in the history of the world.

When he had been settling in at the Front months ago, Chaplain John Phelps had read the names on the muster for the 118th and saw the name Jolly, Caleb, a boy he knew from home. When they met, Jolly greeted him with a hearty handshake. "Glad you're with us, John> Excuse me, Padre. Glad to see you. When we last met we were nothing but kids. You've come a long way."

"So have you, gunner Jolly. Happy to see a familiar face. Are you doing all right?"

"I guess so. I'm still alive, which is more than I can say for some," he said, in the gallows manner of a soldier.

The Chaplain took to dark–spirited Caleb Jolly like a brother. They met often. Jolly held a grim view of matters. The longer they were together the more often it was Jolly who sounded the preacher, stentorious, words bleak, draped in sarcasm.

The night of the 28th they met in private. Jolly said, "This may be the last time we talk. As far as I'm concerned this is the end for me. It's a strange feeling, but strong. 'It's a good day to die!' I heard that the Indians cry this when they are going into battle. What do you think?" Without waiting for an answer, Jolly said, "It is a tradition here to leave a letter and a will with a friend to send to the family in case a soldier is killed." Taking a small packet of paper out of his tunic pocket, he handed it to the Chaplain. "Would you do me the honor?"

"Of course, but I hope to see you the morning after tomorrow at muster."

"I hope so, too, but I doubt it." As they shook hands and pounded one another on the back heartily, Chaplain Phelps said, "Don't say that. God is with you, Caleb."

"So you say. Tomorrow's the day. My section enters the earth. Here the smell of death is always in the air. It disgusts me, fills me with repulsion. Destruction and desolation, death and suffering is all I see, all I've seen since I got here. I think of myself as already dead so when I am, I won't be surprised. I know I'm doomed. Pray for me as if I had died. That will do me the most good."

To his friend Phelps said, "I'll pray for you, Jolly. But as a living man, not a dead one. May God protect you, give you long life."

Tomorrow's prospect brought Jolly's brooding anger to the surface. "If you won't do what I ask, don't pray for me at all." Jolly suddenly turned on his heel and rushed out. You can't even count on a friend, he thought. What the conversation had turned to was so unexpected, so out of the ordinary, the chaplain didn't know what to say. John Phelps worried that he had done a bad job. To Phelps Caleb Jolly was like a living scourge, reminding him of the terrible suffering—physical, emotional, and spiritual—the war brought to men, not only Jolly, but to many others.

September 30's Entry in the Chaplain's Diary

The chaplain kept a private diary, each day entering the observations and meditations that came to mind.

September 30: Much burial and already reburial. Soldiers dig up the shrouds, lay them in a long line of coffins. If we gave as much respect to the living as we do to the dead, how much more care should we have for those alive, and cease this murder. It is hard for me to see any other word for it. I talked with Atkins about this. He told me I was right, but it is too late for that. He was right, too. Too late. Whoever is last standing on the field of battle will be the victor. So it will be more slaughter. In seminary days we never imagined a cataclysm of this magnitude. What are we to do? Comfort the afflicted, give courage, pray with them, bandage wounds, record every death in the record book. Now mostly burials and visit the wounded.

My mind began a kind of catechism.

Who built the coffins and crosses, stenciled the names?

Who dug the graves?

Who recorded name and registration number?

Who sewed the shrouds?

The Army sends bolts of canvas and coils of rope. We have a dozen industrial sewing machines, hired ladies from the village to cut and stitch, shrouds easy to close at the top with a drawstring. Contract with local lumberyards to make up coffin material. Delivered flat. Holes where screws will be drilled in to hold the pieces together. Ready to assemble.

Here the soldiers live with woe and strife and suffering, disease, death, pain, thirst, hunger, humor—much humor—the humdrum, boredom, fatigues of every sort and senseless parades of every kind, constant training, spells of frenzied activity, the morning "hate"—a tradition at the Front—when each side fires off a salvo at the other, a greeting to start the day, and trenching, always digging. Millions of Jobs, a handful of Herods. Christs paying for sins for which they are not to blame. So it seems to me.

I think God looks down in amazement and disgust. He did a bad job with us. But, being here, I wonder. Was it the work of Man?

Chapter 12

Otis Mankins and *100 Games of Solitaire*

To Pass the Time

Otis Mankins—gangly, taller than his fellow trainees, with a farm boy's hanging arms and sloping shoulders—toted a flimsy booklet along when he boarded the train at Sumter station for Camp Sevier. *One Hundred Games of Solitaire*, and a deck of cards tied together with jute string. By no means a social boy, he kept to himself, had little to say when others spoke to him. He fit right in the Army with his "yes, sir" and "no, sir."

He played the first game in the booklet, "Klondike," on the train all the way to camp to pass the time. He played one game, one deck, until each card was in its proper place and he reached the game's object. By the time the train arrived at Spartanburg station he had conquered "Napoleon at St. Helena," also called "Roosevelt at San Juan Hill." Because of the names, he enjoyed winning them.

At Camp Sevier he mastered ten more games, pausing at "Washington's Favorite." The 118th Infantry left Sevier on May 4, arrived at Camp Mill in New York the next day, sailed two days later to Halifax, Nova Scotia. In the days of training and rest before the ship *Glouchestershire* joined a convoy, set out for England and France on May 16, he made his way through several more games—"Napoleon's Flank," "Grant's Reinforcements," and "Idle Year," which took only a day's play to finish. "M" Company sailed along with five other companies of the Regiment. On the ship he had no room to lay out the cards, so his play halted. Ten days later, May 26, the ship docked and then by train to Dover and France. Rest camp at Calais for a few days. Training through the months, nearly a year.

At Recques in France, their first training camp in Europe, Mankins and the others met their instructors, Sergeants Ballwin, Brentwood, and Corporal Atkins. Week after week the 118th Infantry's Lewis gun teams spent in class and practice and nights in study. Even so, in the first several days of training Otis finished four more games, beating "Emperor of Germany." It was a relaxing diversion, seeing the cards fulfill a pattern, a shape, following the rules of each game.

On August 19 the Ypres–Lys Offensive began. Here the "Old Hickory" Division took to the battlefield. They fought under the worst conditions for trench warfare and the worst as well for open warfare. The night they arrived at Ypres Mankins played the twenty-fourth game, "Four Kings." As he drifted toward sleep a voice spoke to him. "Until you reach the object in all one hundred games in order you and your Lewis machine gun section are in danger." This message added new and deeper terror to the already traumatized young man. Every kind of dreadful thought flew through his thoughts. He thought of the cards with remorse and repulsion. How had this innocent pastime produced such horrid consequences? Cards, the Devil's device? Now he saw the truth of that claim that he has so lightly avoided.

What Otis had to do filled the young man with mortal dread. The games, no longer a diversion, now a burden, a curse.

Mankins scrambled from his cot and ran and shook Caleb Jolly awake, the section's card shark, poker his specialty. The private told him what the voice had said.

Mankins' plight irritated Jolly. "You woke me to tell me about solitaire? Not safe? Of course we're not safe. Nothin's gonna make us safe. You're nuts. What makes you think anything depends on you? If you don't finish what'll happen?"

Mankins replied, "The words came into my mind. I don't know how. I heard them plain as I hear you talking right now. After one hundred, we'll be safe for the rest of the war, no matter how long it lasts."

Annoyed, Jolly egged on poor Mankins. "First of all, you didn't answer my questions. Second, how many games you won?"

"Twenty-four."

"I see," said gunner Jolly. "Just seventy-six to go. It took you a year to get this far. Third, I hear the war will go on into next year and maybe the year after that—1920. So you have plenty of time to finish. Keep up the good work. I sure want to live. Want my help? Is that what you want?"

Otis didn't hear the sarcasm. "Plenty of time to get killed if I don't finish all the games is all I know."

Private Jolly kept it up, a touch of sarcasm. "Odds are strong against you. Even this minute soldiers are breathing their last on some battlefield."

Jolly saw that joking deepened Mankins' dread. "If you're so worried go talk to the Chaplain. Maybe you need spiritual guidance," Jolly said.

"I don't need no spiritual guidance, whatever the hell that is."

"You want me to talk to him? He'll put you straight. What you're thinking can't be right. You're an ordinary soldier with crazy thoughts."

"No. It's my problem," said Mankins.

"But it's driving you crazy."

"I know. It's still my problem."

"Well, you're driving me nuts, too. You woke me up to ask my advice, didn't you?"

"Sure. But I'm worried."

Then Private Jolly said, "I told you what to do. Do it or don't. Up to you. We hear wondrous tales of instructor Atkins. Maybe you should talk to him. I'm not doing you any good."

"I heard them stories." Private Mankins said, "They're a lot of bunk, that's what I think."

"Go back to sleep. Don't bother me. Forget about it."

Training filled the Lewis sections' days and nights. Having little time to play distressed the solitaire player, grieved, terrified him. He knew that each passing day more men suffered and died. Him to blame. Him at fault. A black mood followed him. A dark face, an angry look.

Yet the private struggled on, game after game. Even exhausted, Private Mankins played his heart out, concentration drowning out the racket, the shaking ground, the dreadful consternation.

He reached the thirty-fifth, "Blockade," and was blocked. The game wouldn't finish. No matter how many times he tried it, the wrong cards came up. Now they felt cold, dead in his hands. Inside he was empty, hopeless, alone. Otis Mankins despaired of finishing the games. Fear coursed through his frame. Nothing came up right. He began to fumble with the deck. Cards fell on the floor. His vision blurred. Then a few cards would surface in useable order, followed by turn after turn of bad cards. He couldn't advance.

Even though it was nearing midnight, and even thought he thought little of the stories about Corporal Atkins, he felt a need to talk to him, and woke him. "Sir, I need to tell you."

"What is it? It's the middle of the night."

"I'm sorry, sir. Very sorry." The private told the Corporal what had happened, what he heard. Terrified, Mankins ended, saying, "I think God gave up on us. Look at how many of our own kind we slaughtered. He might be thinking let them wipe themselves out. I'll start over. I've learned from my mistakes. Erred for certain, with this war."

"You're worrying yourself to death," said Atkins. "Change your thoughts or you'll invite a bullet." Then, "I'm going to tell you something. I understand the Jews believe there are three dozen people, the pillars of humanity, who make the case to God for saving humanity from destruction. Something like God letting Noah and his family live, I guess. These people give Him reason to let humans live. One of the Ruffians, Palmer, told me about it. He became a Christian and changed his name. Originally Wigdortz I think. A Jew name. Ziggy, we called him. From the East End. That wouldn't mean anything to you. Where the Jews live."

"You think I'm one of them pillars?"

"I don't know. It's an example. You have a job to do. Play solitaire. It looks like that to me. No telling."

Then suddenly Atkins' eyes shut. After a minute of silence he spoke, as if from sleep or dream. "No matter how many times you shuffle after you lay out a foundation, a devil orders them. Be patient, I am told. Patience. Sit with the cards, I am told. A shuffled deck is all you need. Someone will come who can defeat what stands in your way."

"Maybe Jolly. He's good at cards."

Still in a trance, Atkins muttered, "Someone from the Other Side."

"Really? How can that be?"

Atkins was silent again. Then abruptly he spoke. "We will sit outside tomorrow night."

The Ruffian Private Paul Carmichael, BEF, Killed at First Ypres

The next night the soldiers were asleep in their billets and tents. Except for the sentry and Atkins and Mankins who sat out under the night sky. Mankins set a board big enough to hold a game on two stacked empty ammunition boxes, and on it the deck of cards. Two chairs were ready. "Soldier," Atkins said, "Lie on the ground and study the heavens. Keep your attention on the sky. Be alert." A quarter of an hour later as the moon was just rising, a voice spoke. "Hello, sport," it said. "Happy to see you again. Long time."

"Hear anything?" Atkins asked Private Mankins.

"A voice."

"It's Paul Carmichael. I haven't heard it in four years. Help has arrived." When Atkins was an enlistee Carmichael took him under his wing, taught him the Army ways. "Private Carmichael was a whiz at magic. Played in circus sideshows under exotic names. Amar the Great, Mind Master Swami. Names like that."

Tommy Atkins said, "He knew cards. I feel his presence now."

The American looked around. "Nobody's here." He was alarmed, shocked. What was Atkins talking about?

"You can't see him."

The voice resumed. Both men heard it. Mankins was dazed. Where was the voice coming from? Who was it? "I was with Atkins at the beginning. The boy looks old and worn now, I must say. Over here we don't age. They say Death took him and St. George brought him back. But the truth is, if not for me, he wouldn't have made it." He explained. "My skill and knowledge saved Atkins' life." Then, "Before the War I was a circus sword swallower, fire eater, walked on broken glass, stuck knitting needles through my cheeks. Card tricks my specialty, my livelihood. These hands. I don't know if you can see them. I see you. These hands will save soldiers again. This time they are card-player's hands, not surgeon's."

In amazement, Otis Mankins watched the cards shuffle themselves three times, each time with the precision of a fine machine. "A voice with no body," he said. "Hands with no body. How can this be?" Without answering the question, Carmichael's voice said, "I will play in your place." The cards shuffled a fourth time. Private Paul Carmichael, revenant, good at cards.

His voice again: "Atkins, this place is familiar. Ypres, isn't it?"

"Right here," Atkins said aloud. "Right where we are now. The Nuns' Woods."

The spirit spoke in the voice of the broken-hearted: "This shed covers the spot where our good gun, Vicki, stood when we were blasted to death. Four years ago in human time, forever in ours. First Ypres. I'm told there's been many Ypres since. Barely stopped fighting here. But, my orders: I'm to fight, I mean defeat, whatever's against you in the cards. I have to play solitaire." While the voice went on, the cards laid themselves out on the table in the foundation for "Blockade."

Two more voices joined in. Fellow-warriors with Akins and Carmichael, dead at Ypres, too, Catchpole and Palmer, partners in hijinks and humor. Atkins introduced them to Mankins. He spoke to them as if they were present.

"You the comics Corporal talks about?"

"The very ones," the voice of Ziggy Palmer. "Here to josh a bit and joke a bit. Make light of serious matters. Make the trivial seem important." Quick-witted, the two of them.

"Can we play, too?" joked William Catchpole in a child's voice. "What you playing? War?' In what sounded like a stage aside: "A kiddy game?"

Then Catchpole warned, "Poker? Don't play poker with an American. He'll beat you. Their minds are tuned to it."

"Solitaire," said Carmichael, "Is what I'm playing."

"Are you a poof?" joked Ziggy Palmer.

"Patience? What the hell!" said Catchpole. "Might as well play old maid or mahjongg. "

"Or tiddlywinks, for the love of God," bantered Palmer.

"I does what I'm told," said Paul Carmichael. "We're in the Army, don't forget."

Palmer, pouting, "But you called." Then, "Call my name and I'll be there." To Catchpole: "Make that a line in a song, don't you know?" To Atkins and Mankins: "He still writes nutty songs, makes up smutty jokes. Even so, a pleasure to be with, I say." Then, "We were sent to watch you play. Don't know why, but we'll look on and jabber away."

"Mind if we watch?" asked Catchpole. The two spoke in rapid banter, almost breathless, a round in two voices.

Atkins said, "Make yourselves comfortable."

Exclaimed Catchpole, "Young man, we'll entertain you, cheer you along." He said, "Mockery. Derision. That's our usual humor. This time we were sent to encourage, not belittle. Uplift is what you need. I think we'll be poor at it. Not very good. Not our style. But we'll try."

Palmer: "Play on, Carmichael. Win the brass ring for the boy."

Along with Atkins and the disembodied dead, Mankins watched the cards turn and make their way to their proper places on the foundation.

William Catchpole asked, "Unraveling this soldier's fate?"

"No. The fate of the war," Carmichael said.

Catchpole and Palmer laughed. "A good joke. But play on, McDuff," said Louis Palmer.

"Good luck. The war. That's the game to win!" said William Catchpole.

"You against chance?" Palmer asked.

Catchpole, dead serious: "Against destiny, fate, against the Devil. It's no joke." After that, they were silent.

As the cards turned, slowly at first, then more quickly the cards took their rightful places. Hours later the game reached its end, the foundation filled.

"Thus we prevailed," boasted Catchpole.

Atkins joked, "I think your skits and jokes scared the demon off."

Phony weeping from Ziggy Palmer of the "you hurt my feelings" sort ended the performance for the night.

Carmichael's first night's play broke the blockade. Then two games came to good ends, "Robbers in the Night," the name of the second. Play returned to its ordinary turns of right and wrong cards.

Thereafter, cards turned, new foundations laid, new play unfolded.

Carmichael enjoyed the show greatly, said it lifted his spirits—a bit of a joke of his own—kept him alert.

Catchpole and Palmer in word, voice, and sound, gave evening entertainments, one each night. Comic skits, parodies of songs and poems, imitations of officers and staff, mockery of the Kaiser and Fritz, all in jolly humor. Phony fencing competitions, boxing matches, judo, all described for Mankins. All to entertain their card-turning friend, and bring whatever powers or weapons such spirits, such angels, use to battle the adversary. Humor? As "Beaux Belles" they sang in falsetto the love melodies of the day, replacing the innocent expressions of romantic love with ribald lyrics. They perfected skits of the oafish private and the officious colonel—Private Timorous and Colonel Bravado—pungent with witty sarcasm. Mankins thought they were poking fun at him, and they were.

The three revenants stayed and worked for thirteen nights, August 19 through September 1, long enough for Carmichael's spirit to win forty-one games taking him to number seventy-five. The cards assembled themselves in a deck again by suit and number, ready to be shuffled. Jute cord tied itself around them. Mankins pocketed the deck and joined the trek on the road to the next billet, the next fight. The last time Carmichael's voice spoke to Mankins, and making fun of his southern accent, he said, "I come with y'all this far, boy. You leavin' and I ain't. Far's I know, yer on yer own. Twenty-five games to go. Good luck. They say who wins the war hangs on your solitaire games. One hundred games finished or kaput, as the Hun would say. Who knows? Adios amigo."

Otis Mankins told Atkins what had happened. Tommy could tell that in the Realm Beyond the stakes in the game had been raised. The Corporal said, "Do what the voice told you to do. Play each game in turn to its finish." Atkins told him, "Concentrate on your play. Pray for help and help will come."

"Then you mean I'm not crazy? Jolly says I am. You're nuts, he says. But why me?" asked Mankins.

Atkins said, "I don't know why we're picked. Not just you. Not just me. Ordinary men like us. It happens. I would not have believed such things before they happened to me. These things come from beyond the world we know. I don't know everything. In fact, I hardly know anything. I only do what I am told. I don't think you're insane. Chosen."

General Andrew Jackson Comes to the Solitaire Player's Aid

By September 1 the Thirtieth Division had finished its work at Ypres, packed up, left Proven, Belgium and were on the march. The next stop was sixty-one miles and seven days away. The private has no time to play on the trek. The "Old Hickory" Division billeted around St. Pol September 7, stayed there in general reserve until Sept 20 training, training, training, getting ready for the battle. Day and night the 118th Regiment heard the pounding of the guns, the explosions close by, keeping the coming battle in mind.

The first night at St. Pol Caleb Jolly asked, "Mind if I look at your book? Maybe if two of us play you could finish faster." A near-fatal request.

"You can look," said Private Mankins. "I already told you I'm the only one who plays."

"Okay," his fellow gunner said. "But can I look anyway? Just curious."

"Okay. Don't lose my place."

Jolly thumbed through. "Hey, Otis, what about all these variations? Do you play them, too? Do you have to?"

There were thirteen variations for "Klondike" alone, the first game in the booklet. Slightly different rules. "La Belle Lucie," five versions. "Streets and Alleys" had eight, each with a different name. The booklet described variations for most of the games. In his frenzy to finish the one hundred games, the thought hadn't occurred to Mankins that he might have to play all of them, too. The possibility threw him into a black funk. If he had to play out all of the variations, this was the kiss of doom. Doom for himself. Doom for his friends.

Private Mankins ran to Atkins to ask the fatal question.

He ended, nearly in tears, "I will be the one who lost the war. Beyond regret. I'd throw myself in front of a gun."

Then Private Jolly said, "With the dead all around us, and every kind of weapon aimed at us, we'll be lucky to live to the end. I wouldn't mind living to regret something. It can't all be on you, you know. "

The conversation put Otis Mankins completely out of sorts. He couldn't eat. His sleep was broken and fitful. He fretted and grieved.

To make things worse, the first night at St. Pol the voice of his long-dead grandmother, his mother's mother—caressing, but ominous—started Mankins awake. She said, "Soldier, grandson, my Otis, named for my blessed husband, your solitaire games are holy battles in the war. The battle for Bellicourt Tunnel, in which you will fight, will tell the future. Break through the defenses, and the Allies will be victorious." Then, she announced a new stake in the game: Fail, and they lose the war. You must finish the one hundredth before the battle begins, or. . . ." Her voice trailed off into silence. He knew the rest of her pronouncement without hearing it. Then her voice returned. "Pray for help and help will come." Nearly the same instructions Atkins gave him when he learned that he had to win the games to save himself and his section. She said, "So much at stake. So much to lose." Pleading, "Pray to the Almighty for help. Pray to St. George."

Though this happened in the middle of the night once again, he rushed to tell Corporal Atkins about it. After he heard what Mankins had to say, and without stirring from his cot, Atkins said, "Do what the voice told you. She said play cards." Mankins saw the Corporal fall back asleep, or so it seemed. Since he had not been dismissed, the private stood where he was, at ease. In half a minute Atkins sat upright. His body shivered for a few seconds, his eyes still closed in sleep. The instructor spoke in a strained voice, as if his breath pushed the words out. "After morning mess go to the padre's tent. There is a Bible and prayer cloth on his table.   They will protect you. You will play cards there from now on." Atkins fell back on the cot. Mankins saluted the sleeping Corporal and left.

The next morning Chaplain Phelps greeted the haggard soldier at mess. "Atkins talked with me. Come to my tent when you are done."

Mankins began, confessed to the chaplain, "I regret I ever took up these cards. Worse yet, bought this cursed book. It trapped me. I'm a goner." Mankins's family, his church believed gambling, smoking, drinking, and dancing were the Devil's work. The private's sin plagued him. He remembered his preacher's words: "The Devil lives in every deck of cards. When you see the eye of a king, or queen, or jack, the devil's looking you right in the eye. If you play, or even touch a card, the Devil will lead you deeper into sin and Hell." Otis Mankins felt doomed, but unwilling to stop. He had to play.

Chaplain Phelps told him, "You are an instrument of war. Of course every soldier is. But you, more than ordinary. You were chosen. I pray for you. All of this is difficult for me. My religious training. My theology. This is a new teaching, new gospel, you might say. I learned the age of miracles ended long ago when Jesus left mortal life. Miracles still occur. I'm in a state of amazement."

"Am I here to play cards?"

"Presbyterians are not Baptists. It is all right to play. Besides, this is not profane, but divine solitaire, played for a sacred purpose."

From then on every moment when he was not in training the private sat in the chaplain's tent, the deck in his left hand, the right ever turning cards, the Bible protecting him from the left side, the prayer cloth shielding from the right. He prayed, and an agitation, an impatient nervousness overtook him. A sudden fever and chills, nausea and dizziness invaded his body. In ten minutes the spell passed as quickly as it had come.

Andrew Jackson, "Old Hickory"

Suddenly, in his mind's eye Mankins saw a portrait he knew from the South Carolina State House which he had visited with his grade school class years ago. Old Hickory, soldier, Hero of New Orleans, President, the Thirtieth Division's namesake. All Southerners knew the great man's life. He was a symbol and reminder to the native sons of the greatness of the southern soldier, the ones who served with him, to their eternal glory.

Then an old man's voice, accustomed to lead and command, spoke in Mankins's mind: "Who the hell are you? They sent me here to save your scrawny ass. They say we're distant relatives and I owe it to you. I believe that's bullshit. I never heard of no Mankins in our family. With a name like that we'd of likely kicked 'em out. They say I have to play solitaire. What kind of damned sissy plays solitaire? Worse yet, a soldier. Worst of all, a god damn fuckin' general. But there's somethin' about you, they said. They say you need to beat the adversary. When they told me it sounded like the word begins with capital A. Not someone at the poker table they said. I won't see him. He's the Devil, they tell me. I said what the fuck's goin' on? They said just fuckin' do what yer told for once. So here I am. You just sit your ass down in that chair." The general said, "Sit down, you useless stooge. I need your body. No sleep tonight for you. We're playin' solitaire, for the love of God. Hold the damn deck of cards, will you. Do somethin' useful fer God sake."

After a fruitless quarter hour of sitting and holding the deck a shudder went through Mankins's body, a trembling. Otis Mankins felt tremors first in his fingers, then his hands. His arms lifted on their own. At first his hands struggled, as if they were restrained, though after a few minutes they danced with a card player's grace. The hands picked up the deck, shuffled it three times, a beautiful cascade of cards, and laid out the foundation for "Fortress." The voice said, "This reminds me of the rampart I built out of mud and muck around New Orleans. Fortress, but not much of a one."

Old Hickory, gambler and card player, took over Mankins's hands, inhabited him. Always grousing, the General first played one game at a time with one deck. "This is too damn slow. Cards! Bring me decks of cards!" Jackson ordered. He sent Mankins, frantic and frenzied, to get them. Mankins traded souvenirs he had picked up from abandoned battlefields for decks of cards until he had half a dozen. It never occurred to him what others thought of his bizarre request. Several refused to give up their decks, others said they had none, and a few, thinking the boy crazy, thought it best to get rid of him by handing over a deck or two. When he returned with the cards and give them to the old General, "Old Hickory's" voice bellowed in his ear, "Get another table. Get two more. Line 'em up." Mankins moved the meager furnishings around.

The General played with two decks. Then two games at once with three decks each. Then three games at a time, one on each table. He made good progress. "Idiot's Delight." "This one is special for you, you pumpkin head." Then, "I believe when you were born your mother's cunt pressed your head too hard, squeezed it out at the sides. You got a squash face." Mankins's eyes were small and wide apart. "You nose approaches your mouth. You ain't repulsive, but you come mighty close. Pressure must have squeezed your brain. You must be between stupid and loony." The General went on, inspired. "There must be a kind of squash that grows where you grew up shaped like your face. I believe squash pollen got mixed in when your mother conceived you. What do you think? I see the resemblance, sure enough."

Then the general played "Beleaguered Castle." And so on.

The Company was to leave by truck on September 22. When he finished the eighty-ninth game, said the voice of the old General, "Where you from?"

"Sumter, sir."

"Are you the village idiot at home? You must be," and chuckled at his own joke. Then he said, "Yer movin' on from here. I'm staying. You're under special orders. From me. Ten of one hundred games left for you. Solitaire only, till you win." Then in a comradely way: "Soldier, you gave me your body, your mind, and senses. I done a lot in my life, not all of it good. I never thought I could do anything useful again for anybody, a cause again, good or bad. I thought I was a legend fading into the past, a name in a history book. I was done for long ago." The voice faltered, the General taking in the enormity of what he had seen the past few days, then began again. "I never could have imagined what I saw through your eyes. I saw the rankest fuckin' evil men ever visited on men. It turned into a feast for rats and lice and flies. I thought folks were bad and crazy in my day.

They had a lot to learn about evil and crazy, hardly begun to learn. This was an education to me and grave disappointment in humanity's progress."

Mankins, not knowing what to say, "We're still fighting. Reports say the Germans are falling back and losing. I don't know."

Not listening, General Jackson went on to congratulate himself. "I beat the Devil at solitaire! He fought to block me, thwart the cards. But I out-flanked him, feigned, got him lookin' in the wrong direction, thinkin' I was gonna do one thing when I was going to do something else. Like New Orleans and the British. You must have studied up on it."

"We sure did, sir," Mankins spoke into the air.

"By God. All those games. To my immortal credit, I'm sure. That's a triumph I shall relish through eternity."

Then he made a little address, even though Mankins was the only person to hear it. "This Division, the Thirtieth, honored me naming it 'Old Hickory.' The Division will shed much southern blood here, American blood. It will mix with Yankee blood, also fightin' for America. I am proud to have been called to arms. But fuckin' solitaire, for Christ sake. I'll never get over it. No one but you and Atkins know. So keep your mouth shut. Anyway, they'll think you're crazy if you talk about it. And the padre knows. He's not talkin'. I don't mind now drifting back to the place from whence I came. I seen enough."

With that, Old Hickory, General Andrew Jackson's presence faded, until Mankins was alone at the table. He picked up the cards. They warmed in his hands, seemed to return to life. He breathed in the scent of dread. What would happen now? He had ten games to play. With holy cards. He put the deck in his tunic pocket.

Tincourt, St. George, and the Last Ten Games

The Division was shipped to Tincourt, France three miles east of devastated Peronne. When the soldiers arrived at billets it was already dark. Some in the Division thought Mankins was getting religion, which meant he was afraid of dying, because he spent so much time with the padre. Others thought he had been made the padre's orderly. Only his section knew about the cards. And they kept mum. Mankins retreated to the padre's quarters that morning. He untied the string holding the deck together, shuffled the cards, and opened the book to game number ninety and began. As he played, every once in a while his body would jerk and twitch, twist into grotesque contortions. His arms would flail. His hands would spasm into fists. He would grunt and groan, utter incomprehensible words. Then they subsided into quiet and peace. Private Mankins made his way though games, three the first night—"Serpent Poker," "Demon's Fan," and "Phalanx" and two more games the next night. Mankins' confidence grew.

He thought he would quickly finish the one hundredth game. But the next night he finished no games. The following night the same.

For the third night in a row he failed to bring all the cards to their proper places on the foundation. His confidence waned. The sixth night he completed "Rainbow." The name revived his hope. Then he remembered the Biblical prophesy. The fire next time. There was plenty of fire all around. The explosions, flamethrowers, smoke, buildings—houses, barns, everything made of wood, and trees, too. Smoke thick on the air. His hope flagged further.

Tommy Atkins removed Mankins from all fatigues.

The card player needed to finish the last four games in order to avoid utter catastrophe. The Lewis gun section knew when the big attack would go off and that day was drawing closer. Otis Mankins's play became frenetic, frantic.

That night while he tossed in sleepless worry, a voice filled the tent, its canvas sides vibrating. "Struggle mightily against the Demon, the Beast,' it whispered, its volume amplified to a hurricane wind. "I am St. George, patron saint of Mons, come to redeem my pledge of victory and peace." At that instant, Mankins saw the magazine cover Hans Schmidt showed him once: the Angel of Mons, St. George. He saw the Angel victorious at the last fight against the Hun, sending Jerry chasing.

"First at Mons. . . . . Last at Mons." The words came to Mankins. He understood. St. George had fought the Germans at Mons in Britain's first battle. Britain would chase the Germans from Mons in its final battle with the scourge of the world. In his state of mind these thoughts seemed natural, normal, ordinary, the way a dream seems natural and ordinary. He was in the thrall of the words, the voice, and the picture he had of the magazine cover. The voice went on. "The warrior angels who rallied with me at Mons are here to vanquish the Adversary in the battle of cards, solitaire. Fifty-two cards are the devil's tool, and mine, also."

Then, "Soldier, you are the cards' instrument. Sleep now. Rest. To-morrow you will receive a great power. You will have the strength to defeat the enemy." Private Mankins fell into a deep sleep instantly.

What St. George's voice had proclaimed happened the next morning in a solemn ceremony Atkins conducted. Now he, and the two sections of Lewis gunners were "Golden Arrows of God." He had faith that the other part of the saint's words would come true. He hoped that when he next picked up the cards, time running out, he would bring the test to its end, would beat the Devil, too, the way Carmichael and Andrew Jackson had. The clock ticked the seconds. The night of September 27.

Hour after hour he turned the cards. Soon it took a reasonable number of turns through the deck for play to reach the object of the ninety-eighth game. Then the number of turns the deck needed decreased. He finished "Roll Call."

The last game. "Clock." The private laid out the foundation, twelve cards arranged in the shape of a clock's face, correctly ordered. The clock told him he had little time left. The next night the troops would be in the jump-off trench. Two days from battle. He had to finish before the battle. Now Private Mankins turned the cards and every turn brought a successful lay. Done. Exhausted, finished, he dropped asleep in his chair.

In a waking vision Otis Mankins saw each turn of the cards, game after solitaire game laid out in perfect order, the first to the one hundredth, complete. They revealed divine order in the four suits, the faces, and fifty-two cards, beyond games and rules. The Ruffians—Will Catchpole, Lewis Palmer, Paul Carmichael—were at his side. Then Andrew Jackson, "Old Hickory" himself. Then Mankins saw himself, heard himself speak, so softly the listeners had to draw near. He heard himself say, "A voice that was not of my own mind. St. George's maybe? Spoke with authority, strength, insistent. He said, "Saved from death. This is the salvation granted the living. Your play saved a multitude, victory instead of defeat."

When he awoke, he felt he was arising from a stupor. And he recalled his vision. Drained of energy, he visited the latrine, washed in cold water, and trudged along to mess. It was impossible for him to speak without having his chest swell with sobs, so he ate alone and in silence.

BOOK III

BATTLE PLANS ❖ 4

Chapter 13

The Spring Offensive: The Kaiserschlacht (The Kaiser's Battle)

March 21 – July 18, 1918

Germany Comes out of the Trenches

The Kaiser's Battle was Germany's chance to win the war. Russia declared a ceasefire in the last month of 1917. The Bolshevik government of the new Soviet Russia signed the Treaty of Brest-Litovsk with Germany on March 3, 1918. The Soviet government withdrew from the war. In return, Germany and its allies stopped their attack on Russia. Russia gave up much land and resources to Germany. The Germans now were able to ship fifty divisions from the East to fight on the Western Front.

A year after the United States declared war, among the first troops to arrive were II Corps, the 27th and 30th Divisions, 60,000 soldiers. The 27th, or Orion, Division, was almost all New Yorkers. The 30th, Old Hickory, were South Carolina, North Carolina, and Tennessee boys. As different as one American could be from another. Of the million American soldiers in Europe, both divisions were "lent" to the British Fourth Army. Knowing all this, the Germans planned and launched the *Kaiserschlacht*, what the British called the Spring Offensive.

Operation Michael

The main thrust, *Operation Michael*, began on March 21. Ludendorff would have his army drive a wedge between the British and French where their lines met at St. Quentin, France. Then they would outflank the British, push them east, and crush them against the Channel, if they made it that far. Or, if the British stood to fight, defeat them at St. Quentin and the canal north through Bellicourt to Cambrai. Three more offensives, *Georgette*, *Gneisenau* and *Blücher-Yorck,* would drain Allied reserves from *Michael*.

In *Michael* numbers overwhelmed the British. The Germans began their attack along a fifty mile long line fifty miles from Amiens. In two weeks the Germans drove the British back thirty-seven miles to within twelve miles of the British supply center there. Even without reaching the depot, the Germans greatly improved their situation. From March 21 until April 5, the day the German offensive ended, the British suffered 178,000 casualties, more than 10,000 a day. Simple as that. The Germans. 240,000 for the campaign, a massive loss.

Begun on April 7 with a two-day German bombardment, *Georgette*—the battle gained three names: the Lys Offensive, the Fourth Battle of Ypres, the Fourth Battle of Flanders—lasted twenty-two days, ending on the 29th, the Allies victorious. The British, Canadian, French, Belgian, American, and Portuguese armies fought. In the battles each side lost 120,000, killed or wounded. The losses added up, as engagement followed engagement.

Before the next offensive both sides refitted their armies, reorganized and consolidated, issued new uniforms, new weapons, fed, cleaned the men of lice and mud, trained—always training—took them by lorry and train, then march, march, march to the next battlefield, a new position, entrench, reconnoiter, prepare to attack or withstand an attack. Hundreds of guns to transport, camouflage, site on targets. Train-loads of ammunition to haul, fuel, food, clothes, barbed wire, shovels, picks, mauls, everything the soldier needs, and store at depots. This took weeks.

Then on May 27 Ludendorff dealt the next blow, his third attack, *Blucher-Yorck*–the Third Battle of the Aisne. May 27 to June 6, 1918. Here the German Imperial Army surprised the French, rushed through a twenty-five mile-wide gap in the line, passed through thin defenses, reached the Aisne River in six hours. The next days took the Germans closer to Paris. In three days they captured 50,000 Allied soldiers and eight hundred guns. Wounded or dead: 137,000 Allies and 130,000 Germans. A quarter of a million in the three offensives. Since the start of Michael the Allies had 425,000 casualties, the Germans, 490,000, 925,000. Nearly a million soldiers wounded or killed.

At that moment Germany was on the verge of victory. Then, as had happened often before, the Hun outran his railhead and supply train. Food and supplies used up. Ten days after it began, Ludendorff halted the offensive.

In the next battle the Germans planned to bring two major salients that the first and third attacks had created into a new straight front. The Noyon-Montdidier Offensive, 8 – 12 June, five days.

Finally, the Germans began the Second Battle of the Marne on July 15, their final major offensive on the Western Front. The attack failed. French and American forces counter-attacked, overwhelmed the Germans. August 6 the battle was over.

The German Army Wasting Away

The German Army was wasting away. The spirit of defeat spread like the influenza. So many killed, wounded, captured, their own guns and supplies now in the enemy's hands. Fritz was exhausted, demoralized. He was hungry and without food. He emerged from his dugouts in great numbers, hands raised, downtrodden, weary. His face spoke of failure, disbelief, and shame. The hope for German victory died. Thus German Army's great Kaiser's Battle the *Kaiserschlacht* ended.

As Ludendorff planned, in case the Kaiser's battles failed, the German army withdrew to the Hindenburg Line, considered impregnable, unassailable.

Chapter 14

The Allied Offensive (The Great Advance) Begins

General Foch's Plan

Appointed Commander-in-Chief of the Allied Armies on April 3, 1918, French General Ferdinand Foch unified the French, British, Colonial, Belgian, and American armies. The Allies' plans and decisions for the spring and summer battles were in his hands. Realizing that the past four months' exertions had exhausted the German army and expended much of its resources, Foch, Haig and Rawlinson for Britain, the Australian Lieutenant General John, Canadian Currie, and the American Pershing knew that conditions were right for a monumental push. The Great Offensive was to attack the entire ninety-mile front so the Germans could not afford to shift troops from one point to another. The combined Allied armies would attack in the Great Offensive Maréchal Foch directed.

Foch planned four blows, one to begin after the other on successive days. On September 26 French and American troops attacked between the Meuse and Rheims, in the Battle of Meuse-Argonne: forty-seven days of hot, deadly battle. This was mainly a battle of Americans against the Germans, with the French playing a significant role.

The next day, September 27, the British First, Third, and part of Fourth Armies attacked Cambrai at Nord-Pas-de-Calais along an unfinished section of the Canal du Nord. By October 2 the army had cut a ten and a half mile breach in the Hindenburg Line. Compared with advances the Allies had made in battles over the past four years, the victory was stunning and swift. The third attack was along the St. Quentin-Cambrai front in France toward Maubeuge, in Belgium.

On September 28 at Flanders French, British, and Belgian armies set upon the Germans, fought in the direction of Ghent, Belgium.

The Fourth Army—made up of British, Canadian, and the 27th and 30th Divisions of the American army—was assigned the Bellicourt tunnel sector. September 29. Zero hour: 5:10 a.m.

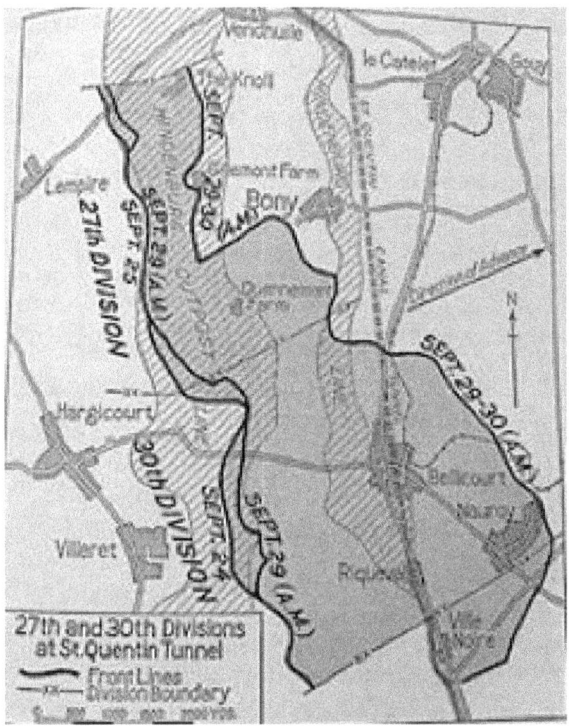

Where the two American divisions would fight the Germans

General Monash, his staff, one hundred officers, planned the Battle of Bellicourt Tunnel. They worked miles away from the battlefield, safe. The staff and generals knew things never go the way they plan. Too much unpredictable. Even so, they have to decide the number of guns, the quantity of ammunition, all calibers, food, where to depot supplies, route of march and travel, transport. They estimate the number of deaths, how many wounded. They decide where to put aid stations, plots for cemeteries. Numbers, not persons, count. Overwhelm the enemy with numbers, ratios. The staff steels itself. It could not be otherwise. They planned every step of the attack on the Hindenburg Line, hour by hour, down to as short as four-minute intervals for moving forward one hundred yards, tanks and infantry to keep up behind a moving bombardment. He had what he needed to overcome the Germans there. The General commanded the American II Corps' 27th and 30th Divisions, 30,000 soldiers each, his own Australian 2nd and 3rd , and 5th, 12,000, 36,000 in all, and the 5th Cavalry Brigade in reserve, plus artillery and corps ancillary troops. 86,000 men for a front only three miles long.

LANCE CORPORAL TOMMY ATKINS ❖   4

Chapter 15

At St. Pol, Sniper Jenks Braddock's Dream

September 8, 1918

Sniper Jenks Braddock came to Private Spears' tent. "Can I talk to you? Just the two of us? You won't tell anyone. Promise."

"Sure. What is it?"

"I had a dream. I want to find out what it means."

"Sure." Said Private Spears, "Something in my book?"

"Yeah. Maybe," Braddock asked, "What's it called? *Dream Book?*

"*Master Book of Dreams.*"

"Yeah. I think so."

"I'll get it out." While he went through his kit, he asked, "What did you dream?"

Jenks Braddock said, "Sometimes I remember parts as I wake up. Always fills me with dread. I didn't dream anything happy since I come over here." The sniper closed his eyes and took a deep breath. "Last night I dreamed more real than anything."

"Yes. I had dreams like that," said Spears.

Braddock went right on. "You were in it. I know what it means. It came in words. And a rat, big as a house cat, spoke to me, said he'd kill me. Spears, what does your book say about rats? A rat with yellow eyes? Look it up and tell me. Maybe it's one of those that means the opposite. I hope so."

Without even reading in the booklet, Spears knew the meaning of rat was dark and grim.

Spears kept *The Master Book of Dreams* wrapped in waxed paper, and canvas. Even so, it had begun to wear. He took it to an armorer, a friend of his from before the war. "I worry it will fall to shreds. Could you fashion a box for it? I saved a dozen casings." He handed them to the armorer. "That should be plenty. I will find a way to return the favor."

The armorer said, "As if we aren't busy enough. They want cases for bibles, pictures of their sweethearts. Pleas and bribes." All the while snipping, hammering, bending, in a few minutes the armorer made the box. "Here. Be careful when you take the top off. It's not as snug as it could be."

Now Private Spears took the booklet out of its case, unwrapped it, and read. He said to Braddock, "Not good news, but not everything happens the way the book says. There's prediction and there's reality."

"All right. Read."

"I'd rather not."

"I don't care what you'd rather not. Then let me read it." Spears handed him the book. Braddock read. "Rat. Impending troubles." He raised his head from the booklet and said, "Who doesn't know that? You don't have to be no fortune teller to know that."

"Yes." Spears went on. "Millions of soldiers dead and the war isn't over. Suffering, death. Life for those alive and whole at the end filled with ghastly memories, I expect."

Then sniper Braddock read on. "Treachery, death if they attack." Dismayed, Braddock said. "Killed by a rat?"

"It must mean a Hun," Spears said. "They're rats, don't you know? Attack must mean you're alive when they come. It's the Huns. What'd you expect? Bad news. But anything can happen. We see it all the time. Anything."

As if he had not been listening, Braddock said, "Trench rats are viscous." He covered his eyes with his hands. "I can't bear the thought of rats eating my corpse."

The talk deflated Braddock's spirits. He hoped to return to his home in the mountains, leave all of this behind when the war was over. Hunting and fishing and enjoying the outdoors. Now he doubted that he would ever get home. He dreaded lying in the devastated land all about. Spears could see the dejection in Braddock's eyes. "You trust me, don't you? Some things I know to be true, others possible. But in premonitions some things seem true, like your dream, or what the book says about rats, and they turn out to be wrong. The wheel of fate is not just one wheel. It is many, each turning at a different rate, different sizes—like gears. See what I mean? What you saw is a possibility, one among many. There is nothing inevitable. Many things are possible."

THE AMERICAN SOLDIERS ❖ 4

Chapter 16

Wounded at Mons, a Shell Fragment in the Neck and No Scar. . .
Before the Americans Learned Who Atkins Really Was

Said William Spears, "You heard the instructors. Look at his neck, they say. See? No scar. As if he was never struck by shrapnel, died, and came back to life."

Hans Schmidt said, "I think it's like the joke in the County 4-H fair kids pulled off every year. 'The Horse Whose Head Grows Where his Tail Belongs.' We tied a horse in a stall with his ass facing the door instead of his head. In another stall we hung tack and saddle and blanket over a wire frame and hung from the ceiling. Call it 'The Invisible Horse.' In a third we put together a horse's skeleton. 'The Phantom Horse' we called it. Low-level, bumpkin humor. The jokes got a smile. People didn't mind paying three cents to go in and have a look. Gave some money for the kids' activities."

"I don't get it. What do you mean?" asked Mankins.

Jenks Braddock said, "Dummy, you don't get it? The main thing, there was nothing in the stalls you couldn't easily explain. It was a joke. Like no scar on Atkins' throat. It's no evidence that anything happened. But the main point of the story is that the Angel of Mons saved him. I doubt that it's true. There's plenty of old Irish and Scotsmen at home who'll spin you a tale like that to get the pleasure of getting you to believe it."

The Lewis gunners took it all as good fun, camaraderie. Accounts about Tommy Atkins, instructor, interested us mightily.

Tommy Atkins Inscribes Red Crosses
Next to the Names of Those He will Initiate

"Swamp Fox"

Next to the names on the muster roll the angel Lieutenant Dease had given him in a dream vision Tommy drew a cross in red ink, not an X, but a Christian cross.

Kendall Haydon   Gunner One   was the first name Tommy marked.

The instructors saw that Haydon keenly observed the world situation and his role in the war. The universal Southerner in character and conduct. If the measures for all the Southern soldiers were averaged—height, weight, hat and shoe size—he would fit almost every measure. He abundantly intelligent. The young man educated himself by study and conversation.

Atkins read down the list until he came to Ezekiel Able Gunner Two Deep-set brown eyes reveal his eager mind. Prominent nose and high cheekbones. He stands erect, as if born to the military posture, commanding and giving respect. American patriot of the highest order. A leader's qualities. Well thought of. Likely to earn promotion quickly. As Atkins inscribed a cross next to his name he foresaw that Able would lead his men across the Hindenburg Line, breaking the Dragon's Vein.

The third name that called for a cross was William Spears Gunner Assistant A boy from the sea and the farm, from St. Helena Island where he grew up among the Gullah Geechee, a Negro culture. The people shared the lore and religious practices with the young white boy which deeply influenced his way of looking at the world.

As Atkins read the report about Hans Schmidt, Gunner Assistant, the South Carolinian's hollow, angular face came to mind. Little flesh between skin and skull. From Sumter, South Carolina, Schmidt was moved by patriotic fervor to fight in the war he foresaw long before the United States entered. The only child of German immigrants, he was a soldier interested in the machinery of war, the workings of the Divine in war.

Otis Mankins, Gunner Assistant, totes ammunition. Corporal Atkins knew that each draft of soldiers contained its complement of dull, dim souls. Such was Mankins. Farm boy. Stirred to enlist because his friend Hans Schmidt read to him about the war from newspapers and magazines. Hoping to leave the farm, work from morning to night in all weathers for his father. And his father wanted him gone.

Atkins scratched a crude cross in red next to Otis Mankins' name.

Jenks Braddock Sniper Strongly muscled from physical work and exertion. A slight squint, probably from aiming at game down a gun barrel since childhood. From where the South Carolina Piedmont dips into old mountains and valleys. Braddock hunts and traps, and lives in the wild outdoors. Eager to hunt the Hun, about whom he had heard ghastly accounts. Atkins knew that Jenks Braddock earned the sniper's position, which he craved.

Red cross near his name.

"Gamecocks"

Atkins came to the name Donald Barton, Gunner One. The Corporal knew Barton's bulldog's scowl, his lower jaw thrust forward, jowls already begun. The instructors suffered Barton's fierce spirit, hoping he would become fit to lead the gun against the Enemy inside the Bellicourt Tunnel. Otherwise, a hard pill to swallow. Tommy Atkins marked a red cross next to his name. The Angel Lieutenant Dease so ordered. Atkins knew he had to have faith, but saw little reason for the choice of Barton.

Caleb Jolly, Gunner Two. Before he dipped his pen in red ink, Tommy paused to think. Jolly's hair a flaming red, like the ink, eyes green. Alert. Irish. His face took part in conversation, one moment jolly, the next serious, even angry. Wit and good cheer. He had the athlete about him, a runner's body. Atkins knew the young man sought adventure in the "Big Blow" "Over There." Handy in the way of a farmer. Jolly read and thought more widely and deeply than most. Thereafter disillusioned and bitter.

A red cross for Miles Mason, Gunner Assistant, the boy from Columbia, the state capitol. His father a laborer, five children to feed, and Miles the oldest. He removed himself from the family board and larder and sent his pay to his father. And he wanted to see the world.

And a cross for Beau Baylor, Gunner Assistant. Quick to learn, and eager to get to the Front.

These and the chaplain and wagoner Elliott Joiner and two other wagoners completed the list of those who Atkins would initiate as "Golden

Arrows of God."

And Initiation at Tincourt

September 22, 1918

On September 6 the Division was ordered to the Cambrai-St. Quentin sector. By stages it reached billets at Tincourt on September 22.

Atkins sensed that soon someone from the Other Side—the Angel Dease, or St. George himself—would order him to initiate the Lewis machine gun teams, the chaplain and the muleskinner, Elliott Joiner, into the "Golden Arrows of God." The signs were present. First Churchill, then Holmes, and Doyle. He long knew that these few under his care and charge stood in a special place.

When they were billeted the message came—a visitation, not from any he expected, but from the soldier who took command of the guns when Dease died. Private Sidney Godley. The godly soldier, who raised the spirits and led the Ruffians, helped the Victors, himself killed with the others at Ypres. He spoke no word and the vision of him was fleeting, but Atkins knew its meaning. He knew to gather the men in the chaplain's room of worship. Then, in the flesh, Godley entered the tent. Only Atkins knew that he was the Godley who died four years ago at Ypres with the others of the Ruffians gun, for he seemed as alive as any. Atkins explained who Godley was, introduced him. Then Godley spoke to the Americans. His voice seemed to come from beyond this world, the words welling like water from a deep spring, thoughtful, with sober tone. Plain, everyday. He said, "The war is reaching its end. Much is about to happen. You will be important in it. When commanders and generals say it they mean everyone in general. I mean you in particular."

He paused. Then, "You already know much about Tommy Atkins' extraordinary experiences. Not the lucky escapes or the brave deeds. You will soon encounter such things yourselves. I mean what you know about the saintly Atkins."

Godley, returned to body, told them about Dease's death and transformation into an angel who served at the side of St. George through the war. He repeated what they already knew of Atkins own death and return, and what had happened at Mons those years ago. They listened, astonished.

Then he said, "You poor, innocent boys do not all deserve to be tested and tormented. But you will be."

Then, "What I teach you will sound strange, but you must accept it. You are being prepared for an extraordinary role in the war."

They absorbed all he said. Out of a leather cylinder he drew a sheet of old parchment marked with ciphers, letters, scrawls, brown marks—old dried blood. "I must initiate you. Each of you will be a 'Golden Arrow of God.' You have each proved yourself worthy of trust."

Then the Lewis gunners stepped forward in turn. Sidney Godley pricked each man's right forefinger with the pin from the back of Tommy Atkins' miniature gold arrow. Do not write your name. Just a drop of blood. None need take an oath. "I have no arrows, no insignia, to give you. Yet you are 'Golden Arrows' in His eyes."

He addressed them solemnly. "Some of you will fight on the field of battle. Some will descend into the tunnel under the plateau, a passage to the world of darkness. No one knows what will happen, though common sense says some will spill blood, some die. Some will suffer wounds and live mangled lives. Some will be untouched. My brother Tommy Atkins has examined your hearts and abilities. You passed spiritual tests he gave you without your knowing it. Even the worst of you. One Lewis gunner will pierce the Le Catelet-Nauroy Line. Who it will be, or what will happen no one knows. It might be a fatal jolt of energy, like lightning. It might be nothing the soldier will even notice, just another step in the direction of Germany. Whoever it is will find out."

Tommy Atkins added, "You will fight the way you were trained to fight. You will fight against demons, devils. The angels who fought beside us at Mons will fight at your side. You may see them. You may not. You are in the hands of the saints and angels, and the sacred Dease."

And Fate and Chance, the skeptical Donald Barton thought.

Then Sidney Godley spoke in a way and a language they had not heard before, inspired, spiritual. "Your actions will harmonize with invisible powers that dwell in the earth. Geomancers, they are called, know these energies, work with them." Then, in plain English: "You will not be the first to cross the Hindenburg line, but first to cross the second line. The greatest power is in the second line." With a pointer, he marked a line on the trench map. "The Le Catelet-Nauroy line." Then, again, in the words of a seer: "Practitioners of the esoteric arts mask their secrets. This secret above all they would hide. You now know the secret and will break the mystic power. The fate of the battle, the war, of armies and nations will unfold." Tapping the map with his pointer, he said, "Across the railroad track the Great Change will begin."

Then Godley indoctrinated them in the role the Teutonic gods' played in the war and the battle to come.

"Around the world men call these gods by different names. The gods and names are themselves, and also stand for cosmic forces."

Tommy Atkins interrupted. "I have been around the German enemy for four years. I sense their gods' presence. You can see them in the Hun's face, his demeanor." Atkins became not quite the professor, but one learned in what he was saying. Not only angry, but grief-stricken. His voice forceful and inspired, he went on. "The Hun hears his gods in the names of their plans and defenses and battles. It fills their so-called *Kultur*. Every German soldier, every German citizen, thinks he embodies the power of the names."

Godley went on with the teaching, the initiation. "You will meet their gods on the battlefield. Or their soldiers, for each German fights for his gods. Each god has a light side and a dark."

"Woton, god of knowledge, poetry, sorcery, healing, royalty. God of the gallows, frenzy, battle, death. An ugly, long-bearded, old man. A spear supports him. Two dogs and two ravens follow him everywhere."

"After him, Siegfried. *Sigu* 'victory' brings *frid* 'peace.' Both sides. War, then peace. Peace after conquest. He is the hero in Germanic legend and epic. This names the line you will break, the German name for the line."

He told them about Kriemhild, in saga, epic, and myth, beautiful warrior whose name mixes 'battle,' *hilde* with 'mask,' *grim*. Battle mask, a helmet with face guard. See what I mean? Not Christian."

Then he said, "Brunhilde, a Shieldmaiden, Valkyrie, decides which soldiers are to die and when. And the beauty Freya, chief Valkyrie, goddess of sex-love, war, and death. She comforts the dying soldiers, eases their passage to the otherworld. The bravest souls she takes to her home to stay for eternity."

Piped up Mankins, "Sir, sorry to say. I can't remember any of this. What's the good in knowing?"

"You only need know that they are in the battle, fighting here, too." Godley paused, listening. "Lieutenant Dease tells me any of you might face them, must fight to the death." In reflection: "Some will die anyway. Bomb. Machine gun bullet. I'm sad to say."

Then Godley led them to secret knowledge. "The Wandering Fluid, Spring of Exceptional Power, can be tapped for the benefit of mankind. In esoteric understanding the line also contains evil energy. One of the strongest fluids on earth runs along the ninety miles we are fighting over. The Dragon's Vein it is called, a beast filled with bile and hatred. You might guess that the ground under the tunnel and in the plateau is a line of concentrated energy. Don't think the Germans didn't consult with geomancers. They know the line is here and put it to their use. You Americans will cross the sacred boundary, disarm the evil energy, a power for evil-doing." Tommy Atkins knew this, but it was Godley's task to teach. Tommy watched his students' reactions, saw that some of the Lewis gunners were amazed, some bewildered by these teachings, some incredulous.

Godley concluded his lesson. "Piercing the Siegfried Line on the earthly plane will be the equivalent of St. George slaying the dragon in the realm of the divine. The Dragon's Vein. Above and below ground and in Heaven above."

Vickers Gunner Sidney Godley, gone these four years, said, "You are ready for what comes." He saluted the men and they, him. About face and he was outside, and gone. The soldiers sat in stunned silence, each absorbing what he now understood. They knew something would happen, but could never have guessed that it would be this.

After the men were dismissed Atkins called Haydon aside. He said, "For you there are special instructions. Godley gave them to me to deliver to you. In turn, he received them from the Angel Dease. Those above know of your skill and temperament. They know your connection to the other Kendall Haydon. Now, your orders, your job. You will receive the power to look, observe, recall what you hear and see. You will see the celestial battle. You will see the gore and blood of angels and devils. It will terrify you, sicken you. Your gorge will rise is disgust and repulsion. Yet you are to take it all in, absorb it. You are to be the receptacle for all of the horror that unfolds. You will survive the war. In every means you have, you will transmit what you take in in hopes of mankind taking to heart the hope that this will be the war to end all wars. You will be like an Old Testament prophet, though I hope your warnings and pleas bear more fruit than theirs did in their days. Go, now, my friend, and prepare yourself."

Haydon was astounded by what Tommy Atkins said. Prepare? Prepare for what? He sensed that he is to be a receptacle, a vessel, a repository. All he could do was worry and fret. The prospect Atkins laid before him brought to mind horrific visions that even now made him tremble. What would it be like in reality? He had hoped only to fight like a soldier, a good soldier. Now?

That Damned Rat

Tincourt, France
September 22, 1918

At Tincourt the Americans, tired from their long trek, sat on the ground while they were being assigned their billets. Some cleaned their guns, some filled bandoliers, some hunted for lice in shirts, tunics, and trousers. Caleb Jolly, like a carnival midway sideshow barker, had caught a dozen fleas that he kept in a little glass bottle. He took it out and got up a little entertainment. "Welcome to the Cootie Canteen! See the show! Watch 'em eat, drink, summersault, swing on a trapeze, pull a cart. Watch 'em dance! Watch 'em fuck! Watch the ladies lay their eggs!" And for part of his patter he said, "These ain't related to the louse. Not at all. You can't train a louse, a trouser rabbit. But you can train a flea. Gather round."

"That's too much," said Private Mankins.

Jolly took a small magnifying glass from his kit and said, "Watch the flea circus close up."

"I never heard of such a thing," miffed, Otis said.

Private Jolly: "There's a lot you never heard. That's what you get for being a dummy."

"You're a laugh," said Beau Baylor, as he caught and crushed the lice between his thumbs' fingernails. "I can give you some of mine if you want more."

"You see, Mankin?" said, Jolly. "Where there's life, something is bound to happen."

Just then a sergeant barked an order and they marched off to their billet. Jolly said, "No show. Sorry, boys. Maybe another time."

In the hayloft they spread out their kits for the night. Jabbered away about nothing. They were moved by their initiation, but were not sure what it meant. During it, Atkins had not been his ordinary self. His talk was unusual, odd.

A gas lamp created a circle of light in the middle of the loft. The edge of the light just caught a corner where a bit of hay moved. Out of the corner of his eye Jenks Braddock spotted the rat, big as a house cat.

"He's looking at me," Braddock whispered to his gun-mate Able.

Zeke answered, "No need to whisper. He doesn't know what you're saying. He's just looking. He ain't looking at you."

"He's not looking around," Jenks said. "He's glaring at me."

Annoyed by Braddock's foolishness, Able said, "So look back. He's just a damned rat. What'd you expect? Rats all over the place. Didn't you notice?"

"Not with yellow eyes. It's him, Zeke. The one I dreamed about. You know what Will Spears told me? His book of dreams says a rat means bad things will happen. Maybe even death."

"It's just a damned rat," Able said. "Forget about it."

"No, it's not."

"What the hell do you think it is, then?"

"A demon. A devil." Transfixed, Braddock said, "Hear him now? He's talking to me."

Exasperated, Able said, "You're nuts. Go see the doctor. Calm your nerves. Think straight if you can."

"He's talking to me! He's talking even now. He says he's gonna kill me. Can't you hear him?" said the boy from the Piedmont, usually full of courage and wilderness skills.

"Jenks, you're talking to yourself," Ezekiel Able said. "Come back to reality. Snap out of it. You're scaring yourself. Besides, you don't need a book of dreams to tell you what might happen. Millions dead now. The most important fact when it comes to our future. There it is, death, if you're lucky. Grim as hell if it's a bad wound. Then you have suffering to look forward to before death. I'm not being mean, just honest. Forget the fuckin' rat. Yes. You might die. I might die. But a rat's got nothing to do with it."

"He's talking to me, I tell you. Ask Atkins if such a thing ain't possible. Ask Spears. They'll tell you."

"Snap out of it."

"He has yellow eyes."

"How do you know he's a he? Maybe he's a she. Eyes are black, anyway, not yellow."

"Don't you hear him?"

Ezekiel Able threw a clod of dry mud at the rat. It scampered into the hay and out of sight. Able thought this was the end of foolish talk.

Chapter 17

The Wagoner's First Tale

(Elliott Joiner)

Saint-Pol-sur-Ternoise (St. Pol), France

September 25, 1918

Trucks Clogged Every Road

Convoy of seventy-seven trucks transporting ammunition to the front

What did we have in common? Donald Barton and Ezekiel Able and me? We fought in the 118th Regiment, "M" Company, all proud South Carolinians. And we were cousins. As different as our Army jobs were, our paths kept crossing. Funny that I would say it that way. I was a wagoner.

When I arrived in France I was Artillery. Now, I was Infantry, a driver. Me, and Privates Zachariah Christian and Philip Mather. We were three in a bunch, like muscadines on a vine. Or scuppernongs if you want. Grapes, anyway. All with the regiment.

Until a few days before the big battle, the main attack on Bellicourt Plateau, I was a wagoner, good at mules and horses. Worked them near every day on the farm at home. Plow, harrow, plant, ride, drive them in tandem. Hitch them and drive. Feed, care for them. Groom, stable boy, mucker.

Here I hauled limbers all around—guns, ammunition. I rode lead horse, left hand side, a second hitched to my right, two riders and four horses behind. It took six horses to pull the steel ammunition wagons, sometimes hauling several hundred rounds of ninety-pound 115 mm shells. We made two and three trips a night.

One Lesson in How to Drive a Heavy Ford Truck

I had one lesson in how to drive a heavy Ford truck. Someone must have thought if he can ride a horse, he can drive a truck.

I told the sergeant, "All they have in common is they locomote. I can't work the gas pedal, brakes, and clutch and steer all at the same time right off."

I told the sergeant, "Not the same as working a horse."

Then I told him, "Entirely different skill. Mechanical, not animal." The sergeant didn't listen. He barked, "Get in this damn truck and drive." I didn't know how to work all the parts together, let alone drive. I was still grinding gears when I was ordered to haul a truck load—three tons of ammunition.

It was rare, unheard of, this close to the line to transport during the day. Now the army would not be ready to fight if we could move only at night. It needed so much ammunition for the artillery, machine guns, rifles, small arms, signal flares, grenades, ordnance, parts, and every kind of supply. For three days and nights we hauled everything battle called for, dumped it at depots behind the front line. You can't imagine how many tons of explosives we hauled. We had forty more hours of draying before the battle began.

As much as possible we drove along paths cut through forests. At night we were forbidden to use headlamps. No lanterns. No cigarettes. It was easy to get lost. Each night an infantryman came to guide us. He walked in front of the first truck, a piece of white paper pinned on his back. We had to keep the trucks close to each other. Near the end, the 25th it was, we drove for forty-eight hours straight. That took us to the night of September 27th, two days before the big blow. That night the convoy stopped at a fork in the forest's dirt path. We walked around the trucks to wake ourselves up. Drank coffee. To show how bad it was, I laid down on a pile of crushed stone alongside the path for a minute and fell asleep. I couldn't believe it later when Zachariah told me an artillery shell hit twenty yards away. I slept through the explosion. I drove the last truck in line, loaded with a thousand fuses, the new 1 0 6's. They get screwed on the tips of artillery shells to blast barbed wire to shreds.

When I woke up I was alone. The convoy had gone off. Zachariah drove ahead of me, but with headlights off, he didn't notice that I wasn't following.

With the light of some wooden lucifers I scoured the ground to see which way the tire tracks went, but there were tracks down both forks. Sometimes we had taken one path and sometimes the other, depending on the dump we were headed for. I couldn't tell which fork the convoy had taken. I prayed for help.

Just then I saw a thin slip of light along the path to the right. I thought it was a Lucas Lamp with its thin slit of light. Even that light was forbidden.

Then I thought a soldier had come back to guide me. The slit became an orb, a globe of light, a glow shimmering in the center and mist-like all around it. A will-o'-the-wisp. And I heard a voice. "I am the light." I chuckled to myself. A piece of scripture talking inside my head in Tommy Atkins' voice, of all things. I had prayed and got this light, this answer. I knew which way to drive. As soon as I started up the engine the light faded and disappeared. Soon I caught up with the convoy, nearly bumped into Zachariah's truck. If I had gone the wrong way the Germans would take me prisoner, capture the fuses, and learn we had a new weapon in our arsenal. Not that the Huns could do anything about it right then, but it could help them later. But for certain I would not have delivered the fuses to our Army.

With ammunition trains and medical trains and service trains and sanitary trains moving back and forth to Bellicourt and depots and nearby villages, it would be hard for the Germans to miss what was going on. It's true, they knew a major attack was coming. Yet, by luck, we escaped their notice. As it turned out, even though worn out with defensive skirmish fighting, they were ready.

No Hun Aeroplanes Set to Fly

Morning of September 27, 1918

That morning's air reconnaissance reported no German aeroplanes set to fly today in our sector. We heard the Jerrys were running out of aeroplanes and pilots. It would be safe to travel in daylight.

The convoy—seventy-seven trucks, the ammunition train—stopped at St. Pol for a midday meal and rest. The trucks clogged every street in the village and the road into, through, and beyond. The main road ran alongside a shallow, wide, sluggish river. We were eating, lounging about, exhausted from two days' work and only a couple hours' sleep. The three of us gathered by the river bank, Zach, Phillip, and me. As I said, the scuppernongs. And me. A bunch of grapes. All from the same part the Midlands of South Carolina.

Some made their way down to the water. Some filled water bottles. Some rinsed mess kits, scrubbed the dust from their arms and faces and necks. Some took off puttees, boots, and socks and soaked their feet, trousers rolled up to the knees. At home we could strip naked, sit in the sun, go for a swim. Not here.

After we ate we stepped into the water to wash and stretch our legs, get whatever relief we could from the strain of driving. It being summer, the river fed by rain, the water was tepid. "Wet, not refreshing," Zachariah said.

Driver Mather: "Wet's good enough for me. At least we can wash."

Dozens of us were doing the same up the bank. Villagers came down, peasants they were, with cheese, meat, fresh bread, wine, beer. We were starting to have a jolly time, a moment of relaxing.

Then, suddenly we got a signal from a spotter balloon several miles down the river. An aeroplane, black iron crosses marking the wings, was flying in our direction. We knew he would see our trucks parked together along the road.

"The pilot's damn map will show a river running alongside the village," Zach Christian said.

"He's on reconnaissance checking our line's disposition. I think he has nothing to do with the village or river," said Philip Mather.

"We're a perfect target," said Christian. "A rich target. When the fighter sees us he'll drop his bombs."

I said, foolishly, "I don't think he'll notice." I changed my mind. "No. You're right, Zach. "He'll come for us as soon as he spots us."

"He'll have bombs in case a good target comes along, like us. If just one shell strikes near a truck, seventy-seven and the ammunition and all of us will be blown to Kingdom Come."

"Then again, he may not have any if he's only on reconnaissance," said Christian, thin hope in his voice.

"We should be so lucky. He'll have 'em, all right." Said Phillip Mather, "Pretty well trapped. We trapped ourselves."

Even though we were not far from our trucks, the first truck in line would have to drive off first, then each follow, like the boxcars in a train, each starting one at a time. Sadly, mine was first in line. I worried about stalling, running off the road, crashing into something.

If the flyer wiped out the contingent the consequences would extend beyond us soldiers, the trucks, and our loads. No trucks, no drivers to re-supply. Even now, after all the hauling they had done, they would have to haul ammunition for each day's fight while the army chased the Huns until they surrender. There would still be days, maybe weeks, or months of fighting. Without trucks and drivers and the supplies they would carry to the soldiers it would be impossible to win the battle. If the convoy was destroyed the General might as well call off the attack or sacrifice everything in a futile fight.

Destruction was the fate of villages we had already driven through, farms, cities as well. Shelling and fire-setting, planted bombs, looting and booby traps in the cleverest places. The Army was here to save people and these countries, the Huns, to destroy them and their way of life, make their countries possessions of the German Empire. Here at St. Pol, one bomb, and done in a minute.

Said Private Christian, "We don't have time to warn the villagers."

"If he drops a bomb it will be the biggest Fourth of July you ever saw, and it won't be celebrating our independence," said Mather.

The men turned poets for a moment. Said Private Christian, "Our independence from mortal life you mean. We would get to see what comes next, Hell, heaven, or nothing."

Said young Zachariah, "Concussion alone would bring down every brick building in this town. Explosions will set the wood buildings afire. The villagers will perish, the town disappear. What is here will be no more."

I said, "No time for prayers."

Mather joked, "If prayer worked, there would be a lot fewer soldiers in the ground."

Soon we heard the aeroplane engine, the sound of a fly buzzing. At this distance if I didn't know better I wouldn't be able right off to tell if it was something small and close by, a fly, or an aeroplane, big and distant. Its throb grew louder, rising in pitch as it drew closer. I said, "Looks like Beelzebub come to plague us."

I thought should we run to the fields around the village? Maybe hide in stables and barns? I asked, already knowing the answer.

Zachariah Christian mocked, "Shelter will be useless if he drops a bomb."

"No refuge, and if any of us survive, the pilot will use us for machine gun practice," said Private Mather.

Fog and Cloud

The earth trembled. It was as if the Titans wrenched themselves out of the earth, or the Hebrew God's Behemoth trampled the earth as prophesy promised for the end of days. Then there was an upwelling of the river. The water churned. A maelstrom formed, a swirl of water became a waterspout lifting water fifty feet in the air. The river flowed upstream, ran swiftly, nearly sweeping the men off their feet. Fish of all kinds and sizes struggled on the surface. The sedges and grasses lining the bank bent and swayed under the water's pressure. When the ripples reached the three drivers, the water turned frigid, and from muddy brown to crystal clear. At first it was refreshing. Quickly it numbed the feet, the cold traveling up the legs.

The cold water condensed in the hot sunlight. Moisture saturated the air. First a vapor, then mist, then thick fog gathered and overlay the river. Droplets light enough to hang in air sent light in all directions. A white veil, a bride's or nun's, masked the trucks' presence. The sky directly over the road, river, and village turned from translucent to opaque, air made visible. The fog climbed into the clear blue sky. All around the air was clear, the view crystal. Christian said, "River smoke, we call it at home." It covered the river like a feather quilt fluffed over a bed. We sensed the presence of forces drawing it over the river. No wind stirred. All this happened in less than a minute. The cloud began maybe twenty yards ahead of my truck, who knows how far beyond the last of them.

Then through the fog smudges, blotches, dark forms, came down. Biting insects, hordes of bluebottle flies thickened the air, and stinging hornets in equal number. Gnats, millions, in clouds, little whirlwinds like dust devils Wagoner Joiner used to see lift the straw before it was raked from the harvest field. We "scuppernongs" covered our faces with handkerchiefs for fear of breathing gnats in, smothered by gnats, keeping them from our eyes. Their buzzing together sounded like the aeroplane's engine. Light from behind threw them into monstrous silhouette shadows.

Then the wagoners saw rays of golden light pierce the fog. At first Phillip Mather thought it was the sun, but the sun shone elsewhere in the sky. Butterflies, thousands of thousands, every color and size, descended through the light. When the butterflies came close the three drivers saw their faces, human, compassionate and fierce all at once. Wings astir, they fluttered among the men. Their wings beat a solemn music, stirred the fog into billows and swirls, thickening the cloud cover.

Beelzebub, it was truly the Fly Devil, Lord of the Flies, leading his troops against the fragile butterflies which contended with power their frail bodies belied, smothering the insects, not with love, cutting off the air the monsters needed to live.

In the midst of the fog vague shapes became figures, putti, baby angels, angels, who looked down on the drivers. Zachariah Christian had seen them on old paintings in a museum. Here they were, benign and weeping.

Cherubim, swift-winged, who carry the Almighty through the heavens, attended: four-faced, human in front, eagle behind, lion to the drivers' left and ox to the right, and three pairs of wings. Each fifteen feet tall, properly proportioned. Grandeur and ferocity.

Equal in size to the angels, insects with faces the soldiers saw on the spouts of churches they marched past, gargoyles and monsters, misshapen faces, evil expressions, fell through the fog and fought.

Angels on fire, the size of worms fishermen use for bait: the Seraphim. Bright spots of flame, their eyes seeing in every direction. The three drivers heard the cry, "Holy, holy, holy," chanted again and again. The Seraphim battled demon rats, fought slavering-fanged demon hounds, crocodile, and savage bear.

All the while the Hun plane came on.

Eagles flew toward the river, their talons grappling vipers who arose in the marshy sedge, making off with the wriggling creatures to the trees across the river. Beyond the circle of the divine battle vultures wheeled on the air, some perched in trees, some on the ground, strutting their lopsided lope. They smelled death.

The demon armies tore at the veil of fog so the pilot could see the trucks below. Immediately angels repaired the rents.

Along the riverbank soldiers resting, stood and pointed. We heard their excited whispers. Those with their feet in the water felt it turn cold, same as us. They saw the river turn upstream, same as we did. They saw the cloud arise from the river and block the sky. "I wonder if any of them see the pandemonium in the sky," said Christian. "I could be wrong, but I doubt that others saw this happen."

"What makes you think so?" Mather asked.

"You may see things that others don't see Atkins told us when he stuck us with his pin. Remember, Elliott?"

I replied, "I forgot he said it. You're right. I remember now."

"Did Atkins stick the others with a pin?" I asked.

"From what he said, it didn't sound like it," Zachariah answered. "But I don't know."

Then, Mather, an echo. "Maybe it was just us."

"Best we keep mum," said Christian.

"We better not talk about it," repeated Mather.

I said, "Witness. He said something else, but I don't remember what it was. But witness."

Then Philip Mather said, "If anyone asks us we say the water turned cold, a cloud came, and the pilot couldn't see us. That's enough of a miracle. They all saw that. Maybe it's for us to have seen the spectacle, why I don't know."

"Not yet, you don't."

Said Zachariah, "Atkins gave us visions, the war on the Other Side. I believe he had a hand in it all together. Joiner, what do you think?"

Though we didn't know where they had come from, little of what they meant, we agreed that Atkins had picked us, for what, we were beginning to sense. Witness. Testify. For me, bury my cousin.

The pilot flew over and away. A cheer went up along the line. Salvation though divine intervention. We fumbled into socks, trousers, boots, and puttees, and put our mess kits together. We were in no rush to get back to the trucks. All were excited about our miraculous escape.

I said, "The angels thwarted him."

Says Mather, "The hand of the Divine brought down this fog. Nothing natural."

"A grave explosion," Zachariah punned. "Seventy-seven truckloads of ammo. Divine fog protected us, saved us."

I said, in the same vein, amazed: "The gift of fog, water suspended in air, hid us."

Christian, "If not for this miracle, there would be no fight tomorrow to cross the Hindenburg Line."

Relieved, I said, "By God, that pilot had a chance to win the battle all by himself before it began."

Chimed in Christian, "You can't hit what you don't know is there."

"It's a pity he doesn't know what he missed. I would love it if he was filled with eternal regret, eat his Hun heart out," I said.

Zachariah: "The Kaiser, blast his soul, would have kissed the pilot's arse, pinned a medal to it, made him a damn general on the spot."

Private Mather said, "I did see gaps in the clouds. Herr flyer must have seen something."

Me: "Some buildings, a few men sitting in the shade of the arbor at the *estaminet*, maybe a lady laying her laundry on the grass. Maybe a farmer harvesting crops, or tending his horses. He couldn't see enough to see us."

When the pilot turned back to his aerodrome our trucks were already creeping along a dirt path through a forest. We drove so slow we stirred up little dust. And even that did not rise above the trees. So we made it safe to our depots and drop-off points.

The Sergeant Sent Me Back to the Horses

When we got to the depot the sergeant took me off the detail and sent me back to the horses. He figured out the truck was too much for me. I had told him, but he didn't listen.

BOOK IV

LANCE CORPORAL THOMAS ATKINS ❖   5

Chapter 18

Sir Arthur Conan Doyle and Tommy Atkins at the Battle of Bellicourt Tunnel

(British IV Army HQ, at Templeux, France)

September 28, 1918

I had not expected to see any more actual operations of the war, but early in September, 1918 I had an intimation from the Australian Government that I might visit their section of the line. Little did I think that this would lead me to see the crowning battle of the war.

It was as if some huge hand had lifted me from my study table, placed me where I could see what I was writing about, and then within four days laid me down once more before the familiar table, with one more wonderful experience added to my record."

Sir Arthur Conan Doyle
Adventures and Memories

(Commentary by Private Sir Arthur Conan Doyle,
Crowborough Company,
Sixth Royal Sussex Volunteer Regiment)

Doyle, the man on the left

Doyle's Reporting on the War

The English public knows me mainly as the author of the Sherlock Holmes stories and other fiction. The *Strand* and *the London Times* commissioned me to write accounts of battles and events in the Great War. I wrote about the Battle of Mons, where my brother in-law, Captain Malcolm R.A.M.C. Medical Officer to Company "C". Wounded at Mons, Belgium and died six days later. I wrote about the Battle of Le Cateau, both fights largely forgotten, having taken place four years ago in the war's opening days. During the war, and at the Army's command, I wrote editorials, articles, opinion pieces, essays, analyses, Army reports, about the war. I was reporter, commentator, analyst, official government correspondent. Letters to the editor offered my views on military matters. I traveled to the Western Front several times to observe, meet with military and political leaders, talk with generals, staff, officers, rank and file—gathering information first-hand to report to my fellow Englishmen.

I extolled the heroes, the grand, the glorious. I was to witness the war's many dimensions, extol the heroism of the troops, put in words how the British peoples and the Americans would hold it in their hearts and memory. I wrote what I saw, heard, learned, knew to be so, and felt in my heart.

I write now as Sir Arthur Conan Doyle, historian. I want you to know where the battle of Bellicourt Tunnel stands in the annals of the Great War. I quote happily from what I wrote in 1923. "I was privileged to see the battle, report on it for all the world to read about the heroism of the British, the French, the American, the Australian armies."

How I Came to be Invited to Bellicourt Tunnel

I had not expected to see any more of the war, but in early September the Australian High Command invited me to visit their section of the Hindenburg Line. The invitation was more of an order. I thought they may think the troops may want to meet Sherlock Holmes' creator, relief and entertainment before the "big blow."as the soldiers came to call it after the war. But, no. I was to observe and report on the battle planned for Bellicourt Tunnel. Little did I think that I would see the crowning battle of the war.

The Battle of Bellicourt was so important to the war—and my life— that I devoted a chapter to it in *Adventures and Memories,* "Breaking the Hindenburg Line." In it I wrote about the Allies penetrating the impenetrable.

On September 26, three days before the main attack, Sir Cook, Naval Minister of the Australian Commonwealth, and his aide-de-camp, Commander Latham, put me under the charge of British Corporal Tommy Atkins.

The Deeper Reason for Private Doyle's Going

> *Under our very eyes, was even now being fought a part of that great fight where at last the children of light were beating down into the earth the forces of darkness. It was there. We could see it. And yet how little there was to see!*

Adventures and Memories

Conan Doyle and Captain Leckie at Windlesham, their last meeting in life

Something beyond the invitation, something profound, accounts for my being selected. St. George, the Angel of Mons. It had to do with my brother in-law, Captain Malcolm Leckie, Royal Fusiliers, BEF, Company "C's" chief medical officer. Details of the battle and St. George's divine salvation came to me in an extraordinary way. I was not free to describe it then. I am now.

The night of August 29, 1914 four years ago at Windlesham Manor, our East Sussex home, my wife's dear invalid friend, Miss Lily Loder-Symmons, studying "automatic writing," demonstrated the art for the evening's guests—Sherlock Holmes, Mrs. Oliver Lodge and Professor Lodge, eminent physicist, former president of the British Psychical Society.

Miss Loder-Symmons entered a trance. The pencil she held wrote on its own over a blank page. When the brief communication ended, without reading the message, she gasped, surprised, and said, "Sir Arthur, the handwriting is not mine." I crossed the room, read over her shoulder. Astounded, I said, "It is my brother in-law's hand." As remarkable as this was, even more remarkable were the words: "I am dead in body. Nevermore shall we meet in the flesh"–my heart came near to bursting, tears rose, blurring my vision. "One moment, please." I wiped the tears, wiped my fogged reading glasses. "Malcolm tells us that he is dead in body, but he lives on. This message confirms that his soul lives on."

Skilled in researching incidents of psychic phenomena, I was quite certain that I should verify the authenticity of the communication — that it had indeed been sent by my brother-in-law. I wrote the answers to two test questions on a slip of paper, sealed it in an envelope, and gave it to the hand of Sherlock Holmes. "I am the only person who knows the answers," I said. To contact Captain Leckie's spirit Miss Symmons-Loder entered a trance again. I asked the questions. Without hesitation, her hand wrote. Holmes opened the envelope and read. The answers were the same. My brother in-law communicated from beyond the world of matter and bodily life.

The BEF and the German Fifth Army clashed first at Mons, Belgium on August 23, 1914. Captain Leckie, wounded at Mons, was taken prisoner then exchanged for the captured son of a German General. My brother in-law died five days later.

Through Miss Loder-Symmons Captain Leckie recounted the divine events that took place at the critical moment in the Battle of Mons. Vastly outnumbered, our soldiers defended the eighteen-mile-long Mons-Condé Canal. Twenty-eight bridges and locks were weak points, the most important being Nimy Bridge. All day two Vickers Machine Gun crews, Royal Fusiliers, Company "C", held off attacks at Nimy bridge, the most vulnerable point at the salient, the place in gravest peril. The Germans were on the verge of breaching the British defense.

St. George

St. George on horseback, treading the clouds, and St. George in the flesh on the ground bellowed command. He raised his sword and angels on horseback flew down from the sky. Angelic infantry rose out of the ground, routing the Germans. The German cavalry horses reared, galloped off in all directions, their riders thrown to the ground, side-arms only. Horses hauling artillery gun limbers bolted, running wildly. The Germans were badly mauled. The angels' attack gave the British hope and courage.

The next night at the Forest of Mormal just beyond the French border the angel Jeanne d'Arc opened a way for the British Army to move swiftly, saved it from being encircled and entrapped. On 26 August at Le Cateau St. George and his host again saved the British II Corps under the most dire circumstances, isolated, one Corps in the place specified, not two, exposed to German artillery fire.

Official dispatches did not report the angels' aid. Unofficially, Sherlock Holmes and I gave an account of the events to First Lord of the Admiralty Winston Churchill a few days after the communication from Captain Leckie. He informed the War Council. Our report of angelic intercession followed one he received from his aunt, Lady Archibald Campbell. Churchill assigned me to report on the war.

To the psychical, esoteric, occult, spiritualist, and mystical societies throughout Europe and England it was clear that the Hindenburg line was an energetic monstrosity, a barrier. One need only read their magazines and journals of the day to see. The Siegfried Line scratched across Europe's face, dug by the hands of thousands, thousands of picks and shovels. The Germans did not call this system of trenches, barbed wire, and emplacements Hindenburg. We gave it that name to let us know who the enemy was. Symbolism, you know. The lines' names came from myths buried in the hearts of the Germanic tribes, names of Teutonic gods. Myth, religion, law, culture. The gods are gigantic forces–material and spiritual—clashing on earth. As in the epics of the world, Humanity pays for the gods' antagonisms. The war in heaven was being enacted below by miniscule mortals— like ants, termites, insects who swarm on the face of the earth, hornets, flies, gnats, mosquitoes in the air. In their sagas and epics arguments between Teutonic gods result in tragedy for mortals. Even the heroes. We are instruments of the forces' wills–evil and good.

Thus, I was present at this momentous event in the world's history.

Sir Arthur Conan Doyle's Initiation

In the years that followed his death, Captain Leckie spoke to me in meditations, séances, visions, and dreams. In the most significant vision my brother in-law instructed me to meet the priest at St. Waudru Church. I had never heard of the church, nor did I know where it was. Not knowing what to do, I did nothing. During an early visit to the Front, I was spirited, pardon the pun, behind the German lines to Mons, Belgium. While the Germans occupied Mons and all of this part of Belgium, none were in the

Grande Place when I was there. As I approached the city hall, out of the corner of my eye I saw emblems, the head of St. George on my right, the dragon's cast in brass on the left, on the stair railing I was about to grasp. Quietly and unseen, a priest came up behind me and spoke. "St. George and the Anti-Christ. The dragon. Notice the letters engraved over the doorway next to the Marie's entrance.

"Sir?"

"Notice the words." Carved in the stone: "Les Messieurs de St. Georges." Then he said, "You are brother in-law to Captain Malcolm Leckie, are you not?" I was astounded. "Come with me, sir."

In somber ceremony I was initiated into "Les Messieurs de St. Georges," and an even more secret order. Robed and hooded men witnessed the proceedings, but spoke not a word. Then the order's hierophant—the ruler—the priest, gave me a benediction.

As we shook hands in parting, he muttered, almost inaudibly, 'Tommy Atkins will find you.'" That was all. I had no idea what he meant. He turned and left, giving me no chance to ask. He did not intend to explain.

Tommy Atkins stands for all the privates in the British army. Like Fritz for the Germans and Doughboy for the Americans. As with such messages, pondering and cogitation were useless. I awaited revelation of its meaning.

Before Officers' Mess that Evening

I was dressing for mess. A knock at the door. An orderly spoke.

"I apologize, Sir Arthur. Sorry to interrupt. Soldier to see you, sir. Said I need only mention his name and you would ask him in."

"His name, then?"

"Strange. He says Tommy Atkins. Thought he was joking but that's his name. Showed me his identification disc."

I rose from the table, eager for the meeting. "Show him in."

When I reported from the battlefield I would always speak with some young men from the rank and file. They shared anecdotes and stories which were of great interest and value to me in my writing. I would introduce myself, saying, "I know you would you like to shake hands with Sherlock Holmes, but I am not he. I merely write his stories. Conan Doyle's the name." It was a chance for the young men to have a moment's chat with someone they might be interested in meeting. I would say, "Not quite so good as a crack cricket batsman or boxer or bicycle racer." But something to remember, a tale to tell. "I met so and so in the war." But this case was different.

"Lance Corporal Atkins, sir." He saluted.

"I owe you the salute. Private Conan Doyle. I am pleased we meet."

"Indeed, sir. I am your escort for tomorrow."

"Very good," I said. "I know there is more to our meeting than that. I knew someday we would meet. Your name has come to me. Its meaning was not explained. So in a manner, I am prepared. I expect you will enlighten me. Pardon me. I invite you to sit. I have mess with my hosts in half an hour."

Atkins took a chair.

"I'll stay only a minute. You are right, sir. I needn't tell you that what I say to you is not to be spoken of."

I replied, "You needn't, but you did. I vow to keep it close."

"Right, sir. No pledge needed, sir. I know your heart and mind."

The young soldier rather rambled in his talk. "All to the good, sir. The Ruffians, we called ourselves, the Ruffians and the Victors, our companion squad. When alive, we worked and fought together, friendly rivals, you could say. Your brother in-law and twelve machine gunners initiates. 'Golden Arrows of God.'" Atkins had been gunner six for a Vickers squad defending Nimy Bridge. He witnessed the miracle of Mons. He was part of the miracle, I later learned. "Captain Leckie was with us when we saw St. George and his angel warriors come down from the sky. We saw it together. Ours was the last emplacement the captain visited. I was the last to speak to him, salute him. On his way back to the medical tent, he was crossing an open expanse. A shard of hot shrapnel struck him in the neck."

"A blow soon to be fatal," I said.

"I was a lad of seventeen. My first day in battle. Since then, he's been with me many times. Sustains, encourages, and comforts me. His kindness is a hallmark of the man."

I said, "And Captain Leckie has been in communication with me. What you have to tell me, I don't know. I am eager to hear."

"Yes. I have something for you."

"A token of my brother in-law?"

"Not exactly, but nearly. Information. Explanation. I believe the thirteen of us were picked to be 'Arrows of God' with the foreknowledge that you would be a proper vessel for the Captain's message."

"Thirteen? What thirteen? And what message?"

"The two Vickers teams and your brother in-law. The message? That the soul lives after bodily death. What you learned when he died."

"Oh, yes, indeed. That message. Indeed, that is the message."

Atkins explained. "We Ruffians, our initiation in 'The Golden Arrows of God' was an initiation into the ground of being and a way to be after death. After the first battle of Ypres I was the only one of the squads alive. I had many encounters with Ruffians and Victors, mostly Ruffians, who came from the Other Side. I am one of them, but on this side. Captain Leckie and the others ferry tortured souls to death's realm. They free souls caught in the throes of violent death. The many souls who still suffer painful confusion the Victors and Ruffians relieve of their burdens. The spirits of yet other dead fight on against the souls of dead Germans over the very battlefield where they died. Corrupted souls whose bodies vultures, rats, maggots have eaten, the Ruffians and Victors cleanse and send them on. Even more, sadly, are past help."

I said, "I hear much of messages coming to families in dreams and sensations, and other phenomena that tell of relatives wounded or dead."

"Yes, sir. Sad news, always. Devastating."

In a Larger Sphere

Thomas Atkins taught Doyle. "The 'Golden Arrows' do other work as well. Mislead and distract the enemy. Create diversions and disturbances. They are *agents provocateurs*, I think you call it. They forewarn the Allied leaders in dreams and visions. Generals credit themselves with ideas that lead to victory. But where did the ideas come from? Experience, certainly. But the ideas the Ruffians and Victors planted in their minds—generals and staffs—grew into plans and strategies. Imagination. Inspiration. Fortitude. The 'Arrows' supplied these, too. Injected into the big generals' minds."

He went on. "The two squads of Vickers' 'revenants' brought friendly relations between the Allied leaders, suspicious of one another, jealous for their own views. The 'Golden Arrows' unified the Armies in resolve. At Le Hamel, unified, coordinated, concerted action became the model for the rest of the war, the way to win."

"You, Sir Arthur, more than anyone, know the Divine lives in the world. This is your testament, your preaching. Your brother in-law showed you the truth of the connection. And your friend Yeats. He confirmed it for you. This is the news I have for you, sir."

Doyle replied, "You bring back memories of my brother in-law. The last evening we were together we played billiards. He rarely won, but that evening he did. Knowing he was going off to war, and in honor of his win, I left the tally for our last game on the wire—500 to 477. It is a memento for me. He is still there."

"Sorry to bring up what is painful," Atkins said. "I am grizzled, you might say, by experience. My naiveté was tarnished four years ago, my first day of battle. It is completely corroded now."

"What took its place?" Doyle asked.

"Stark realism. I have seen too much to harbor hope for humanity, I am sorry to say. I have brought up sorrow for both of us."

I could tell the Divine had touched this ordinary-seeming boy, this soldier. Listening to what he said was like hearing an angel discourse.

Atkins went on. "Yes. That is so. St. George promised the people of Mons and Belgium victory. But, like St. Thomas, I had ample reason to doubt. I have lived through four years of death, suffering, despair, pain, grief. Many times the Germans have been on the verge of victory. Now our victory is near. In church we sang a hymn.

> A thousand ages in Thy sight
> Are like an evening gone;
> Short as the watch that ends the night
> Before thy rising sun.

Atkins paused in thought then went on. "Not to make light of the tragedy, it seems like these four years have been like those thousand ages in God's sight and St. George's."

I told the Corporal, "The Germans call the war 'Der Tag' meaning the day of victory. Victory there shall be. But I believe it shall be ours. Tomorrow we shall see."

Returning to his role as guide, Atkins said, "Remember, I am to escort you, tomorrow. That is all anyone knows. We will often be with others. When we are alone we can speak freely. I know you will write for the papers, and not about these matters." He prepared me for the next day. "Tomorrow when we are on the battlefield, while others will see soldiers fight and die, attune your senses to see the Above and Below in battle. Devils will arise from the great tunnel that runs below, and angels descend from the air and contend here. St. Waudru at Mons will rejoice when the last German crosses Nimy Bridge at the stroke of the end. You will see this."

We saluted again. Corporal Atkins said, "I will pick you up in the morning. We will go out after the first few waves of Americans have made it over. I promise you heavy shelling tomorrow." Then Tommy Atkins told me Lieutenant Dease directed him to initiate the British officers and poets Siegfried Sassoon and Wilfred Owen who would be with us by special arrangement at the mess. While Owen had not yet published his book of poems, it was prepared and its contents circulated and known among officers interested in his writing. Sassoon already had three books of poetry published. It was Sassoon's personal influence on the younger Owen that inspired Wilfred. I needed to warn them that directly after dinner they were to follow the Corporal, though I could not tell them why. Though an unusual request, I agreed to do it, he being, in a sense, my superior in the matter.

Headquarters Mess

September 28, 1918

At Templeux a small farmhouse was Headquarters. My sleeping quarters were there. At mess that night were Rawlinson, commanding the British IV Army, Major-General George Read of the American II Corps, and John Monash, head of the Australian Corps—all five Australian infantry divisions on the Western Front. General Commanding, Lieutenant-General Butler, III British Corps, his heads of sappers, gunners, first and second staff officers were our hosts. My brother, Brigadier General John Francis Innes Hay "Duff" Doyle, DSO, CMG, was Butler's Assistant Adjutant-General for the 24th Division. As a courtesy and honor to Innes and me, Butler wired, ordered him to join the Headquarters mess that night.

And the General kindly freed Siegfried Sassoon and Wilfred Owen, highly respected officers and the eminent poets of the war, to dine and converse with us.

A List

On my way to dinner I passed an easel board, "Improvements Contribute to Winning," paused to read.

1. Ammunition
    A. Have more than we can use of each
    B. Quality of shells
        Uniform loads
        Well-made casings
        Smoke bombs, high explosives, shrapnel
        mixed in attack
        The 1 0 6 fuse
2. Science and Engineering
    A. Formulas for gunners to adjust for wear
    (More use, more wear. Every hundred shells, the gunners adjust.)
Result: fire, accurate and deadly.
    B. Accurate cameras
        Adjust for angle of shot
        Clear focus
Result: produce topographically accurate maps
    C. Accurate cameras produce Accurate Topographical Maps
        Measures elevation for accurate artillery fire
        Slope and depression which cannot be seen from
        an approach (What lies ahead)
    D. Artillery receives reports every two hours
        Wind speed and direction, temperature, humidity
        Artillery adjusts for these factors
Result: improved fire accuracy
    E. Sound and flash detect German gun emplacements
Result: No test bombardment to determine the target location
    F. Tanks
        In great number
        Greatly improved over earlier model
3. Royal Air Force
    A. Many modern aeroplanes
    B. Many skilled pilots
    C. Track emplacements, disposition, movement
4. German Air Force (*Deutsche Luftstreitkräfte*)
    A. few planes, few pilots, mechanics, replacement parts,

little fuel.
Result: Cannot see what we are doing,
where weapons and soldiers are.
5. Staff
A. Plans coordinate the work of all branches to maximum effect.

The Chief of Artillery, also on his way to dinner, came up to me. "Sir, list of improvements. They represent much work over the past two years by every branch of the service. They will serve us well tomorrow."

He observed, "There is a new fuse, the 106. Thanks to Minister of Munitions, Winston Churchill. I've heard it works wonders on wire. I hope so. It would be a great aid if it does."

I said, in good cheer, "Hear, hear! To Minister Churchill. Gallipoli stung the old bulldog. But he always serves his King." Then I said, "The list. I see. Each small improvement, while none alone could do the job, increases the likelihood of victory. All together, they almost guarantee it. The Germans will be surprised, probably not by anything major, but by the result. One thing leads to another. Better camera, better maps, better weather reporting, better knowledge of metallurgy better range and load, better accuracy."

The General said, "Indeed, Sir Arthur. We plan to overwhelm them with surprises and hard fighting. I am sure they have surprises waiting for us. We are going into battle with the same plan we followed before. Frontal attack. The items on the list will spell the difference. By the day after tomorrow we will see the benefits of bringing the Army to new fitness. And, we have their detailed plans in hand, thanks to your friend, Mr. Sherlock Holmes."

I said, "I expected that Holmes would be about in the war somewhere, but never knew where. I am glad that he is of service."

"Indeed, I am sure he is, and has been. Quite the fellow for intrigue and spying. I am sure he will have much to tell you when the war is over," said the Chief of Artillery.

"I doubt it. He is as secretive with me as he would be with the enemy. Secrets are best kept as secrets."

"Sir Arthur, let us go in to mess."

"If this were another place and time, I would look forward to an enjoyable evening."

"Do enjoy it. All we have is the present moment. So war teaches."

The Eve of Judgment

When I arrived at the dining room I saw my brother. We shook hands warmly, glad to see each other. The next day he would join with the American 27th and 30th divisions to attack the Hindenburg line.

Just then an orderly announced Sherlock Holmes' arrival. Dressed in an American private's uniform, he saluted the assembly.

The French liaison was present. Surprised to meet the famous detective, he asked, "Sherlock Holmes, est-ce qu'il est un soldat dans l'armée anglaise?" The whole table waited to hear what Holmes would say. "Mais, mon general," he stammered, "il est trop vieux pour service." There was laughter. Too old to serve. "It is not my uniform," he continued. "I had to trade a German uniform for one of a departed American soldier. But I am here, thanks to a kind invitation."

Before Dinner Sherlock Holmes Recounted what Happened at Domrémy, Jeanne d'Arc's Birthplace and Home

Under ground in the coffins in all the graveyards of Europe was a rich harvest of lead, brass, and bronze, needful for the war. German soldiers dug up the coffins. As spades struck caskets, the metal sang its ruddy song. They dumped the corpses and skeletons back into the holes, stripped the metal from the coffins, and shipped it to the Fatherland. The graves exhaled fetid air. This metal added to the ore miners dug from the earth, smelted, and sent to foundries. Blast furnaces melted the metals and turned them into bomb casings and bullets. They did the same with bronze and brass statues.

Holmes disguised himself as an old German recently conscripted into the Army and took on the identity of a dead German soldier. He carried all the official documents a German soldier needed to identify himself. His pay book and identification cards and disc named him Klaus Mueller, of Aken in Saxony His wallet held photographs of a wife, two grown children, grandchildren, and the soldier himself, in poor focus, but it was easy enough to say it was him. A letter from the wife described life at home and wished her husband God's protection and long life for the beloved Kaiser. Holmes disguised himself, captured every detail of the man in the picture.

Fluent in German, he spoke the dialect of the soldiers whose group he was seeking to rejoin. He seemed bewildered, frightened, fretful. He was withdrawn. He hardly spoke. One-word answers. He gave the impression that he was lost, disoriented, wandering aimlessly, affected by the war, forgetful of much. One observed, "The men newest to war seem the quickest to succumb to fear. You see them quaking, nervous, unable to face the enemy. Frozen with fear in the trenches, unable to climb the scaling ladder and go into battle."

"Maybe their imaginations had gotten the best of them," another added.

Sherlock Holmes joined the crew salvaging coffins in the church graveyard in Domrémy, Jeanne d'Arc's birthplace and home.

On September 4, 1918, not knowing why, Sherlock Holmes was compelled to leave the work and enter the church. Like an ordinary soldier's, his feet marched without will or effort. Passing through a low, thick oaken door and a dark vestibule, he entered an even darker interior. The odor of incense and dust lingered. Dust motes floated in the light that filtered through the stained glass windows. The light struck statues of saints, kings, paintings and sculptures of Jesus and Mary and angels, the darkness and shadow obscuring others. Despite its being the early days of September the air inside was cold. A small, ancient church, unlike the massive cathedrals, many destroyed all over France and Belgium. Wandering about the church, he found himself before the statue of Jeanne d'Arc, the girl warrior clad in armor, sword raised high. He touched her shield. Transfixed, Holmes' mind emptied of thought. Before his eyes she turned to living flesh and spoke. "Sir knight," she said, "I will take you to the German plans for a battle that will soon begin." Then in his mind's eye he saw maps of increasingly greater scale. She said again what she had said at Orleans. "*Courage, on les auras.* Our enemies, even if they hang on the clouds, we shall get them! And we will drive them from France!" Homes understood the ancient French as if it were English. The statue's eyes lose their color, its flesh its luster, and all was as it had been.

Suddenly, Sherlock Holmes stood at the pinnacle of the cross on the church steeple, Jeanne d'Arc suspended in air beside him. He looked out over the lands around Domrémy. Then his body rose up from the steeple into the air to the height RAF reconnaissance flies. He closed his eyes and opened them when he stood still in air in what seemed seconds, the land beneath him not Domrémy. Now he was above the three-mile long Bellicourt tunnel, one hundred eighty miles to the north. As if he was examining a map, he saw below him the German installations.

Then the vision ended and all was real. He was in a German trench at the entrance to a dugout. He descended twenty steps. To the right was an officers' bunker, no one present. An oil lamp shed its light over a circular cherry wood table stolen from a nearby chateau, itself in ruins now. On it, were maps and plans laid out for study. Holmes quickly rolled them into a tight cylinder and tucked them in his tunic.

The next thing he knew, Holmes was standing in front of the statue of Jeanne d'Arc.

He left the church and rejoined the scavenging crew. In the confusion of movements as the Germans maneuvered into new positions, he made his way into a wooded ravine where he hid. He examined his find: the full German plans for the defense of the St. Quentin Canal and Bellicourt Tunnel. At night he slipped from hiding and made his way to the front over ten nights of stealthy travel by darkness. When he arrived at the British line, now dressed in an American soldier's uniform he stripped from a corpse, he waved a white handkerchief, surrendering as had so many Germans at this time. When taken in custody, he made his identity known and was escorted to the chief intelligence officer of Fourth Army. He worked with the officer, interpreting the codes and language the maps and papers contained.

No One Spoke of the Coming Cataclysm

That evening, every now and then a telephone rang in the next room. And every few minutes orderlies called out staff officers who excused themselves, spoke a few words, and returned. Training, self-control. I spoke little about war, once observing. "The Americans are like dry tinder laid upon dying embers." It elicited no comment, though each man in the room had his own views on the matter of the Americans.

Throughout the evening no one spoke of the cataclysm taking place all along the Hindenburg Line and at whose abyss we stood. Late into the night our talk was of literary matters. Literature and war, poetry and this war. As we were at our coffee and cigars and brandy. After the dinner the waiters brought dessert, coffee, tea, a fine port. I was surprised at the officers' appetites, considering what tomorrow promised.

When we were alone for a moment, I asked Innes, "Don't you think my talking about Sherlock Holmes and story writing isn't out of place, even unseemly?"

"Not at all, objected Innis. "You keep their thoughts away from their worries. Fill their minds with stories and pictures."

I argued, "It is of no consequence."

My brother said, "It is good for them. They know what lies ahead. No reason to think about it. Keep it up. But did I tell you I'm joining the Americans, command. Some sprouts, I think I'd call them. Southern boys."

"No telling what this war will bring. This battle."

Mess

The steward rang the chime for dinner.

After toasts to King, Empire, the soldiers, and others deserving of notice, a heartfelt toast from General Rawlinson:

"What lies before us is wonderful and awesome. Terrifying. Like being on the eve of Judgment Day. Germany's defense will come to smash. Then the Fatherland, as they call it, will get the vengeance it deserves. A toast."

A resounding "Here! Here!"

Rawlinson rose to leave, and all rose with him. "Gentlemen, " he said, "All is ready. We have a brutal fight ahead. Always the unforeseen and unexpected. The Germans know we are ready to attack. Their defenses are formidable. They have their own plans for a myriad of contingencies. And they are likely to have some surprises for us. Rarely does everything go according to plan in battle. Too many moving parts, as they say. Courage, skill—these matter. Our American friends are untried and untested under such conditions as we have before us. We must hope for the best, and victory on the morrow."

The Initiation of Poets
Wilfred Owen and Siegfried Sassoon

The dinner over, from a doorway Atkins signaled. Owen and Sassoon rose, followed the corporal into my room. I rose to leave, but Atkins told me to stay. Behind him came Sherlock Holmes. Atkins said to them, "You must wonder why Sir Arthur made so unusual a request of you, me a Lance Corporal. And why Holmes is with us."

"Indeed. What is it then?" Captain Sassoon thought this speech presumptuous and arrogant for one of low rank. "What does this mean, then? Who are you?"

The comment piqued Owen's interest. "Go on, then, please," he said.

The little corporal explained who he was, his role in the affair, and concluded, "Holmes and Doyle are already initiates. They are here to witness the proceedings, which are sacred. It is a blessing for them, and their presence sanctifies the event.

Sassoon turned to Doyle and said, "We were called from our commands to spend a literary evening with you. It has been a delight. But initiation into a mystical society? You've such extraordinary interests, I must say."

Doyle said, "Please listen to Atkins."

The corporal said, "I have been instructed to initiate you into the order of 'The Golden Arrows of God.' Strangely, his words sent them into an enthusiastic thrall, as if a monumental poem was about to present itself. So it was for the two poets. Images and words, entire lines, stanzas, some rhymed, much not rhymed, came to them.

Captain Owen said, "I always felt, no, knew, that my poems came from some spirit, some daimon that lives inside of me." Then, to Sassoon. "You, too have sensed that presence, have you not?"

"Indeed, I have."

Now, with authority, Atkins spoke. "One of the Order has been working with you from within. All the great poets have this inner working."

I added, "I have spoken with the great Yeats and he swears to it. He has met his daimon in dreams and vision. He even has a name and a history. Leo Africanus I believe, a spirit from the past. Dictates, forces, draws

Yeats along, willing or no. You are, as all true poets know, the vessel from which the poem pours."

"Indeed, sir. Though more like the furnace in which ore is smelted," said Sassoon.

"True," said Owen. "True for me at least. Cogitation and rational thought have their place, but there is something else, something extra, the poem's seed and germination, its soul and essence, something beside myself."

"So it is," said Atkins. "That you know far better than I." Then Tommy Atkins conducted the rituals of invocation and instruction. With his pin, he stuck the index finger of each man's right hand and pressed it to the parchment. He closed his eyes before he spoke. Now his voice seemed to emerge from another realm. He intoned, "You are the inspired voices of the poet. Your words will be immortal reminders of war's horror and folly." This he repeated two more times, as if he needed to speak, but nothing else came. Then, freed from whatever restrained him, he told them their fates, their futures. As if speaking in the language of long ago, he said, "Yea, your names shall be inscribed on the stone floor in the hall of remembrance, in sacred Westminster Abbey."

Then, to Owen. "Captain, Sir, you will play a role that will last long after your passing. In the realm between life and death a multitude of souls are trapped. These blind, ravaged souls howl, like the souls in hell. You will be a path, a circuitous and unexpected way to free their spirits. In the future you will direct men and women in the techniques of retrieving, restoring, and releasing soldiers' souls. These people will not have read your poetry. They are not students of literature or history. That is not what will move them. In years to come they will travel from England. Some of the dead need only someone to look upon the gravestone and the soul will ascend. Their graves have never been visited by relative, friend, or comrade. Others need prayer, yet others, rites of release. And finally some whose remains are soot and ash, bodies obliterated, strewn on the field of battle, need special intercession. Rites of retrieval and gathering shards of souls. All this will be done through your prompting their hearts."

Atkins foresaw clearly the sad fate of this gallant officer and profound poet. Dead at Sambre–Oise Canal in France. And the double grief that would come to his mother—oh, agony of the weeping mothers—the telegram announcing his death delivered to her hand as church bells tolled the good news, the war's end.

Turning to Sassoon, he said, "Sir, not everything is given to me. Your future was not made clear. I can tell you will live to a ripe age, always remembering your harrowing experiences, but offering inspiration and hope to coming generations."

The Trek across the Battlefield with Atkins

September 29, 1914

There was the battle—the greatest of battles

Adventures and Memories

"Under our very eyes, was even now being fought a part of that great fight where at last the children of light are beating down into the earth the forces of darkness. It is here. We can see it. And yet how little there is to see!" These were the very words I spoke to Atkins and the spirit of my brother in-law.

The fog finally cleared by 11:30. We had a car and driver. Atkins and I. The driver parked the car behind a hill out of view of the Germans. The corporal and I took a path through a farm to a British anti-aircraft battery, chatted a moment with the gunners, passed the heavy guns far behind the line, and reached the field guns where we paused to see the loading and firing. Then we crossed an open plain, made our way forward through old trenches, passed acres of rusty shredded barbed wire. The noises of hell's pit rose from the land. The blasts from our side were deafening. We stopped by a howitzer battery. The soldiers had shelled the enemy for six hours already. Under a rain of our own shells we went forward, crossed a devastated farm field, and, 1,000 yards from the Hindenburg Line, reached an advanced dressing station hidden deep in a gravel pit. Within, doctors and medics treated American wounded and injured. The dressing station backed up against the wall closest to the Germans for protection from bombardment. The Huns the Americans chased out of the pit were now shelling it.

Captain M. Leckie, D.S.O.

R.A.M.C. He became a lieutenant
in February, 1908, and was promoted
to captain in August, 1911.

A wraith, a shade arose in the midst of the doctors and nurses and medics. Many saw. It took on substance. I recognized the image of my brother in-law, Captain Malcolm Leckie. It was him in every detail. Short, slight. His hawk's eyes, trim moustache, erect posture. A doctor soldier. He did not speak, yet I heard his voice, his words. "I will give you safe passage and the gift of vision. You deserve it. You will see, my brother, what is invisible to others, but there nonetheless."

Ahead was Bellicourt, fields of rusty wire between us and the village. Americans crouched in the sloping fields, advanced slowly. Germans crept out from dugouts to cut off the attack. Salvos of shell-fire fell closer and closer to where the three of us crouched, too.

I thought Atkins had done well getting as close as we did to the Hindenburg line. But now came the crowning bit of good fortune. My brother in-law spoke to us. "Ahead is a rare vantage point. I will guide you. And my young friend, Atkins. Though not as young as when we met." Captain Leckie rushed us forward.

The Line where the Americans—South Carolinians, North Carolinians, soldiers from Tennessee—forged through, was now only two hundred yards ahead.

Over a gentle rise and up a hill ahead we saw a tank at the ridgeline. That was to be our closest approach to the German trenches. With spanners and levers, the crew repairing its track. The American infantry platoon it was leading had gone beyond and now occupied the trench. I saw them with my own eyes. We crawled forward in the face of heavy artillery and machine gun fire. Suddenly a German shell struck the tank. In an instant it was aflame. Petrol spewed out. I began to run toward it. Atkins tried to throw me to the ground. "It might explode at any moment!" But I would not be held back. We both ran forward. When we got close we could tell that those inside were already dead, burning. But two had been thrown free, one, his uniform, soaked in petrol, and flesh on fire. In a frantic, piteous voice, the gunner, lying on his back, his eyes fixed on a cloud overhead, mouthed the words, "Shoot me! Shoot me! Shoot me!" He begged. Aghast, I saw the heart of this horrendous dilemma. Kill a man, or let the fire bring him agony, then death? Only one thing to do. I drew my pistol from its holster. "No! Not you!" I heard my brother in-law's voice boom. Atkins knocked the pistol from my hand, rushed to the man, knelt down, his own pistol in hand. Atkins looked the soldier in the eyes. Bringing the pistol toward the boy's temple, its muzzle not touching the skin, out of the soldier's range of vision, he fired.

"It is done," said Atkins. Then, "I have killed maybe hundreds of Germans, but they are the enemy and far away. I couldn't tell if it was my bullets that did the killing. But to kill one of my own. This tears at my heart. A brother-in-arms." Tender-hearted compassion, nearly saintly. He knew the soldier's suffering, as great as it was, lasted only a few minutes. Sad to see another life wasted, gone for naught. So it is in war.

Captain Leckie said again. "Thomas Atkins, you will see a golden sphere, transparent, arise from this soldier's chest. As you saw when Dease's spirit rose. I will convey it to the abode of the blessed." He said, "Because of you, this soldier is given this gift." My brother in-law spoke again. "This was your final initiation, 'Golden Arrow of God.' I ordain you in the name of St. George. When next you die, you will ascend to the heaven of saints. St. George, your beloved Dease."

Tommy Atkins Reveals More to Conan Doyle

Ordained, Atkins could preach a deeper doctrine. I was his pupil. Perhaps he would teach others, but I do not know. He said, "Sir Arthur, under our feet at this battlefield are cosmic forces at work for good or evil, the outcome to determine which. You know about gravitation, magnetism, electromagnetism."

"I know something, but very little, really."

"Here they are instruments of war, unseen and unnoticed. The ancients speak of ley lines. The Orientals use them in deciding where to build and where not to. Where to build military defenses. Where to attack. It is a detailed, complex system. You might know a bit about dousing, but that is baby knowledge compared to these systems. We know nothing about what lies one hundred, two hundred miles beneath our feet."

Captain Leckie said me, "Brother, I give you the gift of vision."

And in an instant I felt heat arising from the earth, as from a blast furnace. I smelled burning brimstone. I saw energy coming out of the ground, black against the day's blue sky, energy melting like molten rock. An apotheosis, a fulfillment of divine will and command. I was filled with joy inexpressible. A new order would change the world. As if this massive sacrifice appeased the gods. The future would reveal what this foretold.

That day the Allies broke the Hindenburg Line and, as at Mons, angels in all forms and manifestations fought their enemies.

In spite of all the advantages that lay on our side, the Germans withstood the attack that day. We advanced and they abandoned the strongpoints and several trenches, the tunnel as well. On our trek back to headquarters we saw the wounded making their way to aid stations on foot, in carts, on limbers. Defeated Germans carried injured American and Australian infantry on litters, four prisoners to a man.

A Great and Necessary Feat

Breaking the Hindenburg Line was one of the greatest feats of the war. Its being overwhelmed devastated the Germans. Though they fought valiantly up until the last, hope of victory evaporated. Duty carried them on and much fighting lay ahead. Slowly, the Allies pushed the Germans back. Their impregnable line had been pierced. With my own eyes I saw it.

But the cost of war—a generation of men. Metals, oil, steel, minerals became weapons and ammunition, resources of the earth squandered. Machinery built to feed death. The aching hearts of those whose husbands, sons, friends, brothers were buried in the dirt, dismembered, scattered over the surface of the earth, mired in mud, buried under collapsed trench walls and bunkers, bodies laced on barbed wire, men crazed with shell shock. Missing limbs, missing senses, missing minds. The seething, living, festering enmity between people who hated and fought one another for four years.

Even so, for me the adventure was the culmination and the beginning of a path to follow—the life of the spirit everlasting—the rest of my days.

I thought I would write about this Tommy Atkins after the war. He spoke like a prophet or seer. May I live to write it. May many live to read it.

BATTLE PLANS ❖ 5

Chapter 19

Facing the Hindenburg Line

September 29, 1918 5:10 a.m.
Zero Hour

(Account of Private Kendall Haydon)

Blue and Yellow, Red and Black

We rode train and bus to concentration points then marched to the front following painted wooden posts to our positions. Two roads to the north—Blue and Yellow for the 27th Division—and two south—Red and Black—for the 30th. While engineers built and repaired the roads, they sledge-hammered in the posts along the shoulders.

On September 18th Monash made the first attack against the outer Hindenburg Line defenses on the front of the British III and IX Corps. An attack on September 19 failed. He tried again on September 21, attacking the northern half of the sector. On September 21 Monash attacked the sector's northern half again. Again the next night under a full moon.

The night of September 23 our Division relieved the First Australian in the Le Catelet-Nauroy sector, facing directly west.

At 10:00 p.m. on September 25 the British began an eight-hour bombardment followed by a gas attack the next night. The guns fired 3,000 shells of the new "BB", the same as German Yellow Cross, "mustard", or yperite gas. At 6 a.m. that morning the artillery switched to high explosives and shrapnel. From then until "Zero Hour" 1,044 field guns and howitzers and 593 heavy guns and howitzers—forty-four brigades of field artillery, twenty-one of heavy artillery, and four long-range siege batteries—fired without cease.

On September 26th the 118th attacked the Hindenburg line and held a two-mile long front line, the 117th supporting. The German defense, heavy with artillery and machine gun nests, kept the ground, stopped the 27th Division the next day. The 118th had to fall back to a line with the 27th.

Under the circumstances, an attack by fresh troops the night of September 27/28 would have killed some, wounded some, worn the Krauts out, discouraged them. The next day they would have been beaten. We would have taken strong points before fresh German troops got there. This would have straightened and connected the objective line for the next day's main advance.

But there was no attack. Instead, in the dark from the heights northeast of Vendhuile Hun relief troops pushed through the many approach trenches and reinforced the points at The Knoll, Guillemont Farm, and Quennemont Farm to counter-attack the British.

The American Second Corps' objective was the line Le Catelet-Noury, the strongest part of the Hindenburg Line.

Before the attack, by dark of night the Allies massed troops and materiel. Aeroplanes flew over the enemy lines doing their usual reconnaissance, bombing, strafing, taking photographs for the cartographers and planners, and harrowing the Germans. But the real purpose for the raids on this occasion, their engines masked the noise of tanks and trucks hauling men and material into position. The tanks rumbling to their start line, out of sight and hearing of the Germans. The soldiers kept quiet, moving with care.

The night of September 28 we dug a shallow jumping-off trench in front of the main one. Only three feet deep, the dirt piled and packed in front. Much easier to get out of and over than the deep trenches behind us. We assembled here before going over the line. The night before that we waited in the deep trenches. Two machine gun battalions, our two teams among them, were along the trench line ready to fire on the Hindenburg Line.

On Y/Z night crackling volleys of machine gun fire and bursting shrapnel shredded the darkness.

"M" Company was ready. Atkins last words were encouragement. "Get through the wire. Go down into trenches. Clean them out. Up and over the wall and onward. Keep going. Some of you will die, even more wounded. Be valiant, brave. You are Americans. Fight with your brain and body. This is what you trained for, what you came to do." Then he shook hands with each of us. "It's up to you. I must stay behind, observe."

Finally, he reminded us of the good news. "Remember the Bellicourt Tunnel surprise for the Germans. The new fuse on the tips of the bombs shreds wire. Look for places you can get through. There will be torn up wire all over the place. The Germans will not have their guns on those spots. Look carefully. This is to our advantage if you are careful."

The night before the big blow the Australians gave us a jug of rum. Grog, they call it. We poured a good helping for each in our tin mugs. The two Lewis machine gun crews together.

A toast from Donald Barton: "To the rest of your days, however many there may be."

"A cynic's toast, wouldn't you say, Haydon?" said Caleb Jolly.

"I agree. More like a curse than a toast." Gloom entered the trench.

"Heartfelt is how I meant it," growled Barton. "But take it however you want."

That night I didn't sleep. Many slept soundly, as their snoring attested. Others were awake. Talk ranged from the personal and private to the battle we would fight next morning.

Bats through Binocular and Periscope, By Coordinates, Compass, and Landmark

Meanwhile, at dusk that evening the Gamecocks had been ordered ahead, not to fight, but to observe. Barton saw what looked like thin smoke coming out of the ground. The British already knew that the tunnel under the plateau must house German soldiers, how many they didn't know. So at first Barton thought it was smoke from cooking fires. He picked up binoculars. "I'll take a look. We're far enough away, concealed." Gunner One Barton saw multitudes, clouds of bats, their swooping and flopping, falling and rising, turning, twisting. Soon the men heard a faint squealing, a squeaking. Clouds of bats rose up, darkened the sky for several minutes. Thick concentrations came out of spots about one hundred yards distance from each other. And some came up in narrow streams. "Just bats," he said. "Pass it on to Intelligence. Might be useful. Who knows?" We took the coordinates, even the narrow streams.

The Telling Battle

Caleb Jolly came to join the party, the rest of his section already asleep. He said, "This could be the telling battle, the last day to fight, risk dying, stop killing," his voice dripping sarcasm, "Maybe the day the Germans surrender."

"I doubt it," said Private Haydon. "There's a long way to go before this is over. If it goes on I won't be surprised."

"But if we break through," said William Spears.

"Just getting through, there will be a lot of dead hanging on barbed wire," Hans Schmidt said. "Across the way is thick with machine guns and artillery. If we don't bust through maybe we'll wipe 'em out next year. Let 'em freeze and starve in the trenches."

"But what about us? Ain't we in a tough spot, too?" moaned Mankins. "We'll freeze, too. They're close to home. I bet a lot of them get leave, go home, get warm and fed."

Hans replied. "I hear the Krauts are low on coal. Use it making bombs and weapons. Not enough miners. They're soldiers now. Blockade keeps them from food. Hungry ain't the best way to fight. Plus their folks at home eat grass and roots. They mix sawdust in their flour for bread. We got 'em in a tough spot. That's what I hear."

Asked Jolly, "Who'd you hear that from?"

"I just heard it" said Schmidt. "I don't remember who."

"Hearing don't make it so."

"But it makes sense. Look at the skinny prisoners," the private from Sumter said.

There fell a pause in the conversation, each man quiet in his thoughts. Then, up spoke Jolly. "Look at all them young soldiers, sound asleep. Peaceful as dead men."

"You're a gruesome bastard, ain't you?" said Hans.

I joined the conversation. "This is the 'all or nothing.' The whole pot in on the gamble. We trained and rehearsed. So it's not really a gamble."

Jolly had a quick answer. "But we're fresh to the game, Kendall. We fought all right at Kemmel Hill and Ypres, but this is different."

I said, "Fresh, yes. But ready. I'm going to sleep." The others got ready to do the same.

All the soldiers already asleep slept on peacefully through the chatter.

If I Die before I Wake

(with the Gamecocks)

Private Miles Mason said, "For all I know this might be my last night alive. I remember the bedtime prayer I recited 'If I die before I wake' going to bed each night."

Barton said, "Cold feet? Wake up dead? Dead same as asleep. That's what the prayer tells me. I think those millions of dead soldiers are sleeping. The only thing they know, they are not awake."

Mason said, "Who knows what they do? They can't tell us."

"I'm not worried about not waking," said Mason. "The Germans hardly ever attacked at night. It's tomorrow that keeps me awake, not tonight. The Hindenburg Line sits right in front of us. The name alone is frightful." Then he topped what he had just said. "The line itself is worse."

Otis Mankins listened. He had played and won the one hundredth game of solitaire just hours before. He was exhausted. His hands trembled. This talk did him no good. He said, "Shut up. Shut the hell up. Morbid talk, morbid thoughts."

Barton said, "Listen to Otis, now. Sweet dreams. Sweet dreams. Stop scaring yourselves."

September the Twenty-Ninth

(Private Miles Mason Has His Say)

On Z day we Doughboys dumped our overcoats, blankets, and kits—impediments in battle—at company headquarters. Each of us carried 220 rounds of rifle ammunition in his bandolier and two hand grenades. Each regiment carried 600 smoke bombs and 2,500 ground flares into the fray. The division had ninety-six machine guns, nearly six hundred gunners. Each infantryman carried his own food for the next day.

One hour before zero we reached the assembly line. Somehow knowing that the Americans' would strike, at that moment the Germans, in the shroud of fog, fired Verey lights, flare rockets, and SOS rockets, and lit up the sky. As if to say, "We know you're coming. So we turned the lights on for you." As was intended, it surprised us. Would the Germans swarm out of the trenches and attack? Had they pinpointed our location, set the range for their machine guns and artillery? A rumor went round that the British had got hold of the German layout. If we had done that to them maybe they had done the same to us. Had the Germans got hold of General Rawlinson's plans?

5:00 a.m. Ten minutes before zero hour the artillery bombardment began. Lurching forward toward the Germans, the tanks' treads clanking, hungry prowling monsters loomed out of the mist, their guns' snouts, six pounders, sniffing for prey. As the tanks lumbered forward, billowing smoke swallowed them up.

The new artillery fuses tore the barbed wire entanglements apart the way they were supposed to. Now the infantry could get through. Each of us was with his thoughts. Ready to go over the top. The barrage struck the German artillery emplacements. Observers' spotting was accurate. Our shellfire obliterated many batteries in the first few minutes.

Then the guns filled the Hindenburg fortifications with high explosives ad shrapnel and mortar.

The creeping barrage. A curtain of bursting iron. Once we headed out, every four minutes our artillery fire moved forward 100 yards. The infantry was supposed to advance behind the shells and shrapnel. Sometimes barrage worked and sometimes it didn't. Often, the infantry could not keep up with the pace of advance. They would encounter obstacles, or find themselves beset by enemy artillery and machine gun fire. When the shelling barrage outran us the barrage did us no good. The good part: The enemy's infantry could not come out of its trenches to fight. Not even stand on the firing step to defend themselves. Before they could climb out of their trenches and advance shells rained down on them.

Ten minutes later, zero hour. The British Fourth Army—Australian Corps, American II Corps, and the British 46th North Midland Division—assaulted the Hindenburg Line at the Bellicourt Tunnel sector.

Before the whistles blew we saw the low, thick clouds, deep murk. Barton said, "The fog of war. I think Napoleon came up with the phrase."

"Think he said it in French?" asked Mankins.

Donald Barton said, "Of course, you dummy." He went on with his address. "General confusion of war. Not knowing exactly where the enemy is, how many of him, what he plans to do. Turmoil once a battle begins."

"Plan, and when the battle starts, the unexpected happens and everything changes," chimed in Beau Baylor. "Orders misunderstood. The runner carrying orders gets killed. Even when orders arrive, understood, followed, things go wrong. A platoon wanders off, lost for good. The enemy delivers a surprise. A hundred misfortunes."

In this case, the fog was real.

The whistles blew. Over the top from our support trench. Once we went over it was forward only. No turning back. We realized the peril we faced.

That instant the Germans shelled the position. We escaped with our lives. At least for the moment.

The battlefield. The best and worst conditions. British artillery fired smoke bombs at the German trenches' left and right flanks. The enemy knew we were coming. Dense fog and low-lying smoke clouds blinded his machine guns and artillery. They had nothing to shoot at. We gunners were not in the smoke, and still couldn't see beyond ten yards, sometimes just a few feet. We couldn't take advantage of the Germans not seeing us. Infantry didn't dare fire—strange thing for a soldier—for fear we might shoot our own. Artillery couldn't rush the guns forward, couldn't get the horses up to a gallop. Shell holes.

The truth is, the fog and the smoke saved us from disaster. On a clear day we would have been easy targets, many more killed. Not that disaster didn't lie ahead.

Artillery fire lit the sky. I thought the world had reached its end. As far as the eye could see in all directions the earth looked like it was ablaze. Earthquakes shook the ground, volcanoes, geysers erupting. Hurricane winds, lightning and thunder, a tornado's ferocity. It jarred my head, just about shook me silly.

We were high strung, high pitched. All the senses were assaulted. Without cease, the concussions from artillery fire pounded my ears. The pressure and sound jumbled thought, my brain's ability to hear and think having passed its limit. Every tortured sound you could imagine struck our ears—the roar of bursting bombs, the whine, the scream of shells punishing the air, rattling doom-fire from machine guns, their staccato bark, the sizzle of shrapnel breaking into a thousand shards and splinters, bullets' whistle, the shriek of bursting grenades, the mortar's poom poom, the rain of dirt and rocks pounding the earth, the shouts of soldiers urging one another forward. Hell's flames came from exploding bombs. Devils were the creatures in the trenches opposite. Hell itself had come to earth. Inside the roar of the explosions and angry clatter of machine gun fire I heard a symphony of horrid human noises, the wounded and dying. I am sure others experienced this in the war, but it was new to us.

As we advanced we saw every kind of atrocity. An arm here, a leg there in the barbed wire, balls and prick hanging from it, a head accusing me and all civilization for what we had done to him. I found a stomach in the grass, intestines twisted around a tree limb above it. Repulsive, disgusting, fascinating. All around, everywhere we looked, the dead mocked, "Stay longer, and you will join us." I saw body parts from earlier days' fighting everywhere. Every grotesquery, every unhuman gesture. I saw an arm sticking straight up out of the ground, the fingers gone except the forefinger, pointing heavenward.

The stench worsened the ghastly sights. The smell of cordite. Sulfur. Brimstone, the preacher called it. Smoke from our own smoke bombs. The sickening smell that every dead thing gives off filled the air. Putrefaction in the hot weather was well along. I don't know a stink as repulsive as the sweet, nauseating smell of rotting flesh. I wretched and gagged. Many vomited. There was no escaping it. If you ever smelled a dead animal on a farm, or a piece of rotten meat, multiply it a thousand times, if you can imagine.

When we fought at Kemmel Hill, our first battle at the beginning of August, the stench near killed me. I needed something to mask it. Up until then I was not a smoker. My minister preached against tobacco and drink, dance as well. One day early along a field agent from the Knights of Columbus gave me some cigars, Prince Albert pipe tobacco, and a corncob pipe. He said, "This might help you. The cigars especially. Smoke all you want. It might help." I thanked him. It made me sick. At first it did. Then it helped a bit, but not enough. I got used to smoking. I smoked all the time after that.

Caleb Jolly said, "You didn't used to smoke before you came over."

"No," said Mason. "But I do now, all right. Just like you."

Even taste. Open your mouth and there was every kind of chemical on my tongue, in my nose. I spit and choked, but couldn't get rid of the taste.

At the Front

The west bank of the canal, heavily fortified with dugouts and machine guns. Allied artillery would fly over and leave these emplacements un-harmed.

German emplacements on the west bank.

Corporal Atkins came with us when we went to the line that morning. Still teaching us. He repeated what he had already said many times, as much as anything to keep our minds from the day's prospects. "Dread the bayonet. Half of them German kids and broken down old men. You have seen them. Prisoners. You don't have to worry about them. The rest. Those are the one's to dread. Dirty, vicious fighters. All sneers, snarls, their talk loaded with spit and gargle. He'll come right on you. Run you through with a dagger to keep his bayonet clean. Look you in the eyes while he plunges in the blade. The most honorable way to fight, they say. Though the bayonet is the worst for you. Man to man. Face to face. Not like a bullet or shrapnel."

"Gentlemen, this is as far as I go with you. I am to accompany a dignitary, escort a writer who will report on what he sees. Let us shake hands again." He clasped each man's right hand and his arm with his left. They felt the warmth of his feeling for them.

William Catchpole, Louis "Ziggy" Palmer, and Captain Malcolm Leckie Come to the Aid of the Lewis Gunners

(In the words of Kendall Haydon)

Advancing on the German Trench

We were advancing on the German trench. Two gunners, Able and me, two riflemen—mainly pack mules—hauling stacks of ammunition magazines and ammo, two spotters, Schmidt and Otis Mankins and sniper Braddock with us. We made our way to a little hump in the ground, some dirt thrown up by an explosion. Set up our Lewis. Braddock spotted a Hun machine-gun nest in a shallow depression. I let loose a burst. One Kraut keeled over dead then two more toppled to the ground.

Then Jenks Braddock's quick eye spotted another nest. Before I could take aim another of their guns had us in it sights. There were plenty of shell holes by then. Then farm boy Mankins surprised himself. Words came out of his mouth. "Run like hell ahead to the shell hole and jump in."

Three of us down the hole. Schmidt and Braddock found another right next to it and rolled in. Comrades, corpses, from their insignia, engineers, lay at the bottom. Germans, too. The shell hole was shallow around the rim, steep farther down. "Thank God for craters," I said, then ordered, "Scoop up dirt and pack it firm." We built a crude fire-step. We set the gun and went after the Hun. Plenty of ammunition.

Bullets from the gun Mankins had spotted shaved the ground. I said, "Keep down. Turn your backs to the wall." I snuck a peek over the rim back the way we had come and saw a wave of Americans coming toward the trench fall, cut down.

A poor lad at the crater's bottom heard us talk. He did all he could to make us know he was alive. In the midst of the shouts of guns, his voice came to us, low, soft. Then a wordless whisper, then a whimper, then just moaning.

I said, "One of those guys must be alive. If he's one of us pull him up. Otherwise, leave him. Hurry." Able and Mankins slithered down and hauled him up. He was a mess.

"Water," was all he could manage. Zeke Able unscrewed his canteen's top and raised it to the boy's lips. He drank, nearly choking. When he recovered, he drank more. Choked. Coughed again.

"Your name?"

"Private Barker. Thomas. 105 Engineers.

"We thought you was dead. You look dead."

"I nearly am," he whispered. His voice was nearly gone. I put my ear close to his mouth. "Give a minute. More water."

"How'd you end up here? How long you been here?"

"I don't know. A few days, I think."

Three nights before he and two others crawled out at night and reached the Hun's wire. They lay still to make sure nothing was moving. Barker whispered to his sergeant. "I hear Huns talking. If we understood German we could bring back useful information."

He told us, "Sergeant, may he rest in peace, whispered, 'Well, to begin, we don't know German. And what makes you think what they are saying would be useful? For all you know they might be saying if only we understood English we could get intelligence from the doughboys.' His last joke. He's down there."

Above the hole the battle went on.

Barker rested between each phrase, each sentence. I couldn't tell if he was gathering strength or putting his thoughts together. Probably both.

"Ran into a German cutting crew. Or they ran into the three of us. We fought 'em near this hole. Pulling and pushing, we all tumbled in, fought like wild men. All we had was side arms and wire cutters. They had the same, and spades. Didn't dare shoot in the dark. No telling. Might hit our own man. Went at it pistol butts and fists. Punching, gouging, strangling. I killed one, smashed his skull with a cutter. Heavy thing, thank God." He said a German swung a spade, broke his leg. The Hun swung again. The blade, like an ax, cut Barker's thigh. The fight a bloody mangle. Private Barker said, "Tussled all the way to the bottom. Dead Germans down there, too."

"Then I was the only one alive. Everything has been here to feast on the bodies. As long as I could, I chased off rats, birds. Maggots got the best of me. Couldn't crawl out of here if I wanted to. No sense trying. Dare not. The Krauts would pick me off in a minute. I was lucky." He ended, "Didn't cut any wire that night."

William Catchpole and Louis "Ziggy" Palmer, Both Deceased, Materialize

Then we saw a ray of light bright as the sun fall to the bottom of the crater. Two shapes took form, at first a blur, as if we only needed to rub our eyes and they would disappear. Then the blur took on substance—two British soldiers. They scrambled up to where we were perched. Saluting, they spoke. "Private William Catchpole. Dead before my time." Then adopting the voice of an American gangster, he said, "We're comrades of Corporal Atkins, see? You know Atkins? Machine gunners he fought with at Mons, see? Two bombs go off and five of us gone." Then the tone of his voice changed, sober, sad. "The child Tommy Atkins was getting water for the guns. He's the only one alive. The rest of us live in spirit." Then, bowing, the other fellow introduced himself. "Ziggy Palmer, private, AEF. Killed at First Ypres. Specialist in comic bits. Along with my partner here."

In a theatrical aside, Catchpole, beanpole, said, "There've been many Ypres since. Even a comic newspaper. *Wipers Times*. Heard of it? We did the writing. We worked on the living writers' brains, the writers who could hold a pen and strike typewriter keys. They didn't know anything about us." He went on. "Thought they came up with the jokes and humor and sarcasm and foolishness themselves. Let them think what they want, I say."

"As if they were capable of such a thing themselves," chimed in Palmer.

I recalled. "Ruffians. Isn't it?"

"You know about us? Atkins blabbed to you, did he? What do you think, William?"

"Well, he must have had a reason. But a good knock on the head for each of 'em, and they'll forget they ever heard the word."

"You medics?" Barker croaked.

Palmer heard. "Lord, no. Clowns, comics from the London stage. But we'll find a way to put you back in fighting fettle. That's what the Army wants." Palmer, his hair done up in a clown's corkscrew hairdo: "We used to see our names on leg-house billboards. Our character names, anyway. Performed as Sir Edward Twaddle of Tweedledale and his valet, M. T. Head, as Stout and Sturdy, Lout and Dirty, a routine about Milord's trickster gardeners, then Cheese and Sweets. We are whatever concoction of characters we can throw together to get us on the stage and in the money. In the Army we were the Beaux Belles. The boys like the ladies. Had big busts, brassieres stuffed with bandage, cleavage to go with, and short skirt and heels."

Catchpole: "What the soldiers call us now is high grade names, better quality. Soldiers call us 'Friends of the Wounded.'"

Back and forth.

"Brothers of the Dying," said zany Ziggy.

"'Angels of the Covenant,'" said Catchpole. "'Comrades in White'. Is keeping them alive a blessing? Bring them back to fight and die again? That's what medics and doctors are for. But we're not here for small talk." To the wounded soldier: "Got a name, Doughboy?"

"Thomas Barker, Private. 105 Engineers. Don't call me Doughboy."

"Yank, then."

"Worse than Doughboy. Don't ever call me that."

"Blimey, I won't call you nothin' then," Palmer said, in phony cockney dialect. Then, "We're waiting for the doctor. We're the entertainment till he gets here." Mimicking what he thought was a Southerner's accent, Palmer said, "Been doin' it nigh onto four years, as y'all Americans would say." Then his voice returned to normal. "We've joked up many a bloke. Keeps us busy day and night. This being dead, at least for us so-called 'Golden Arrows of God,' it's hard work. We've yet to hear the twang of a harp or smelled the roses of Paradise."

Catchpole: "Toil without end."

Added Palmer, "I hope when this is over we'll get our rest."

Catchpole, tall and wiry, bowed at the waist. "What we do mostly is greet the wounded or dead with a joke, a riposte, a funny saying. And we've plenty of 'em."

"Like the laugh of a lifetime. We call it The Laugh of an Afterlife-time."

Ziggy joked, "Nothing cheers a dead soldier like wise cracks and bel-lyachers."

Catchpole added, "A bit of smut thrown in—if it raises a blush—added pleasure all round. No end of laughter. Let's give 'em one."

"You start."

"No, you."

"All right, then." Ziggy Palmer cleared his throat. "Say, I was offered a promotion to sergeant and turned it down."

Catchpole, with a look of mock astonishment: "You were offered a promotion, but you turned it down? Why did you do that?"

"I didn't want to give up my privates," he said, and grabbed his testicles.

For a moment, the soldiers were not thinking about war, but the remarkable thing that was happening. Where did these beings come from? And comics? The last thing they thought dead soldiers returning to life would be. Comedians.

Seeing that the doctor had not arrived yet, Private Catchpole said, "Here's another. A situation we know well. You start, Ziggy."

"Which one you mean?"

"The rich man with St. Peter."

"All right, then," Palmer said. With the air of a man of great wealth, "I had a peculiar dream last night."

"Indeed? And what did you dream last night?"

"I dreamed I died and went to heaven. While St. Peter was showing me the sights I asked him how long a minute was up there."

"You asked St. Peter how long a minute was in heaven? And what did he reply?"

" He said that a minute in heaven is as long as a million years on earth."

"A minute up there was as long as a million years on earth. Wonderful! Is that all you asked him."

"No, sir. Then I asked him how much a shilling was worth in heaven."

"You asked St. Peter how much a shilling was worth up there. And how much did he say a shilling is worth?"

"He said a shilling was worth a million pounds on earth."

"Wonderful! A shilling in heaven is worth a million pounds down here on earth. What then?"

"I told St. Peter I found a good investment. I asked him to lend me a shilling."

"You asked him to lend you a shilling? Not pound? What did he say, pray?"

"He said he would." The comic's beat. Then, "In a minute."

"Everything here a surprise, a joke just waiting to be sprung, don't you agree?" said the two, taking a bow.

Captain Malcolm Leckie, R.M.A.C. Saves the Dying Soldier

Then a sphere bloomed in the bottom of the pit, clear quartz, the size of a baseball, turning to a golden globe, it grew to the size of a man—and became a British officer. The two Tommies saluted. Could we call them privates, them not being exactly human?

Palmer said to the officer, "Why, it's our old Brother in the Spirit, Captain Leckie. First to leave. First to come back. Ain't that so?"

Catchpole to Barker: "Doughboy, you're in good hands now. He's the doctor. Doctor to our Company. Shrapnel at Mons. Dead in body six days later."

Ziggy Palmer took up the conversation. "Once in a while we meet. It's that way in the spirit realm. Especially those of us with jobs among the living. If we had a sense of time I would say it's been a long time since we've seen the Captain. But no telling, really. We might have seen him a few moments ago. Such is our lack of sense."

"Of time, you mean?" asked Captain Leckie.

"Yes. Sense of time."

Said Palmer, "Besides that, we do lack sense. Dimwits we might be, but no way to know, is there?" his question rhetorical, in the way of the English.

"We bump into each other, reminisce, talk about old times, our doings. Beyond that, I don't know," said Will Catchpole Thrilled to know a relative of his favorite writer, he said, "But Captain, tell the boys who was your brother in-law."

Said Captain Leckie, sharply, "A soldier here needs a doctor now. Let me get to it."

Ignoring the doctor, Palmer said, "Young Haydon, the doctor was Conan Doyle's brother in-law."

"Conan Doyle? Who's that?" I asked.

"Why, don't you know? Sir Arthur Conan Doyle. Tell them, Captain."

"Author of the Sherlock Holmes stories," said Captain Leckie. "Now let me get to work."

"It never struck me that someone wrote them," I said.

Palmer, filled with pride and knowledge, said, "Most people think Dr. Watson wrote them, or Holmes himself. Or that they just came into being like newspaper reports. Sir Arthur Conan Doyle wrote them, and Captain Leckie was his brother in-law. He's a celebrity."

Irritated, the captain said, "I'm here to save a man's life. I need to get to work. Not much time. A few minutes more and it's too late for the lad."

Barker's trouser leg was caked with dry blood. Without another word, Catchpole ripped open the trouser. Palmer knelt down, gently unwound the poor soldier's puttee.

The thigh was green and grey, the wound festering. Crimson lines snaked up the skin and beyond his trousers. Palmer coaxed the cloth away from the scab. Barker wrinkled his nose. "Gangrene," he muttered. "I thought I smelled it. I'm a goner."

"Not so fast, young man," said Palmer. "The doctor's saved worse than you."

Captain Leckie opened his medical bag, took out what he needed. "This will hurt," he said. While the doctor cleaned and stitched the wound, and bandaged the leg the comics chattered away.

Catchpole: "Atkins is our link to the living. So we only meet wounded, maimed soldiers, guide some to the underworld."

Followed on Catchpole's heels, Palmer: "You're our first Americans. Welcome to the war."

Ziggy added, "We give 'em solace. "A lot of lost souls floating about. Some in the dirt, some in the air, some just lost who knows where. You should have seen the mess at the Somme. Multitudes drowned in mud. A ghastly way to perish. Every kind of death, I say."

"In other words," said Will Catchpole, "We guide soldiers' souls who can't find their way. We escort them to a place we call 'the abode of the fallen.' Classy name for what we can't describe."

Squat and round, Ziggy: "Salvation for some. Resurrection. The Caldron of Rebirth. Passage to the underworld."

"The truth is, most stay dead."

"Why doesn't God save us all?" asked Private Barker.

"Too many to handle. The Divine can handle scores, even hundreds maybe. But millions is beyond His capacity. We humans outdid God. Outshined the Lord, we did. The battles in the Bible. Maybe a few hundred, a thousand soldiers. Even in the last century. But millions."

"Enough of this gloom. We're on the battlefield. Tell another joke while we wait," the doctor said.

"Wait for what?" asked Palmer.

"You will soon see. We need a joke or two, a laugh. I've not laughed in a long while. A few limericks?" And the two recited half a dozen. The men laughed, all except Barker, contemplating his fate.

"No more jokes," said Palmer. "They lost their savor. Our bits grow stale."

"We got a bit of gallows humor, black humor left. But not much taste for it anymore," Palmer repeated.

Captain Leckie looked at his wristwatch. "Speaking of waiting, enough time has passed." Then, as if he was unhappy with the bandage's wrapping, the captain said, "Palmer, unwind the dressing." When it was removed, to our astonishment we saw that the flesh was whole and fresh, as if there had never been a wound, let alone infection.

"See?" said Catchpole. He went on. "Divine help and healing. That's the joy we bring. Not just laughs, jokes. That's the good news."

Palmer asked Catchpole, "Is there bad news?"

"If there's good, there has to be bad. Every silver lining has a dark cloud." To the soldier, "Here's the bad. You'll go back into battle. Give the Bosch another chance to kill you. If that happens you won't have the luck. No third chances. That's the rule."

Then Catchpole bowed, saluted, and said, "Gentlemen, we would join up with you ourselves, but it's not permitted. Against regulations. Besides, we're out of practice. Never shot one of these light guns. We were Vickers. You're fine young men. May you prevail in the battle."

Palmer waved goodbye. "Ta, ta," he said. Then the two comedians sat down in the dirt, slid on their backsides down to the crater's floor and faded into ground beside the bodies of the corpses.

And when we looked, the doctor had disappeared. We sat for a moment in wonder and amazement. Then I said to this Barker, "You stay where you are. You're too weak to move. I'm sure the Germans won't be coming this way again. You'll be rescued before the day is over." Then I said, "To the gun! We have a trench to take."

And that will be another kind of miracle, but a miracle for certain.

The Damned Rat in the Shell Hole

While the others jumped into the crater where they found the dying engineer, Sniper Braddock and Gunner Spears ran and slid into an old shallow shell hole. The two peeked over the edge, scanned what was ahead, ready to fire at any Huns they spotted. In a rare moment of silence Braddock heard a loud scratching in the dirt. He looked to his left and saw a rat perched at the lip of the hole three yards away, its eyes glowing yellow. In his brain, Braddock heard a voice, high pitched and soft. "You are in your life's last moments." The rat scrambled across the short distance, leapt the remaining yard, its claws grabbing the cloth of Braddock's puttee. It scratched its way up his trousers and tunic and, squealing loudly, bit the thick of his left cheek. In terror, Braddock jumped to his feet and tore at the creature, tore it free of his face and threw it to the ground. In the next instant a bullet shattered Braddock's skull and he fell to the dirt, instantly dead. Keeping his head below the level of the ground, Private Spears looked in horror. His comrade-in-arms was dead. Strange as it was, Braddock was right about the rat. Sadly, *The Master Book of Dreams* prediction was right.

Ezekiel Able Pierced the Second Line and
Went Far Beyond the Hindenburg Line

Private Spears ran out of the crated and joined the others in advancing on the German trench. Lost in the gloom, Hans Schmidt asked, "Where the hell are we?"

"Which way?" Able echoed.

The squad leaders were supposed to have compasses. Few got them. Of those, most were broken. The Swamp Fox crew had none. And they could not see ten feet ahead. William Spears told Haydon to keep moving forward. "You'll reach the railroad tracks."

"Are you guessing?" a voice asked. Whose it was no one knew. By now soldiers from other lines had stumbled upon the Foxes and joined in the advance. They knew nothing about Spears' knowledge.

"Instinct," Spears said. "Intuition. Like the Swamp Fox used." Soon they reached the tracks which would lead them to Bellicourt and the Le

Catelet-Nauroy line, their objective. But in the gloom of fog and clouds and smoke, they couldn't tell which way to go. Were they north of the village, or south? Left or right? The wrong way would put them in the hands of the Germans.

"Go left, Haydon," William Spears declared.

I said, "Follow Spears."

"Or is it right? Who says so? How come?" the voice asked.

I said, "You don't know about Spear's ways of knowing. We count on it."

At the Le Catelet-Nauroy Line, the enemy trenches, the Swamp Foxes and their new friends killed off a Hun machine-gun nest, took it over. Firing the Germans' heavy Maxim machine gun, the soldiers fought off a counter-attack and killed many more. Finally the Germans surrounded them. Haydon had the men put their weapons down and put up their hands. Atkins had taught them if you're dead you're no good. If you are captured you can get away and fight again. Don't die for no good reason.

In the momentary muddle and confusion Ezekiel Able grabbed the Lewis, a pan of bullets attached, and ran off. At that moment Otis Mankins, who hauled the canisters, the pans loaded with bullets, grabbed two out of the magazine and ran after Able. Catching sight of Mankins out of the corner of his eye, Ezekiel shouted, "Go back! Go back!" But on came Mankins, intent on dying heroically. Able ran to a second nest, poked the Lewis in the firing loop, sprayed the inside with the magazine's bullets, enough to kill the entire crew. By then Mankins was sprawled in the dirt, dead, his arms stretched forward, the canisters held out toward Able. Ezekiel entered the pillbox and took over the Maxim. Immediately he sprayed bullets from inside at the Germans. None knew what happened to Able after that, since the rest alive took for the trench that lay ahead, their objective.

And me? Kendall Haydon? Atkins told me I would see the battle in the heavens. At first aeroplanes scudded about the sky. I thought maybe he meant I would see an aerial fight. As soon as Able left, the sky became a brightly painted canvas like I had seen in museums. colors, fancifully shaped clouds. Rays of sun falling from gaps in the clouds lighting patches of ground ahead. I couldn't look for fear of being shot. But then, first as glimmers and shapes, transparent, I began to see the tumult Atkins had predicted. Every form of demonic being began to crowd the sky. In no particular order, they wheeled and tumbled. Then I saw the intended victims. Angels looked like babies, pudgy arms and legs, short torsos, heads out of proportion to their whole size. How, I wondered, could there be a fair fight. If the angels were to protect us, to fight on our behalf, we were lost. Innocents to the sacrifice. And so it was. They fell from the sky, blood spouting from vicious cuts. Decapitations. Bodies shorn of limbs.

A ghastly sight. I recalled stories from history and legend of the killing of innocents, the rape of women and girls.

Suddenly, though, a rumbling as of a herd of horses assaulted my hearing. And a whirlwind descended from a cloud. Shouts and hoarse cries of an avenging horde. Twisting and writhing, angels of vast size and proportion took form in the air. And at their head, astride a massive white horse, St. George, crying his war cry once again. At his side, I knew it was Dease, dead and alive, his face red with rage. Fear filled the baby-murderers, the demons. They looked about seeking help or a place of escape or refuge. What they had done to the babies was now done to them. Limbs severed from bodies. Eviscerations and decapitations. Shouts and mayhem. The stench of blood and putrescence, unloosed bowels, filled my nostrils. How long the onslaught lasted I could not tell. But its meaning was clear to me. After all the death and grief, the suffering and privation, the fear and starvation, the good would win over the evil. That is what I would report to Tommy Atkins. And the hope that war would be gone from the earth, mankind living at peace. No enemies, no reason to kill. I felt it in my bones' marrow. Would that this be mankind's future. This would make the sacrifice worthy of all that was lost. I hoped this was humanity's future. Even so, there lingered a doubt which I hoped to quell.

Caves, Quarries, and Tunnels

Canal Tunnel entrance

The German military engineers made good use of the land. Abandoned mines, craters, shell holes, excavations, gravel pits, burrows, crevices, cellars, holes, ditches, troughs, places to lurk and hide.

But throughout the war the armies used caves, quarries, and tunnels to hide depots of weaponry and ammunition, hospitals, prisons, vast populations of soldiers, command headquarters. Towns and cities underground. In the Battle of Arras twenty-six thousand British soldiers, their presence undetected, came out from caverns under the city, attacked the Germans from behind. At Lens a massive cavern system. Underground easily camouflaged. Entrances easily concealed, impossible to see. Impervious to bombing. Nearly impossible to attack. Excellent protection. Hid soldiers. Added to natural fortifications, the underworld of the Somme and Flanders was alive with sappers and miners burrowing and tunneling. Each spring hundreds of miners came from Wales to dig tunnels for the Allies, stuff the farthest end with explosives and blow up enemy trenches and depots, headquarters. The Huns did it, too. Once in a while one side would break into the enemy's tunnel. Then the miners and Germans fought with picks and shovels. Grim and bloody, hand-to- hand.

Town soon to be destroyed, directly above the south entrance of the tunnel

Tunnel entrance, the concrete wall removed

Towboats converted into billets

The German Army occupied the canal and tunnel and the plateau above. They commandeered the fleet of towboats and barges that served the canal, moored them to the towpath inside the tunnel, turned them into storage and living quarters. Many of the other German soldiers lived in the cavern itself. Along with the trenches' construction, at the south end the Huns carved chambers into the tunnel's east wall to a depth of one hundred yards and a mile and a half long. This subterranean world sheltered Fritzes by the thousands who lived like moles—underground creatures.

The tunnel had a power-generating system, electric lights, and telephone network, plumbing. The Germans built hospital wards, operating theaters, kitchens, store rooms, refrigerated caverns filled with beef and pig carcasses ready for the butcher, refrigerated food lockers, ice generators, laundries, class rooms, latrines, bath houses, depots filled with weaponry and ammunition, a massive armory fully equipped to repair weapons, billets, officers' quarters.

The morning of September 29 the thousands of Huns lined up in the passageways, ready to join the battle, their presence unknown to us. With their kits and weapons it took a while and an effort to climb the steps, double file. They must have come up winded. How they assembled, the British and the Americans couldn't figure.

The British knew the Germans were using the tunnel for storage and protection. What British intelligence figured was mostly accurate, though they did not predict that thousands of the Hun would swarm out like African safari ants to join the battle, swelling the numbers.

Chapter 20

Underground: Fighting inside Bellicourt Tunnel

(Private Jolly's Recollection)

Four Lewis Machine Gunners Found Our Way Down

Donald Barton, Gunner One, picked three of us to go down into the tunnel with him. The rest he left behind to find their way in the fight the best they could. On September 29, considering our assignment, there was no good in our going forward until the fog lifted and we could read the co-ordinates and spot the landmarks. But we were not certain that the land-marks would still be there, with all the bombardment and debris. In these battles the landscape changed quickly. A building, a prominent feature, could be obliterated, and all around it gone, too, in an instant.

After following the coordinates and several minutes searching, we found a shaft and made our way down the steps the Russian and French and Belgian prisoners cut in the clay and rock. We each carried a flash-light, electric torch the British call it, but covered the lens with folded handkerchiefs, so only the barest light came though. The place was almost empty, the soldiers now above, giving battle. We found a few Germans on guard. It was clear that they did not expect us to find our way in. "Shush," Barton whispered. He crept up on a sentry he found at the foot of the pas-sage, sliced the Hun's throat from ear to ear with his bayonet. Barton spun him around before he could fall, shined his flashlight on his own face, fast enough for the Hun's eyes to see and his brain to register the image of the man who killed him.

"You nearly took his head off," I whispered.

"Don't give 'em a chance to make a sound. Jolly, you're next."

Barton pushed me then each of us in turn to the front of the line. "Cut his head off. Dead on the spot. A man without his head doesn't make a sound."

He baptized us in the blood of the enemy, a rite. Being in this hell brought out the demon in him. He said Atkins told him to initiate us this way, but I don't believe him. Not like Atkins. We were fighting demons. This was war. Anything goes. That's what he believed. Made him a good leader.

Stealth and cunning were partners in the affair, here in the pit of blood.

More than a dozen Kraut sentries died silently without realizing that unwelcome company had arrived.

And so on into the cavern.

The Battle Below

Debris inside the tunnel

Railway into the tunnel

"'Abandon hope all ye who enter here,'" I said when we reached the level of the canal. "I read my grandmother's book *Inferno*, illustrated by the great Gustav Goré. She also has a Bible with his pictures."

"Dante wrote in I-talian," said Beau Baylor.

"Ain't you the educated one," sarcastic Barton said.

Baylor: "This place has the look of Hell. No fire. No brimstone. The cold version. Damp. Dark. Rank. Devilish. What do you say?"

No one answered.

The Hun soldiers slept in wire cages on wooden racks stacked two high. Animal meat hung in the ice room. Venison, squab, duck, goose, good beef, and pork, even boar, sheep, goat, and animals we couldn't identify, probably wild.

I said, "They could withstand a siege of many days down here."

"Are you crazy?" said the crafty Barton. "We'd gas the bastards."

"They sure weren't expecting us to find our way down here or they would have had a stronger guard," Baylor said. "We should turn the place into useless stuff."

Barton said, "There's a lot we can salvage. An arsenal to turn against them. We'll send a salvage crew to haul it up once we chase the bastards past the trenches."

"Jolly, how many soldiers do you think live here?" Beau Baylor asked.

"I guess ten thousand," I said.

Barton laughed. "I think more. A lot more."

"More wouldn't surprise me. Who knows?" I said. "It doesn't matter now. They'll never return. This is the beginning of the end. We'll push them all the way to Germany. They'll run for it soon enough."

"Tommy Atkins prophesized this, didn't he?" said Beau Baylor.

"He did. Even so, we need to be damn careful," said Mason. "I wouldn't be surprised if there aren't some of 'em hiding anywhere. All them towboats and barges. They could easy be lurking in 'em. And any moment they could come on us and we'd be done for."

Barton barked, "Well, keep your damned eyes peeled. Better yet, hope we got 'em all. Or at least enough to scare the others off. They know we mean business. Pitch dark. These couple of lanterns and electric torches don't help much. Somewhere is the center of the electrical system. We got to find it and shut it down."

Sure enough, we ran across the remnant in the tunnel, a couple dozen cooks in the privates' kitchen, lounging about, eating. Close up they were more like criminals than professional soldiers. Devilish, they were. They never expected to see the enemy in the tunnel. They didn't even have side arms, but went at us, fists flying, cast iron pot covers for shields, butcher knives, long skewers for lances. These men were brutes. I put on my knuckle buster with a thick, pointed prong for gouging and got to use it.

Barton said, "Wound 'em and let 'em bleed to death." Then: "Changed my mind. Give 'em a fightin' chance." Soon enough we had 'em all corralled.

Miles Mason spoke some German he had learned in school. Barton told him to ask each one, "Any more?" The Huns knew what he meant. "Nein," they said. Each time Barton said, "He's lying." Then, "Why should they tell the truth? Lying to the enemy is no crime."

Barton had them march to the edge of the canal. He set up Lewis. He said, "Mason, tell 'em face the water. I don't want 'em to pull you in." Mason told them in German. Then Barton said, "Tell 'em jump. Maybe some can swim. Maybe all. Maybe they couldn't. I'm not gonna shoot 'em, just scare 'em. Tell 'em jump. If they don't, push them in. We'll see what happens. If they swim away, who cares? If they drown, so much the better." And soon the two dozen floundered in the canal. A few heads bobbed up and down a few times and never came up again. Others might have been swept away by the current. And some might have swum under the wall that blocked the tunnel entry. The wall did not go to the bottom, leaving room for the water to flow under.

Barton went to the gun and sprayed the opposite wall with bullets from left to right and back again, like he was watering a garden with a hose. The cavernous walls amplified and echoed the ear-shattering gunfire. His native brutality came upon him. Or maybe it was good sense. Give them a good scare, so they wouldn't want to come back. He didn't try to shoot them. It was more like good, bullying fun to him. He laughed his way through a whole belt, not continuous fire, but quick bursts, enough to scare the hell out of the poor buggers.

There was no telling with Barton. His streak of meanness was as wide as a river. The men had seen the way he treated his poor cousin and many others.

He said, "I'm pretty sure we're alone down here now. It's only us."

First We Eat, Then We Work

In the Boche officers' quarters, we found pipes and Turkish tobacco, Havana cigars, armchairs pulled round in a circle, at the center a kerosene heater and kerosene lantern. An upright piano filled a corner, sheet music lying on the music rack, the latest German songs, patriotic, romantic, comic. In the sleeping quarters comfortable beds and cushioned chairs. All pilfered from prosperous houses in Bellicourt. Maybe even from the church. The Germans held nothing sacred that wasn't German.

Baylor said, "They've been down here long enough to make themselves damn comfortable. Cold, but comfortable. In this summer weather, the cold is better than sweating in the sun and heat."

Then we came upon the officers' kitchen, pantry, and dining room. "This is more like it. Officer food," I said. In the ovens we found cooked roasts of beef, pork loins in sauerkraut and dried cherries, chickens grilled on spits, ready for the eating. "The Krauts cooked for us," said Barton. "First we eat, then we find the communications center. Food first. Don't work on an empty stomach."

Already rats scampered around, pilfering the cheese and bread, as if they knew the Hun rats were gone for good.

Miles Mason spoke up. "What about the boys up above?"

"Dummy, they've got their own look-out. We've got ours," Barton grumbled. "Chase the rats and get to serving,"

Mason kept on. "The boys upstairs need our gun."

To Mason Barton said, "You're in a big rush. Maybe you want us to skip this food and break into iron rations? Some corned beef, hardtack, crappy coffee? Or what's spread out in front of us?"

Miles Mason said, "Take it easy, bud. I just think we need to get going. But it would be sinful in the eyes of God to let this good food go to waste. We can't lug it all to the top, so we need to do the best we can."

"Get at it, then," said Private Baylor, rubbing his hands together. We scrambled to lay out a feast for ourselves. Bayonets sliced beef and pork, skewered fresh tomatoes and cucumbers. German pickles and sauerkraut, mustard, rye bread, pumpernickel, beer, wine. We opened bottles of preserved cherries, peaches, brandied fruits. Ate them by the spoonful. We had what I would call a sumptuous repast. We even discovered a stock of champagne and gave it a taste. Mighty good.

"I'd like to spend the rest of the war here. It's like heaven," I said.

Private Mason said, "It'll stink down here, Jolly, when the corpses rot."

"Oh, don't take me seriously. Of course we won't stay here. Just wishful thinking, all the food and drink. I'm joshing."

While we ate in luxury the ferocious battle raged sixty feet above our heads. As we ate, we talked. "These Boche officers live a life of pleasure," I said. "Real silverware, china plates, glass tumblers, and goblets. They might even be crystal. I don't know."

"Pleasure and ease," said Mason. "Aristocrats don't suffer, even in war. Take a look around. There's a big difference between them and the infantry. Bigger than the difference between us and our officers, I would say."

"Pass me a beer. Do you think our officers eat much different?" I asked. "Maybe we just don't see it. Before the war this is how life must have been. All this fine stuff stolen from the rich of the town, from their homes, probably rubble now."

"Our officers didn't do badly, either," Mason said.

"Nothing like this," said Barton. "German officers are aristocrats, the nobility," he said, raising his nose to show their manner. "We don't have them. No, we got the wealthy, but they're willing to fight. At least some of them."

I said, "Well, it ain't the ordinary bumpkin who becomes an officer. He comes from somewhere and knows something."

"Says who?" grumbled Barton. "They're rich, but there's a lot of 'em dummies."

To avoid a row with Barton, I changed the subject. "Being down here, I can see why the Huns don't want the war to end."

Beau Baylor: "Especially, they don't want to lose. When they get home to their beloved Deutschland, things won't be so rosy. I figure once they can't steal food from the poor Belgians and French any more there won't be enough for the soldiers to eat and all the Germans waiting at home. Just a theory. What do you think, Caleb?"

I said, "I believe you're right. I hear they make coffee from acorns, beechnuts, roasted barley. Fake meat, fake fat. Now what's gonna happen?"

"Let 'em starve. That's what I say," said Barton. "Up till now they've been lucky bastards. Mason, give over some beef. I never tasted cheese like this. Cheese this good."

Miles Mason, impatient for action, worried what could happen if we waited too long. "We need get Lewis up to the battlefield. He's hungry for meat, too. And blood."

Barton said, "Patience, Mason. I said we'd go soon enough."

After the hearty meal we went back to the officers' quarters, sat in comfortable chairs, smoked cigars. Bit off the tips and lit them. Sampled more of the champagne.

Then We Went to Work

It wasn't hard to find the massive communications center—telegraphs, telephones, switchboards, lines—that served the Germans all the way from Cambrai to St. Quentin. Barton let me spray the place with a couple of magazines. That was enough. "No more communication from here," Barton said.

In our last days of training Tommy Atkins told us the Germans had discovered in ancient Teutonic texts on energy instructions on how to tap power directly from the earth. Here under the canal, the Dragon's Vein lay sleeping. The Germans awoke the serpent. The instructor told us to look for something that might be the key to such energy, a switch of some sort. We didn't know where to look or what to look for. As we went deeper into the tunnel we heard a humming that grew louder, louder and with several pitches and rhythms. Layers of sound. Almost a chant, a persistent refrain. Some of us heard the words "run away, run away." Some heard "run awry." Some, "run this way." We came upon a steel plate, a square yard, set into the wall. It vibrated and pulsed. The sound came from behind. "Jolly, shoot it at the center," Barton said to me, "We'll see what happens." I took aim from five yards distance. When the bullets struck, there arouse an eruption of sound that deafened us, and a blast of lightning. The walls shook. As if a river flowed alongside the canal several feet above and behind the wall, water gushed from where the plate had been. It nearly swept us from our feet. We were lucky to hold our footing. Then a moan, deep and, if it could be said, sorrowful, arose and died. Eels and snakes and creatures we had never seen thrashed in the water, biting at the air, grabbing for our legs. The water thickened to a black sludge, like sewage. The stench of rot and decay, brimstone, corpse smell. We felt a darkness, the darkness of a cave, darkness within darkness, a dank evil and malevolence harboring a hatred of humanity. Then a light shone with the intensity of lightning itself. We had to shut our eyes and still we could see red through our eyelids. Our hearts and spirits lifted. Then the light faded and our flashlights seemed too dim to do any good.

We were possessed, began to see worlds beyond the real. Each of us had a vision, brief, strong.

To me, despairing Jolly, a message came in words. Witness. Treasure. The words rang in my ears like church bells. I became a pond, then water passing through a dam, down a spillway at a mill, now me the turning waterwheel. The wheel's grinding and squeaking said, "Impossible not to believe. I believe. Impossible now not to believe. I believe." When the vision spoke no more, I knew I had bathed in the River Styx and was now in the Breath of Everlasting Life. My mind's eye saw patriotic posters, the goddess Victory holding her torch, the Huns trampled at her feet. I knew the Allies would win. A few more weeks or months and thousands of deaths and maimings, the war would be over. Still I had a whiff of the despondent in me. I was given an order and I carried it out. Because of the Vision, live or die is all the same to me. I know there is a place in the Beyond for me. I have been there.

Private Beau Baylor's thoughts: "I heard the church bell peal at home, the organ's roar. The choir sang such lovely melody. I couldn't distinguish words, though I knew whose voices they were. My mother, my sister, the voice of the girl I adore and hope to marry if I outlive the war. Other voices. The words sound like an ancient tongue, lovely and haunting, angelic. Each face wore a look of happy peace."

No vision for Miles Mason, he firmly connected to ordinary reality, he, wanting report on the success in destroying the communication center, to bring the gun to the surface and fight there.

Barton wanted to speak to us, but his mouth would not move, though he thought we would have heard him. In front of the us he wept. When he was finally able to speak it was as if he was someone entirely different. "I tremble when I think about it. I was with angels above looking down from the roof of this tunnel. I saw myself with all of you. I don't know how to describe it. The 'me' above experienced where I was, not the 'me' on the tunnel floor. Can you imagine such a thing?" Donald Barton said he heard his Grandfather's voice, he, long dead. Religious. Baptist. Bible reader. Prayers morn and evening, meals. "My grandfather spoke. 'Pray as I taught you. Love your cousins. Love all mankind. Follow the merciful angel who leads you along the road of life to death.' I don't know what that meant. Will I die in the war, or was he saying that life leads to death?" His usual certainty about his own beliefs disappeared, replaced by perplexity and wonder.

All of a sudden Barton buckled at the knees. "Hold me up, please." Please? We had never heard him ask politely, or even ask. Orders and demands were his way. In the tunnel's cold Donald broke out in a sweat. His breath took over, occupied his body. Gasps and wheezing and involuntary grunts and howls came forth. Barton went into a fit. I said, "He's having a heart attack or stroke. Look at his eyes. Bulging and bloodshot. Something's mighty wrong." His eyes closed shut. Gunner Barton moaned and gibbered. His frame shook in a grotesque palsy, then stiffened in paralysis. In a second vision he was on the battlefield a dozen feet away from his cousin. He saw Ezekiel rush forward, plunge his bayonet into a Hun's stomach, stomach sliced open, intestines snaking out. At the same time, the Hun's pierced Able's throat. Barton saw them fall to the ground, each impaled on the other's weapon. He saw their death struggles. He knew without reason, but without doubt, that the place Able died was the farthest forward an American soldier reached, first soldier to cross the second line, Le Catelet-Naroy. "My cousin," he muttered, and gasped, withholding a sob. "My own blood." His became a sorrowing soul.

What Barton saw, heard, felt was more real than the real. Knowledge immediate, full, all-encompassing. Insight after insight. Judgments he held about others evaporated. He instantly he felt genuine brotherhood. "My brothers," he said aloud, and came near to weeping. The gunners were astonished. This was not the Barton they knew. The paralysis passed, the trembling ceased. His breath returned to its ordinary pace and depth. He opened his eyes. Baylor and I helped him to his feet.

Then he said, "Ezekiel came to me, surrounded by light, placed his hand on my chest. The light entered my heart. It was as if a curtain of darkness fell away and sunlight streamed in. I was changed. I changed." Then Barton saw a globe of fire arise from his cousin's body and ascend to the sky. He knew he was watching a soul rise to the realm of the angels. All at once a welter of tears and deep sobbing. He managed to say, "I believe if I let myself, I would sob in grief for all the meanness I brought into life. I would sob for the rest of my days."

We did not ridicule. We did not joke. We watched in awe and amazement and wonder.

We couldn't measure time. An instant, a minute, minutes on end, however long it was, we did not know. Then we returned to normal, and would never be who we were before. Witness. We all witnessed. Each his own memory, his own vision. And saw Barton become a different man. But now we were be soldiers again.

Leaving the Tunnel

First we filled our kits, whatever room we had, with Hun documents, all the orders, instructions—who knew what?—we could carry. We couldn't read German. The intelligence officer would make good use of it.

We picked choice souvenirs. I took a brass pocket compass, brass cigarette lighter inscribed with the German curse, *Gott mit uns*, a wristwatch, a dagger in a fine leather sheath. We stuffed our tunics with tins of goose liver pate, canned meats, sardines in olive oil, herring pickled in wine sauce. "This is the best salvage party I've been on," said Mason.

In a lighthearted tone, not meanness, Barton said, "Aren't you ashamed that you griped about going too slow. For all we've already suffered this is small payment. Plus, we had to steal it. They didn't give it free gratis."

We made our way to the passage we had climbed down. Barton led the way. We let him get far enough ahead so that he was out of earshot. We all had something we wanted to say.

Said Beau Baylor, his eyes aglow with hope and promise, "I never seen a man so changed. Even at the sinner's bench where folks give up their evil ways and take Jesus Christ as their Savior. I have to tell the chaplain what happened. It will do his poor heart good to hear. The suffering he's seen, poor man."

Miles Mason said, "I've heard prayer and repentance at revival meetings, but nothing like this. He's a different man."

"Let's see if it sticks," I said. "Let's see."

After that we scurried ahead to catch up with the man. We didn't know what we would find when we reached to top. We might be in the midst of battle, and easy targets. We hoped that there would the Australians mopping up Huns. But we worried that we might be taken for Huns, since we were coming out of the ground with German documents and booty.

After the long trudge we saw light above. Barton poked his head out like a woodchuck and took a quick look, then snaked out and lay on the ground. A sniper used Barton to gauge his target, and fired. I was next in line. As soon as my head popped up it was over for me. Reconciled to my despair by a vision then dead half an hour later.

The Night of September 29

Since just after sunrise our day was nothing but vicious fighting. After our ordeal scores of filth-covered soldiers lay about, exhausted, many in a stupor of sleep. Others, suffering from strain and shell-shock, were wide awake. Silent men, they stared at nothing. They thought about what they had seen, what the enemy had done to them, and what they did to the Huns. They were changed from who they had been just that morning.

The officers knew that the soldiers had done all they could. They knew that more and impossible demands lay ahead. An officer came along, said, "Stay where you are, soldiers." He said, "You weakened Fritz's resistance. He is dazed. You pricked his pride, made it bleed, broke his morale. You messed up his defenses."

He told them that in the first day's fight the Thirtieth Division killed one hundred Germans, wounded two hundred, took sixteen, captured two machine guns, a *grenadewerfer,* or grenade launcher, ammunition, and stores. They fought over a square mile of ground. Two of the division's officers were killed, two wounded; thirty-five enlisted men killed and 126 wounded. The officer went on, "A modest beginning, but Old Hickory's Division showed pluck."

For all the fighting, the Hindenburg Line had been pierced, but was far from broken. It would take more to clear it out. And the soldiers fought on for a couple of weeks, each day, more killed or wounded. As they advanced they passed corpses strewn here and there.

The night of September 29 the sounds of the day's battle sang the men to sleep, their lullaby. Their dreams carried day into night, the waking world into nightmare.

BATTLE PLANS ❖ 5

Chapter 21

The Wagoner's Second Tale

American Cemetery at Bony, France in its earliest days

September 30, 1918

At night supply details hauled ordnance loaded on limbers to front line depots, the front having pushed toward Germany. The limbers came back with corpses tied on. I was bringing four, each wrapped in a shroud. My cousin Ezekiel Able was one.

Along a path through the woods not far from the cemetery at Bony I came upon Barton. He was there waiting for me. He hailed me. In the dark I could barely make him out.

"What are you hauling?" Who's inside? I saw Zeke get killed. Anyone I know?" he asked.

He must have meant he heard Zeke was dead. Killed the oddest way.

"I can't lie or hide the truth. Our cousin. Stabbed in the throat."

"Which one is him?"

"In front on the left."

"I need to see his wounds."

"Why should I l let you? You were a torment and plague to Zeke. You want to spit in his dead face? Tear him off the limber and leave his corpse by the side of the road? Besides, it's pitch dark."

"I have to see its him. The family would kill me if I was this close and didn't make sure."

"I've seen him. I'll make sure they know. Don't you think I won't."

"Never mind." He took matches out of a waterproof case and struck a light.

"Blow that out!" I whispered loudly. "You'll get us killed."

"I will pray over him." Then, "I must see his wounds."

I said, "What's come over you? Family doesn't mean anything to you. You despise it. "

"You'll never understand. You won't believe what I say. When I was in the tunnel I had a vision. I was taken away. I was a few yards away. I saw him killed. I don't believe it myself, but it's true. My heart came to life for a moment, then died with my cousin. I must sound like a lunatic or liar, but my heart came to life and now it's broken. Please. Let me see him. I would be ashamed to say I was near his body and did not see him."

Cousin Barton went on: "It was Atkins who made it happen. 'Golden Arrows,' don't you know?"

But at the moment I said, "I don't know what you're about. You don't need to see his wounds to pay respects."

"I'm enough a soldier, now, have enough sense of honor, to know that I must. Even if I tell nobody, he deserves this of me."

I was damn near flabbergasted. The man in front of me, talking to me, had never existed before. Tears ran down his face. He sobbed. He clutched at me. I had never seen the like of it. What the hell, or heaven, happened?

"All right. Be quick. I have to get the mules going. More corpses to haul, more ammunition to turn into corpses."

With his bayonet Barton cut the cord on the shroud, opened it.

I said, "Look, say your prayer. I'll pray along with you. He's my cousin, too. I was a hell of a better cousin than you. He was a hell of a better man than you."

"Ezekiel," I heard him plea, "Forgive me. I see now through your eyes. Atkins gave me the gift. I don't deserve it. I came from the tunnel different. It was you who broke the mystical line, fought the spirit of the Siegfried line."

Then Barton turned to me. "Elliot, what should I do with my life? I am a monster. I hope to die in the war. If I'm lucky, if God forgives, me I will."

"I don't know. I sure don't care. I gotta get going. Get on the limber. You can travel alongside your cousin."

Barton bent, kissed our dead cousin's cheek. "Seeing him killed changed me," he said. He tied the shroud shut.

We were close to the cemetery at Bony. We hear spades digging the earth, long trenches, wide and deep.

Suddenly his old self broke into a fury. "I'm going to the Line. I'll kill every Jerry I can! For what they did to my cousin."

"Now, don't you go doing nothin'. Stay on the limber." I grabbed him by his tunic. "You'll be court martialed."

"I have to go," Barton said. And leapt off and ran toward the battle line.

"Them's not your orders!" I shouted as he ran off.

Howled Barton, "The bastards killed my cousin. I'll be dead before you can report me."

I tried to calm him. "This war is coming to an end. We'll be home soon."

"I'm not going." He went on. "Bury me with my cousin."

"Get a hold of yourself, cousin. You need to tell the relatives about Zeke and Tommny Atkins. I would be happy if one of us reach home. You cut the odds in half of one of us getting there."

Donald Barton calmed down, stared at the shroud. Then he talked.

"Tommy Atkins told me the tunnel would change me. At first it spawned ruthlessness. I wish I killed more Huns and in worse ways to kill 'em. I drowned some there. But not enough. At that time I wished I had more to kill."

I couldn't imagine what had happened.

Donald went on. "Then, after we opened the wall and water shot out, I chanced again. Regret. Remorse. I knew the words but not what they meant. That's what I feel about my life, the way I lived it. Atonement. Contrition. I knew those words, too, and thought them silly, for old maids and the churchly sort. Can I ever achieve them?"

I thought, who is this talking? This was not the Donald Barton I knew all the years. "I heard, all of us heard, about Tommy Atkins. His name cast a spell over those he made 'Golden Arrows of God.' Never really knew what it meant. Tommy Atkins. I do now."

I said, "I think Atkins brought it about. Yes, I do. Atkins? Dease? St. George? They lead to God." Then I told him to cover Ezekiel's face and tie the cord tight on the shroud. "Time to go. Step aside. Hope to see you at home if we don't meet again over here." We clasped one another in a confusion, a welter of thoughts and feelings.

In parting I said, "Don't let the wheel run over your foot."

Next day. True to his word. I wasn't the driver who hauled him in. I saw his name on the record file. I don't know how many Huns he killed, but the word is a prodigious number. Machine gun emplacement after emplacement. Medal of Honor, without doubt.

Hun prisoners on October 12, the day the 30th Division was sent to rest camp

September 30, The Morning

The next morning, combing the battlefield, burial parties found the bodies of many killed, but not Able's. They thought, reasonably enough, a heavy shell might have wiped him out, or buried him in the debris and dirt. Later in the day they found his corpse beyond the trench in a German sap, an observation post beyond the second line trench. A Hun sentry and Able had gone at it with gun butts, then bayonets. In an instant, each impaled on the other's bayonet. When they found Ezekiel Able's body one of the burial crew said, "Furthest forward, impaled on a Hun bayonet, impaling the Hun who stuck him. If he ain't an emblem." Gloom. Able was admired, and if it could be said, loved, by his compatriots.

And Able, who cut open the Dragon's Vein on the earth's surface. The power Godley described to us.

Even odder. The crew searched the body of the Kraut he killed. His identification book: First name—common among Germans—Siegfried. Coincidence, it must have been. The Siegfried Line—German name for the line. Maybe there was no lightning bolt. Maybe there was no enlightenment. Maybe no ascension to heaven. Maybe it was nothing more than a coincidence that a Hun named Siegfried killed him. But there was more to it than that. As Atkins prophesized.

LANCE CORPORAL THOMAS ATKINS ❖ 6

Chapter 22

Tommy Atkins after Bellicourt, His Ascension

My Americans fulfilled their missions. They were ordinary soldiers again. The extraordinary was over. Thereafter, back with my old company, Machine Gunner One, Vickers machine gun. Battles from then on. First Cambrai. Then LeCateau, the forest of Mormal, and Mons again. We were pushing the Germans back the way they had come. At Mons four years ago I fought, died, and came back to life. Back where I began. At the foot of this bridge, Nimy Bridge I passed my first belt filled with bullets to Gunner Two. I stood here again.

November 11, 1918 time: 10:40 a.m., Greenwich Mean Time. Armistice to be proclaimed at 11:00 a.m. we've been told. But here, far from working telegraph lines, we knew nothing certain.

I am in sight of Nimy bridge once more. Germans run across it he bridge, leave behind the grieving Belgian people. We in chase. I stand at the same abutment where the Ruffians fought those years ago. Where Lieutenant Dease met death, transfiguration, apotheosis. He speaks to me now. "Yes, the end is near, brother 'Golden Arrow of God.'" I touch the golden arrow bent, worn, on the back of my lapel again, a talisman, an amulet.

The last German soldiers, bedraggled, slovenly, scurry toward home. They are old men, mere children—now taking a final stand across the Nimy Bridge. The water in the canal seemed the same brown water that flowed along the canal four years ago.

November 11, 1918 10:50. Few bullets come in our direction. A few feeble mortar shells, most of them squibs, duds, the German factories producing poor ammunition. No miners now to dig saltpeter. Not enough men to smelt brass for cartridges. Yet, here and there an explosion.

10:55 Nimy Bridge. Five minutes to the final "Last Post" and "cease fire." A bullet, without aim or intention, more a salute in parting than a salvo, pierced my heart.

I had died before, so I knew Life after life.

Dease's voice rang out. "Tommy Atkins, it was not your time, my brother. You had to live to bear witness."

I ascend from my body. I see my corpse below, growing smaller as Dease and my brothers-in-arms carry me aloft. At first my body the size of a dog, than a mouse, now a bee, an ant, then lost to sight in the depths of the land. Then billows of golden cloud enwrap me. My ears ring with the whine of wind tearing through trees, the baying of hounds, lions roaring, the shrill groan of bagpipes, and penny whistle shrieks. As if struck by vertigo, I spin into the darkness of night, enshrouded in the cloud of gold.

Angels swarm about me, like humming birds around nectar-filled lilies. Certain angels reveal themselves to me in voice. Their names blossom in my mind: Ananyal sang, "I am blessed by God; I have plenty, more than enough, rose branches in bloom." I see the angel Piel teaching Jacob, bringing home his lessons with resounding slaps. Then, the apocryphal angels presented themselves. Before each I bow as low as I could bend. Jehudial shouted, "Praise the Lord." His right hand cradled the crown of acceptance, the left gripped a three-stranded whip. The apocryphal angel Barakiel was a statue of gold. Angel Salathiel declaimed, "Your soul belongs to God." And next to God—Mittaron—once Enoch, son of Jared, father of Methuselah, Noah's great-grandfather—in the flesh, a living man. He sat on a flaming column beside God's Throne. Before the apocryphal angels, each the size of Leviathan, I prostrate myself. I see the angel Uriel wrapped in smoke. I see the angel Gabriel, himself fire. I watch them bury Adam in the ground when his life had circled through his days, again, here as they did on earth. And now by my side, in a swirl of drops of molten lead, as if falling from a shot tower, a statue shaped itself, became St. George incarnate.

Angel St. George proclaimed, "Tommy Atkins, 'God's Golden Arrow', you are the alpha and the omega, the beginning and the end, tied end to end, the ouroboros, the snake circled, its tail clasped in its mouth."

In that instant, I saw all the souls of all the soldiers who died through those terrible years. I saw their tears a torrent, a river spilling from end to end–Le Havre to Luxembourg, three hundred and fifty miles long, a fifty-mile wide swath. I suffered the agony, terror, pain, suffering of every soldier, every refugee, every citizen of every ravaged and occupied town and village, each city. A scourge from which there was no surcease.

My ears ring with the devil's laughter. No greater joy, no greater triumph has he tasted since his fall from Heaven.

Tommy Atkins:

Angel of Grief, Memory, and Tears

All who claim authority from God, God curses for their arrogance and stupidity, their fraud, lies, disbelieving his Word. Next time, and there be a next time, the shrieks of pain, the cries of grief that shall arise from the soldier, refugee, and citizen shall deafen God himself. I tell you, this very ground will reek again with the stench of dead men's flesh. Disease shall desolate the ground. Millions, I say truly, millions will fall, destroyed in ways not yet formed in fiendish vapors in the minds of men. There shall be factories whose fuel is the bodies of the dead, whose product shall be misery and tears, ash and bone. There shall be clouds, monstrous mushrooms exploding out of the ground, the heat of the sun blooming forth. Men shall turn to thin air, and buildings disintegrate in an instant. The earth shall feed on flesh and drink blood, as in days of old when they were the gods' food and drink.

These prophecies surpass what you can believe. Nonetheless they are true. You shall see this come to pass. Write it in your log, journal, your diary, commonplace book.

Dear Reader

And at the end, I, Tommy Atkins, the angel of grief and memory, shall roll the Heavens together, and with them, the realm of Hell. I will call on the angel Dease and my brother Golden Arrows. Other angels shall help us–some no bigger than fleas whose wings beat loud as thunder, some the size of men and women, robust and smelling of work and long flight, some big as stars, showering the dark sky with threads of light. Then, like one skilled in knots and cloth, a sail-maker, or one who coils baskets from plaited straw, I will wind and furl the air, shall twist the universe. Others will grind the demons we conquered as in a mill press. I shall call the angel St. George and the angel Jeanne d'Arc and name God from the least name to the most secret. When I say the last the universe shall be born anew, Eden again a blooming garden, man and woman, innocent once again.

CAST OF CHARACTERS

Company "M", 118th Regiment, II Battalion
30th Division, American Expeditionary Force
(Assigned, IV British Army)

Chaplain Second Lieutenant John Phelps

Served the four companies of 2nd Battalion, 118th Regiment. Joined the Battalion on the day the division won its first victory. Two years' graduated from Columbia Theological Seminary of the Presbyterian Church.

Lewis Machine Gun Teams

Team "Swamp Fox"

The men chose the name to honor Francis Marion, South Carolina Revolutionary War soldier who fought using guerilla tactics—quick attack and quick withdrawal by a few soldiers.

Kendall Haydon   Gunner One
Head gunner, keenly observant and deeply thoughtful, fully aware of the world situation and his role in the war.

Ezekiel Able   Gunner Two
American patriot of the highest order with the qualities of a leader. Well thought of, likely to earn promotion quickly. Sociable. Friendly. He will lead his men across the Hindenburg Line, breaking the Dragon's Vein.

William Spears   Gunner Assistant
From St. Helena Island where he grew up among the Gullah Geechee, a remote, isolated Negro culture. Their lore and religious practices were part of his experiences in the war. On St. Helena the farmer was also fisherman, the sea surrounding.

Hans Schmidt   Gunner Assistant
From Sumter, South Carolina moved by patriotic fervor to fight in the war he foresaw long before the United States entered. The only child of German immigrants, he was a soldier interested in the machinery of war, the workings of the Divine in the war.

Otis Mankins   Gunner Assistant, totes ammunition
Every contingent of soldiers contains its complement of dull, dim souls.
Farm boy. Stirred to enlist because his friend Hans Schmidt read to him
about the war from newspapers and magazines. Hoping to leave the farm,
work from morning to night in all weathers for his father. And his father
wanted him gone.

Jenks Braddock   Sniper
From the South Carolina Piedmont where it dipped into old mountains and
valleys, Braddock hunted and trapped, and knew the wild outdoors. Eager
to hunt the Hun, about whom he had heard ghastly accounts.

Team "The Gamecocks"

The team named itself to honor Thomas Sumter, "Carolina Gamecock,"
Revolutionary War hero famous for his fierce fighting against the British,
some say in revenge for their burning his house down.

Donald Barton   Gunner One
A fierce spirit that, the Instructors hoped would be fit to lead the gun
against the Enemy inside the tunnel. Otherwise, a hard pill to swallow.

Caleb Jolly   Gunner Two
Sought adventure in the Big Blow Over There. Wit and good cheer and
handy in the way that farmers had to be. Jolly was a bit of an intellect,
having read and thought more widely and deeply than most.

Miles Mason   Gunner Assistant
A boy from Columbia, the state capitol. His father a laborer, five children
to feed, and Miles the oldest, he removed himself from the family board
and larder and promiseato send his pay to his father. And he wanted to see
the world and this was the way to do it.

Beau Baylor   Gunner Assistant
Quick to learn, and eager to get to the Front.

Transport

Private Elliott Joiner   Wagoner
Good with mules and horses. Hauled limbers guns, ammunition. Then
drove truck loaded with ammunition.

Privates Zachariah Christian and Phillip Mather, wagoners.

Vickers Machine Gun, Company "C",   Royal Fusiliers, British IV Army
Vickers Machine Gun, Company "C",
Royal Fusiliers, British IV Army

Lance Corporal Tommy Atkins   Gunner Six at Mons, then Gunner One,
Now Lead Instructor on the Lewis Machine Gun

Assigned to teach and stay with the American troops following them
through to their mission, Lead Instructor on the Lewis machine gun for the
118th Infantry Regiment, Atkins fought at Mons in the first battle between
the British and the Germans in August, 1914. Before the battle his team, a
Vickers machine gun crew, and a doctor were initiated into the "Golden
Arrows of God." At Mons Atkins was killed. St. George, patron saint of
Mons, brought him back to life. At First Ypres his team was killed, he the
sole survivor. Elevated by St. George to "spirit soldiers", they helped Atkins throughout the war and especially in the battle to come. While he and
the other instructors were British soldiers, now they would aid the Americans at Bellicourt. He is the connection between the revenants and the mortal world and the story's main character.

Other British Instructors

Sergeants Harry Ballwin and George Brentwood, two fellow British Instructors, training the Americans for the ordeal that lay ahead.

British Army Revenants (Souls Who Return)

"Golden Arrows of God"—a secret order within the mystical "Messieurs
de St. Georges" in Mons, Belgium. All of the revenants are initiates and
several others become initiated.

Captain Malcolm Leckie, R.A.M.C. Medical Officer to Company "C" that
the Ruffians belonged to. Brother in-law to Sir Arthur Conan Doyle.
Wounded at Mons, and died six days later.

Team "The Ruffians," also Revenants

Lieutenant Maurice Dease   Section Leader
Directed two Vickers machine gun teams—the Ruffians and Victors. At

Nimy Bridge four years before met death, transfiguration, apotheosis. Serves alongside St. George.

Private Sidney Godley   Gunner One
Killed at First Ypres. A kind man in life and death.

Privates Louis Palmer, William Catchpole   Gunners Two and Three
Escapees from irate husbands whose wives they. . . . No more need be said—and the London burlesque and leg-show comics, revenants tired of war and yearning for Eternal Rest.

Private Paul Carmichael Gunner Assistant
Quit the circus for a life in the Army. Left behind a life of melancholy when he was killed at Ypres. Thereafter he was confident, relaxed, sported a jaunty air. A revenant, good at cards.

Historical Figures

Sir Arthur Conan Doyle, Sixth Royal Sussex Volunteer Regiment

Brigadier General John Francis Innes Hay "Duff" Doyle, brother to Sir Arthur Conan Doyle

Winston Churchill Commander, 6th Battalion, Royal Scot Fusiliers and Minister of Munitions

Sherlock Holmes

World War I poets Siegfried Sassoon and Wilfred Owen

Works Consulted

Mark Adkin *A Western Front Companion*
American Playing Card Manufacturers *100 Games of Solitaire*
Dale Blair *Diggers and Doughboys: The Battle of Bellicourt Tunnel*
Hereward Carrington, *Psychical Phenomena and the War*
George Coppard, *With Machine Gun to Cambrai*
Cyclopedia of Illustrations for Public Speakers
Sir Arthur Conan Doyle "His Last Bow," *Strand Magazine*
    Adventures and Memories
    The Somme: an Extract from 'The British Campaign in France and Flanders'
Byron Farwell *Over There: The United States in the Great War, 1917 – 1918*
Fritz Hamer, Editor and writer, *Forward Together: South Carolina in the Great War.*
Meirion and Susie Harries *The Last Days of Innocence: America at War, 1917 – 1918*
History of Co. F. 118th Infantry, (Hampton Guards) 30th Division, Digital Version
Ernst Junger *The Storm of Steel: From the Diary of a German Storm-Troop Officer on the Western Front*
John Laffin *A Western Front Companion: 1914 – 1918*
Nick Lloyd *Hundred Days: The Campaign that Ended World War I*
John F. Lucy *There's a Devil in the Drum*
Andrew Lycett, *The Man who Created Sherlock Holmes: The Life and Times of Sir Arthur Conan Doyle*
R. Jackson Marshall, III *Memories of WWI NC Doughboys on the Western Front*
The Master Book of Dreams
Gary Mead *The Doughboys: America and the First World War*
Nick Nichols *Discovering Truth: Proof of Intelligence Beyond Individual Physical Conscious* https://www.dropbox.com/s/cnwqcxkr1gj0aza
Nigel Pennick *The Ancient Science of Geomancy: Man in Harmony with the Earth*
Andy Simpson, *Hot Blood and Cold Steel: Life and Death in the Trenches of the First World War*
Elmer A. Murphy and Robert S. Thomas *The Thirtieth Division in the World War*
Mitchell Yockelson *Borrowed Soldiers: Americans under British Command, 1918*

About the Author

Jerred Metz has had six books of poetry and six of prose published. He lives in Columbia, South Carolina with his wife, Sarah Barker. They are proud to be honorary citizens of Mons, Belgium, the city written about in this book and the setting for *The Angel of Mons: A World War I Legend.* Jerred and Sarah are the parents of two grown, married children who have children of their own.

Recent Books from Singing Bone Press

Poetry

A Hermit Has No Plural by Gabor Gyukic

My God, How Many Mistakes I've Made by Endre Kukorelly (translated from Hungarian by Gabor Gyukic and Michael Castro)

How Things Stack Up by Michael Castro

Two Gardens: Modern Hebrew Poems of the Bible (Poems by twenty-four Israeli poets translated by Jeff Friedman and Nati Zohar)

Poems from the Buddha's Footprint by Sunthorn Phu (translated from Thai by Noh Anothai)

Double Identity by Allison Joseph

Doubled Radiance: Poetry and Prose of Li Qingzhao (translated from Chinese by Karen An-Hwei Lee)

We Need to Talk: New and Selected Poems by Michael Castro

The Heart Attacks of the Soul: Gypsy Cantos by Attila Balogh (translated from Hungarian by Gabor Gyukic and Michael Castro)

Butter in a Jar: Days in the Life of Iola Thomas by Jerred Metz

The Melody Lingers by Shlomo Vinner

Prose

Uncle Duke Gathers His Wits: Truths and Heresies by W. K. Haydon

The Angel of Mons: A World War I Legend by Jerred Metz